Finch Books by J.S. Frankel

Single Books
The Menagerie
Port Anywhere
The Window to Tellkar

The Nightmare Crew
Beginnings
Law & Order
Integration

I0658869

THE WINDOW
TO TELLKAR

J.S. FRANKEL

The Window to Tellkar
ISBN # 978-1-80250-519-1
©Copyright J.S. Frankel 2023
Cover Art by Erin Dameron-Hill ©Copyright March 2023
Interior text design by Claire Siemaszkiewicz
Finch Books

Published in 2023 by Finch Books, United Kingdom.

THE WINDOW
TO TELLKAR

Dedication

To my wife, Akiko, who makes my existence
worthwhile, and to my children, Kai and Ray.

And to Jennefer Rogers, Sara Linnertz, Joanne
Van Leerdam, Eva Pasco, Toni Kief, Gigi
Sedlmayer, and so many more, thank you.

Most of all, thanks to my late sister,
Nancy Dana Frankel, who never gave up on me.
This one's for you, sis.

Chapter One

The New Girl

Carson High School, Portland, Oregon
Homeroom class, June first
Seven days before summer vacation.

"Class, close your books. I'm about to give you your final grades for the year."

So said our homeroom teacher, Mr. Osborne, in that semi-aristocratic, snobbish voice that only the truly annoying possessed. Osborne was a short, bald man, well over fifty, with a testy, impatient manner and a caustic way of phrasing things.

Nine-oh-two a.m. and my heart was already beating fast. I'd been sweating out my test results for the past week. Today would either be a 'yay' or a 'nay'.

I could only hope for a 'yay', although a person could never tell what Osborne would do or say. In his mind, if a student wasn't worthy, he said so.

In front of the class.

In a loud voice.

Yes, he was a jerk.

However, today, Osborne must have been feeling generous, as he simply called up the students one by one, spoke to them quietly and gave them the results in a printout.

It was easy to pick out who passed and who failed. Those who passed had that secret smile working, something that imparted a repressed feeling of elation and an unspoken shout of joy, as in, "No summer school. I'm outta here!"

On the other hand, those who failed—below a collective score of seventy-six—had a stone-face thing going on. At least, most of them did. Some of the unfortunates broke down in tears and were comforted by their friends. A couple of them ran out of the class, crying uncontrollably.

"Mr. Catton."

Osborne called Joel Catton up, the self-described resident brain. He was a genius at everything—or so he said.

In contrast, I was a genius at nothing, although my grades were decent enough. The only reason for that was because I pored over my homework night after night until the concepts and facts and figures were firmly etched in my mind.

For me, it was a matter of pride. I was a washout at sports, save swimming, noted for being sort of introverted, but I never gave up on anything. Through sheer determination, I passed my tests and did well.

In contrast, my best bud, Nick Walker, was one of *the* true geniuses, even smarter than Joel. It was a given that Nick didn't have to worry about summer school— ever.

At barely five-four, he weighed two hundred pounds, a perfectly round Humpty-Dumpty lookalike, with button eyes, a moon face and pudgy hands with fingers like sausages.

He sat behind me, murmuring, "Mark, you got this," over and over, and that took away some of the nervousness.

Of course, Nick had to mutter that his grades would be the highest in the class, higher than Catton's. They'd had a scholastic rivalry going on for the past year.

Catton walked back to his seat, which was behind Nick's. Joel's smile was on full display, and he slumped down with a happy sigh. I overheard him whisper to Nick, "Hey, ninety-four percent in the regular courses."

"What about gym?" I asked in a low voice and turned around to catch Joel's expression. He couldn't even do five pushups without passing out.

His face turned red. "Phys ed doesn't count. Ninety-four percent. Beat that, Walker. And I know you're nowhere near me, Cornish."

Catton and our teacher were equal opportunity asshats. Joel never had a decent word for anyone. Tall and skinny, with spotty skin, halitosis and the attitude of a smarmy geek, he lived to make fun of those with lesser grades than his.

Beating him up wasn't an option, as he had no fighting skills. Moreover, his uncle was the principal. Smacking Joel around was guaranteed to earn anyone who did so a suspension.

Secretly, I had the feeling that one day, someone would level his loser ass but good…

"Failure's around the corner, Cornish," he whispered, breaking into my reverie. Maliciousness coated every word. "Summer school is waiting."

Toolbit. I ignored his noise. Seventy-six was the cutoff. That number meant everything.

"Mr. Cornish."

Okay, the teacher had called my name. "Go get 'em," Nick murmured and gave me the thumbs-up sign.

He could afford to be calm. My heart was going a million miles an hour. I whispered, "Yeah, right."

At Osborne's desk, I got the printout—eighty-four. "Well done, Mr. Cornish," he said in a quiet, even voice. "Consider this a window of opportunity to better yourself. You may get into a university, after all."

Some compliment—not. While my grades were decent, my mother didn't have the cash, so forget about getting a scholarship. However, a person had to show gratitude, so I bobbed my head and said, "Thank you, sir."

A quick U-turn took me back to my seat. Once there, I returned the thumbs-up sign to Nick. Joel glowered. His day was ruined. Perhaps today wouldn't be so bad after all...

The door opened, and one of the students came in. 'Late' wasn't the right word to use in Glenda's case. 'Rare appearance' best described her.

As always, she wore a green hoodie and a pair of torn blue jeans, along with a pink T-shirt with a picture of a unicorn on it. Ragged black sneakers completed her outfit, and her outfit could only be described as a cross between 'grungy' and 'funky'.

Two months ago, she'd transferred in from a school back East, and since then, she'd established a reputation as someone who A, didn't like conversation, B, knew more than anyone else, even Nick and C, knew way more than Joel.

Glenda was my height—five-ten—and gangly, with pixie-like features, reddish-gray hair, jade-green eyes, and the ability to turn heads wherever she went due to her appearance.

All the female students thought her stuck up and strange. All the male students simply thought her totally undatable.

I thought she was cool, in her own way. On her first day here, she'd introduced herself in a monosyllabic voice, then she'd found an empty seat next to mine. "I'm Mark Cornish," I whispered. "Nice to meet you."

Glenda gave me the onceover and asked in a neutral tone, "Do you have any of the textbooks?"

I had all of them and showed her. She flipped through them at lightning speed, then she handed them back. "Thank you. I can apply this knowledge."

Uh-huh. And I'd thought that Joel and Nick were brilliant—not. Whenever Glenda came to class— usually two days in a row then she didn't come for two—she knew the answers perfectly. And she always showed up on test day to blast through the questions and essay sections.

It went without saying that she got stellar results— perfect scores…every time. If I hadn't been so fascinated with her, I might have hated her. But I couldn't. Some people were just incredibly bright. She was one of those people.

Glenda walked quickly over to the empty seat beside me, sat down and whispered, "What letter are they up to?"

"They just called my name. You're next, I think."

Glenda's last name was Cron—C-R-O-N. That was how she spelled it, and woe unto anyone who mispronounced it. One guy called her crone—once. She leveled him with a left hook.

No one ever dared mess up her name again.

"Ms. Cron," the teacher intoned. "So nice of you to attend."

No reaction came from her, not so much as a twitch. However, she did apologize. "Sorry for being late. I'll come on time next time."

Osborne consulted his ledger. He used a computer for official stuff, but he liked to keep an old-fashioned notebook to record attendance.

"Considering summer vacation will commence in a few days, Ms. Cron, I doubt there will be a next time until September. You've attended only fifty-two percent of the classes since you transferred here."

"Er, well, at least I didn't attend forty-two percent. The internet says forty-two is the magic number, doesn't it?"

Oh, burn! That got the class laughing. Osborne's face turned red, and he growled, "Come up and get your grades."

In an unexpected and rare display of friendliness, Glenda winked at me and went up to the teacher's desk, her hands clasped in front of her body, head bowed to indicate humility.

Osborne's voice drifted over. "Ms. Cron, despite your attitude and your rotten attendance record, as always, you never fail to surprise me. Your grades are perfect."

Murmurs ran around the class, like ripples through a pond after someone had tossed a stone in it. *Perfect? Impossible.*

But it was true. She returned to her desk, holding her printout, and she showed it to me. One hundred percent in every subject, except Phys ed. I had no words.

"Guess no summer school for you," I whispered.

"I have places to go," she answered somewhat smugly.

What places? Whatever. Glenda had never been the talkative sort. Our lockers were on the first floor, hers being five over from mine, but she rarely went there. She never ate lunch in the cafeteria and spent most of her time in the library, which was on the third floor.

In short, she was a loner, and the other students considered her too weird to hang out with. On the flipside though, Glenda didn't seem to care.

After our class finished, I went to my locker, and she cornered me there to ask me about Portland. "Why?"

Her answer was simple. "Oh, I'm interested in new cities, places to go, to live...that kind of thing."

Since I'd grown up here, I told her what I knew. After I finished talking, she thanked me and asked one question. "If someone offered you a chance to go somewhere interesting, would you go?"

Call that strange...then some, but okay, humor her. "Yeah, sure, I guess."

Glenda seemed satisfied and walked off. The window of opportunity opened and closed fast—or something like that. It simply meant that if you had a chance, you had to grab it.

Reality intruded. With no cash and no connections, my future was set—working in some office or a warehouse.

Thinking about it just got me depressed, so after school let out, I went home to an empty house, cleaned up and made myself dinner, then bored with television and with nothing interesting online to watch, I went to bed, wondering about places to go and people to see.

Before I drifted off, I thought about what my seventeen-plus years had been about and came up with only one word—empty. Being an only child with an absentee mother had never been fun. My father had died long ago. I'd been four at the time.

I barely remembered him. According to the wedding picture that sat on the bookshelf, we shared the same traits—same height, a slender build with wide shoulders and a narrow waist, dark hair, brown eyes and plain features. That was it.

It also happened to be the only picture I'd ever seen of him.

My mother—barely five feet, plump and quiet—never mentioned him. She was too busy working. As a software salesperson-slash-coder-slash-troubleshooter, she often traveled around the country, and she sometimes went to other cities or countries to attend seminars.

She'd left yesterday on another trip. "Two weeks plus," she'd said as she packed, her hands moving quickly and deftly to lay out then fold her clothes.

"Where to this time, Mom?"

Her answer—six days in New York, five days in Toronto then four days in San Francisco to attend some seminar. "I left money for you, but you have a cash card, don't you?"

"Yes."

I rarely used it. I'd saved money from my summer job the past year, working in an ice cream parlor. It wasn't much, but it was enough. I didn't like relying on my mother for handouts.

"So, you'll be fine."

As usual, her voice came out quiet and even, and her expression was unreadable. I wondered at times if she'd ever cried over her husband—my father—dying.

"Yeah, I'm used to it."

My mother's hands stopped moving. "Meaning what?"

This time, her question came out tinged with anger. We hadn't spoken about this for a long time. Her standard answer was that we needed the money. She didn't care for traveling, but she went. "Meaning... what?" she repeated.

Call that spoiling for a fight. Usually, I backed down out of respect, but not that day. "Meaning you're never around. I know the neighbors better than I know you," I replied, not being snarky, but being honest. "What are you running from? Me?"

It wasn't as though she had a boyfriend. She never mentioned any relationships. With her, it was work and more work.

Her face reddened, and she stammered out, "It's not that. Just...just that we need the money. That's all."

I tried a different tack. "Mom, how about you stick around and find out about me."

Now, confusion competed against embarrassment for supremacy on her face. "What?"

Oh, you know. "I mean, you've never met my friends, and you never ask me about my grades. Do you even care?"

The red hue on her face deepened even more. "Mark, I care, but face it. We need the money. I don't work because I love it. I work because it brings us in what we need."

With anyone else, her little speech would have sounded almost noble. In my mother's case, it was simple lip service.

Since she didn't know about my grades and couldn't have cared less, I gave up. "Have a nice trip. See you next month."

Yes, it was a flip answer, and no, she didn't respond. She'd departed the next morning, and a note on the table summed it all up.

Mark,
We'll talk when I get back. I promise.
Mom

I put it in the drawer. There were ten other notes with the identical message written on them. Each time my birthday rolled around, she always forgot. I'd quit reminding her three years ago.

I came to with a start, staring into the darkness. Glenda's words came back to me. Go somewhere if I had the chance? Call that a yes…then some.

Chapter Two

Strange Things Are Happening

School, four days before summer vacation.
Tick, tick, tick.

Lunchtime, eight minutes past twelve, and the cafeteria was crowded. Nick and I got a table near a window that overlooked the field. "I like to look at nature when I eat," he said. "Hey, by the way, congrats. Eighty-four is solid."

Yes, it was, and his overall grade score happened to be ninety-seven, three points ahead of Joel's. Unlike Catton, though, he didn't get angry over Glenda scoring perfect in every subject. Nick wasn't the jealous type.

I was hungry, so I took out my lunch of two tuna fish sandwiches and finished them off quickly. Then I sat back to wait for Nick's grand unveiling of his lunch. Food-wise, he always came prepared.

A small but sturdy mini suitcase sat on the table. Since we'd met in junior high and become friends, I'd gotten used to his daily eating ritual.

More amazing was his suitcase. No one else had anything like it, but then again, no one was quite like my best bud. Nick was probably the most easygoing person around. Because he was short, fat, and unathletic, everyone knew that he wasn't much of a fighter, or they assumed that he couldn't fight.

Up against someone bigger, he didn't stand a chance if the fight was over a girl — and he wasn't that interested in girls — or a seat in the cafeteria or something trivial.

But if someone touched his suitcase or tried to steal a sandwich — and some students had been stupid enough to try it — he acted like a tiger chasing down its prey. Many kids had gotten punched over committing that transgression.

It was an understatement then, to say that lunch was a big deal for him. Invariably, his suitcase held mostly sandwiches, lovingly prepared by his mother, although he sometimes had quiche or goose pâté or French food.

Sandwiches aside, his suitcase held an oversized thermos of chocolate milk or regular milk, three different kinds of fruit and dessert.

But not any common dessert like a chocolate bar… Nick got only the best — lemon meringue pie or perhaps chocolate mousse from one of the finest private dessert makers. It helped that both his parents were wealthy.

Call that living high. If I ate that much food every day, I'd end up obese. I carried about one-seventy-five on my frame, only because I stuck to regular food, worked out in the school gym and went swimming as a reserve on the swim team.

Still, some morbidly curious part of me wanted to see what Nick was eating today. "Showtime," he murmured.

In a grand gesture, he pulled a large floral napkin out of his pocket, laid it on the table after swiping some crumbs away, then carefully patted the cloth down, making sure the edges were straight and not intruding on anyone's space.

Then, it was time to eat, and around twenty students came around to watch. First, out came three monstrous BLT sandwiches, each almost three inches in height. They'd been kept cold by frozen gel-packs. Food poisoning wasn't on the menu.

Next, a thermos. "Fresh milk from the local creamery," he said.

Fruit was important, so he had an enormous Tupperware container of freshly cut mango, one banana and a softball-sized apple. As for dessert, today's goodie topped anything he'd brought so far, an entire chocolate cheesecake that came from the finest cheesecake maker in the city — Mallordi's — a place that catered only to those who had serious coin to spend.

Once Nick had set everything up precisely, the onlookers gave him an ovation then they went back to their tables, their simple lunches and their talk of summer plans.

Me, I had nothing. My summer job at the ice cream parlor had gone to the owner's daughter, and my search for work had so far been unsuccessful.

Nick didn't have to work, so, as he put it, "Movies, food, pizza, food and movies. Books, too."

Food was his life. In addition to the massive meals he ingested, he loved pizza and considered it a separate food group, something above and beyond other edibles.

All that food-love caused him to weigh about sixty pounds more than he should have. He sweated all the time, no matter what the season, and yet he remained in perfect health. Call that a mystery to end all mysteries.

Sandwich number one got unwrapped, and while smashing through it, Nick asked, "So, any plans this summer?"

"I've got to get something," I said, trying to sound positive. "A decent summer job, save money, that kind of thing."

Once more, thoughts of my future called, which then led to depression setting in. If I couldn't get into university, then I'd go to a community college or enter the workforce, doing whatever, and that sucked bigtime...

"Hey, there's Glenda," Nick said as he finished off his second sandwich and carefully dabbed at his mouth, shoving in an excess crumb or sixteen with a pudgy forefinger.

Nick was a precise eater. He adhered to the credo of waste not, therefore, want not. Everything that was in a sandwich went into his piehole. If anything fell from the sandwich, he got upset. Once, in junior high, he'd dropped a slice of pizza on the floor and cried uncontrollably for an hour.

I didn't turn around. What for?

Someone tapped me on the shoulder. I swung around to find Glenda standing a yard away. Call this a first. "Hi," I said, surprised. "What brings you here?"

In a change from her usually confident demeanor, she stammered out her answer. "Oh, I, uh, I wanted to talk to you. You've been nice to me, and, er, I haven't been so friendly."

The term was almost finished and now she wanted to be friendly? Was this an attempt at a pick-up? Not that I was so experienced — I wasn't — but all the same, was it?

She pointed at the ceiling. "Listen… Can we talk? Upstairs, in the library."

"My favorite place," I said in an obvious attempt to get Glenda to see me in a new light. Sure, call it brown-nosing, but not many of the other girls here were interested.

Maybe it was my generic looks. Hatchet face, a mop of brown hair — call me totally unprepossessing. I looked how I looked and never worried about it. If a girl wanted to get to know me, then she had to look past my exterior. I'd do the same for her. That was how I rolled.

Nick had his third sandwich out and ready, but when Glenda took my hand to lead me away, the surprise was too much, and he dropped it.

A millisecond later, his cries of gastric want and need filled the air. So did the laughter from the other students. At least Nick had his fruit and dessert waiting.

Upstairs, Glenda and I made our way over to the library, but before we entered, Valerie Morton intercepted us. If Joel Catton was the school snob and self-described genius, Valerie was the school's self-professed queen.

Queen of the cheerleading team and photogenic to the max. Turned heads wherever she went. Incredibly attractive, with a head of raven-black hair and a face and body that every guy in the school wanted to get to know better, she was also known as the Queen of Preen.

Valerie always carried a pocket mirror and regularly checked her appearance. Make-up, hair, accessories — they had to be perfect.

And they were. Valerie was pretty, she knew it and she wanted everyone else to know it. Yet she'd never been mean to anyone in the sense of lording her looks over them.

In fact, she often went around to the plainest girls in the school and helped them with makeup and fashion tips. Valerie meant well, but she still came across as the living, breathing stereotype of a vain and self-centered beauty queen.

"Hi, Mark," she called out with a toothy smile. "Ready for summer vacay?"

Ignore her and keep going, or be nice and start a conversation? I went with what was behind door number two. "Yeah, just about. Uh, you know Glenda, right?"

Valerie gave her a brief nod, something civil and yet dismissive. She then frowned. "Girl, you need a makeover."

Glenda blinked. "Makeover? Are you saying I'm ugly?"

Uh-oh. Valerie didn't mean to be coarse, but sometimes the other person didn't get what she was trying to say and got offended.

In this case, Glenda had taken it the wrong way. Valerie backed up a step. "No, uh, not ugly, but I'm thinking, if you dyed your hair, put on a different wardrobe and talked to people, you might become more popular. I mean, summer vacation's almost here, so why not push the attraction button?"

Perhaps Valerie thought she was being helpful, but Glenda didn't seem to appreciate it, at least at first. Her face remained expressionless, but after a few seconds, a tiny smile emerged.

"I have to go to the ladies' room," she said. "How about we talk about it in there? Maybe you can give me some pointers."

Request given, Valerie bobbed her head and gave her a smile of relief. "Yeah, sounds good."

Glenda turned to me and offered a cryptic smile. "Excuse us, Mark."

"Uh, yeah, sure thing." At least there wouldn't be any violence today—or so I hoped. After that smile, I couldn't be sure of anything.

Once they disappeared into the washroom, I took a walk along the corridor. As I reached the end of the hallway, the sound of footsteps made me turn around. A few students had come up, probably to get in some relaxation time as well as study time.

I turned away. They could have their study time. They had friends and I didn't, and that was life...

A scream rang out from the lady's room. *What in the...?*

Something must have happened, as Valerie ran out of the bathroom, yelling about a green elf. One of her friends, Carla Needham, ran over to her. "Val, what's going on?"

Valerie pointed at the washroom. "There. Elf... I saw an..."

That was all Valerie got out, as a moment later, she shoved Carla out of the way and tore down the stairs, yelling at the top of her lungs.

Elf?

Naturally, everyone loved a good piece of gossip, and they followed her downstairs, chattering at high speed. Finally, something to talk about, another student flipping out over grades or tripping on drugs or whatever.

Pretty freaky, and while I also wanted to talk to her, now wasn't the time. Perhaps tomorrow would be better. All the same, what had she freaked over? Valerie wasn't into drugs. They would have messed up her looks too much.

Wait... Glenda had been in there with her. Maybe she knew. The hallway was empty, so I called out, "Glenda?"

No answer.

After looking around to make sure no one was coming, I poked my head into the ladies' room, just in time to see what looked like a green individual wearing a brown robe slip through an opening in the air. That opening then vanished in a burst of light.

Mind...blown. I backed out of the washroom and rubbed my eyes. "No way," I muttered. "Absolutely no friggin' way."

What I'd witnessed, that simply wasn't possible. People weren't green, although I'd seen a few people turn green if they drank too much.

But green-all-over people...? Call that odd...no, something even funkier than beyond weird was going on. Upcoming summer vacation or not, I intended to find out what.

Chapter Three

Oh

Seventy-two hours to go.
Twelve-fifty, the cafeteria.

Nick was still eating. What else was new? I ran over to him, half-freaked out by what I'd seen and told him what had happened. His mouth was full of cheesecake, but once he'd finished chewing and swallowing, his response was exactly what I figured it would be.

"Mark, does the expression 'seeing things' resonate in any way, shape, or form?"

He would say that. I was sweating and shaking… This was news! "Nick, I saw what I saw. And what I saw was a green, uh, *person* disappearing into the air."

He took another chunk of cheesecake but didn't bite into it. His eyes grew round, and he gave me a look that could only be described as skeptical. "And you think that was Glenda?"

Good question. "I don't know, yeah…maybe?"

"Man, who can figure out women?"

Right, like he knew. "Yeah, but, Nick, think about it. Glenda just disappeared, then there was this green person there."

Didn't he get it? People simply didn't up and vanish. It wasn't possible. I got more and more wound up the more I spoke, and finally Nick said, "So, ask Glenda about it when you see her."

"That's your answer?"

He nodded as he took another bite of his cheesecake. "Mm-hmm."

My best bud swallowed, smacked his lips then he gave me the Bert look, a snarky, funny stare that puppet always sported. "Yeah, that's my answer. Duh. C'mon, Mark. Maybe it was someone dressing up to freak out someone else. Maybe it was for a student movie."

"Maybe." I still didn't believe it, though.

In between bites of cheesecake, Nick expounded on his theory. "Listen... You were probably imagining stuff. I get daydreams, too. But think about it. There has to be a logical explanation for this. There always is."

With that, he went back to demolishing his dessert. I left him to his trans-fats and asked various members of the student body if they'd seen Glenda or if they'd spoken to Valerie.

Half the kids I asked didn't know about the incident, while the other half wondered what I was doing with Glenda in the first place. "She's just weird," was the consensus.

All right, no one knew anything. Then the bell rang, signaling the end of lunch, and I went off to calculus. Halfway there, Carla came over to inform me that her bestie had experienced a snap. "Snap?" I asked, confused.

Carla twirled her left finger around the side of her head. "Yeah, you know, she went nutso, that kind of thing. Val's a little flaky, you know?"

Flaky, maybe, but going bonkers at the end of the school semester? Totally different story.

"Carla, she's into self-love and being beautiful, but she's never acted, you know, cray-squared. She isn't into drugs. Valerie's always been straight edge. Something happened."

Naturally, I left out the part about seeing a green person climb through a window and disappear. Had I said that, then the attendants in white suits would have soon shown up to take me away, and I'd be in the same rubber room as Valerie.

Carla nibbled on her lower lip before replying. "Yeah, that's true. I know Val. She's all about herself. Okay, you're right, but still, what did she see that freaked her out so much?"

"Search me."

Of course, it was a lie, but I had a reason for it. I wanted to know what Glenda had done or said to Valerie in their brief time in the ladies' room.

Carla said that she'd try to find out what she could. She was off to American history. "Have a nice one, Mark."

After that, she walked off to catch up with her friends down the hallway, and I was alone with my thoughts. This entire scene was a major cup of weird.

Even weirder was that Valerie didn't return to school. Since our term was almost done, I'd see her in September, but her absence didn't stop everyone from talking about it.

As for Glenda, I didn't see her either, so something had to have happened. How could she have disappeared? No one had any answers, because no one had seen it happen.

Or not happen.

Or something.

The next morning, while getting my books from my locker, I tried putting my thoughts in order. Three months from now, I'd enter my second term at my wonderful high school. I'd also be eighteen in a few days, and the state would consider me an adult.

And that meant doing adult things, like getting a job if I couldn't get into university, paying taxes and doing what everyone else did.

Negative ideas, negative concepts, worries and more circulated through my head. I shook it to clear it. No more negativity. Then Glenda's words about travel resurfaced — get away and go somewhere…

"Hey, Cornish, you got lucky. You know that, right?"

I didn't have to turn around to know that it was Joel Catton. His whiny voice gave him away. Mentally sighing, I wondered what his endgame was, then decided that it didn't matter. I'd passed the year. No summer school for this cowboy.

On the other hand, I needed cash, and that meant finding a summer job. Anything would do if it paid the bills. Hell, I'd even scrub toilets, if that was what it took.

"Cornish, c'mon, man. Admit that you got lucky."

Fine, get this over with. I swung around to find Catton's grinning, pimply mug a couple of feet away. "Tell me how I'm lucky, Joel. Go ahead and tell me."

His grin disappeared. "You got lucky," he repeated for the third time, and his halitosis made my nose hairs wilt. "You're not university material."

What a moron. "Whatever, Joel. Get a life. I got one, thanks."

He opened his mouth, but a hand came out of nowhere to spin him around. It was Glenda, wearing her usual grunge outfit, but outside of that, her eyes were purple and full of pure wrath.

Purple? What was going on here? Glenda didn't explain the eye-color change. However, she did state her position most succinctly. "You say Mark's not university material. Well, you're worse. You're not *societal* material."

Joel started to protest, but Glenda clamped down hard on his trapezius muscle in a nerve pinch, which had to hurt—a lot.

A few of the students stopped to watch. Yeah, why not? Get in a show before vacation started, one last fight, and what better way to start the summer holidays than by seeing the school's chief nerd and asshat get taken out by someone everyone considered to be totally weird?

Poor Joel. Glenda's hold made his knees buckle and he fell to the floor, his voice coming out in a strangled gasp. "Hey, let go."

Glenda wasn't about to. She ignored some of the students who were chanting for a fight and bent over to shove her face close to his.

"Listen very carefully," she snarled. "I'll let go when you've grown up. That'll take you the rest of your miserable life. Now, apologize to Mark for being a jerk."

He grunted and shook his head. "Bite me."

Her grip tightened and his face turned white. "Say that again. I dare you."

This time, her message hit home. He mumbled, "I'm sorry."

Glenda picked her head up to grin at me, then she locked gazes with the sweating, hapless Joel again.

"While we're at it, apologize to me for thinking you're more intelligent than I am. You're not."

His appeal for mercy came out even louder this time. "I'm sorry!"

Glenda released her grip. "That's better. You can leave now."

Everyone stopped to watch as Joel took off like a spanked puppy with its tail between its legs. A round of applause went up, but after a few seconds, everyone went back to their lives.

In Glenda's case, she watched Mr. Halitosis go — probably to complain to his uncle — and waved goodbye, to add insult to injury. Then she turned to me, sporting a smile. "Hey, listen... I'm sorry I cut out so soon the other day."

Cut out? She'd disappeared. Was it worth telling her about the green person I'd seen? No, after thinking it over...not. "Uh, you vanished."

For her part, Glenda didn't crack. She neither denied nor confirmed her great escape. "Did you see me vanish?"

She had me there, and her eyes had gone back to their usual green color. "Well, no, I was at the end of the hall...took a walk, and — "

"So, you saw Valerie run out?"

"Yeah."

"Did you see me slip out after her?"

No, I hadn't. My back had been turned, and there'd been a crowd of people. "Well, no, but — "

Glenda's smile went beyond winning. She had beautiful, perfectly shaped white teeth, something I'd never noticed before. Then, again, she'd never smiled before. "Look... I came to ask you what you're doing this summer?"

"Uh, well — "

"Hey, some show," Nick said as he waddled over and gave me the high-five with a pudgy, sweaty hand. "I just caught the finale, but it was prime. So, what's the word?"

I wiped the sweat off on my jeans. "Glenda rocks, and I have nothing else to say."

At that compliment, Glenda bobbed her head and said, "Listen... I'm not into class today. Who wants to get in some reading time in the library?"

Nick glanced at me and inclined his head ever so slightly. I caught the hint. "I'll go," I replied.

With that, we went upstairs. The library was empty, save for the librarian, and she was at the far end of the room. "Nice here," Glenda said as she took a seat. "We have time."

We'd just cut class, which meant we had about an hour. I grabbed a novel from a shelf and began to flip through it. I usually read online but liked having the feel of a book in my hands. Glenda took one as well, and we began to read.

At least, she did. I soon grew lost in thought, and it was always about the past. Other kids who said that they remembered their parents as far back as two? Well, they had that special connection. I never had...

I used to wonder what my parents had in common. Perhaps my parents loved each other, because they stayed together until the day my father died from cancer—or so my mother told me. But after he'd passed, she rarely said more than ten words at a time.

She did, however, start with the old 'you-need-to-chip-in' speech when I was around five. That, and the similarly old 'you-owe-me' spiel. "Mark, I need you to help me out. We don't have much, so that means I have to go to work. Do you understand?"

What did I know? My mother looked so serious. As a little kid, I thought all adults told the truth, and so I nodded solemnly and told her that I'd try. That got a rare smile from her. "Good. If you understand that you owe me a little for doing for you, then that's all I can ask for."

My mother invariably left for work early. In the morning, she prepared my lunch and saw me off to school. When three-thirty rolled around, I walked home, and our neighbor, Mrs. Levine, watched over me until about six.

Mrs. Levine was a kind lady, short and stout, with a wheezy laugh. She always had a smile on her face, and she was good to me.

In the evening, after my mother came home, she and Mrs. Levine exchanged a few words then Mrs. Levine went home. Dinner was something fast and hot and good — then more homework waited. "Extra assignments," my mother had said.

In reality, they were chores in cooking, cleaning, paying bills and more. They were simple tasks, and my mother made a game of everything. It never occurred to me she was preparing me for a life without a parent.

Naturally, at first, I screwed up. What little kid wouldn't? If I did, she scolded me.

"Mark, you're not trying hard enough."

"Mark, I'm counting on you to think for yourself."

"Mark, can't you do this one simple thing?"

It was enough to give me a complex. As a little kid, I didn't know what a complex was, but all the same, I felt bad. I'd let my mother down, so I'd tried harder. Over time, the putdowns stopped, but my mother replaced them with the same 'you-owe-me' line.

Me owing her meant being on my own while she went on her work missions across the country.

Me owing her meant feeling grateful that she was doing so much for me.

Me owing her meant not questioning her commands.

Hindsight had to be the dumbest thing around. If I'd known about her plan, I'd have said something—but then again, to whom? No one was going to listen to a little kid.

After I turned eight, Mrs. Levine died, and my mother figured I was old enough to get along without a babysitter. Initially, it was frightening. I was scared of the dark and often had nightmares, waking up crying and in a cold sweat.

Of course, telling my mother was out of the question. At first, she came into my room, but she never comforted me, only said, "There's nothing here."

Then she went back to bed. Over time, I got over my fear, telling myself that the doors and windows were locked, there were no ghosts or monsters under the bed and that I was safe.

Call it a mental game, but that was the only way I could cope. I learned how to deal with life in other ways, too. Since my mother was away so often, if I fell and cut myself or if I had a fight, no one was there to pat my tears away or clean me up. I got used to dabbing on antiseptic and slapping on bandages by myself.

As I grew older, it all became clear to me. My mother wasn't running to something. She was running away from her responsibility to me, trading a relationship for money. It bothered me to think about it, so my thoughts turned in a different direction.

Then there was Glenda. While she never showed much in the way of emotion, there was a certain ineffable sadness about her. Perhaps she missed her old life out East. At our lockers one day, she'd asked me, *"Do you ever miss anything that you used to do?"*

Although I'd never spoken of my relationship with my mother, something in Glenda's demeanor had compelled me to answer. *"I don't talk much to my mother. She's always busy. You?"*

Glenda's mouth had twisted this way and that before she'd answered. *"I used to be able to walk around. I can't, not anymore."*

Call her answer cryptic — then there was…

"Hey," a voice said.

I looked up. Glenda stood in front of me and chuckled. "Mark, stay in this reality, okay?"

That was the first time she'd ever used my name. "Oh…yeah."

The book I'd taken was on the floor. Damn, I had been spacing out. After I picked it up and placed it on a nearby table, I glanced at the windows. They were dirty, and apparently, Glenda thought the same thing as she walked over to the window and said in a guttural tone, "Windows."

What? "Well, yeah, you look out of them. So what?"

"They have another purpose."

Oh, hell, she'd just gone there. This was whacked out, but a moment later, it suddenly stopped being wordplay. No, something else was going on, and I slowly got out of my chair.

"Uh, Glenda, you're not thinking of doing something crazy, are you?" Suicide was no way to solve a problem.

Her laugh sounded like the tinkling of chimes. "No. But I'm serious about windows having another purpose."

"Like what?"

My initial thought was to run to get the librarian. But that meant leaving Glenda, and I didn't think it was a good idea to just run off and find help.

Glenda expounded on her topic by pointing at the dirty glass. "Well, it's true that windows allow you to see out of them at the world before you, right?"

From the calm expression on her face, she was serious—and sane. "Yes? So what?"

"They can also provide a pathway to other worlds. Watch."

With a shake of her head, she tossed her hair back the way a movie starlet would toss her hair back to reveal her perfect profile. In that situation, it was only a pose and nothing more.

In Glenda's case, it served another purpose. Her hair went from reddish gray to green, a brilliant jade green, to be exact.

And in a lightning-fast display of genetic shifting, her eyes changed color to deep purple, her skin went from white to a jade green that matched her hair, her ears went Vulcan and silver sparkles appeared on her face and neck.

Oh, holy crap! Things like this only happened in the movies, but this was real time, and it was happening right in front of me. How she looked was one thing, but skin tone and color…that was something else. She then shifted into a more compact and womanlier five-three frame—and did she have six fingers instead of five?

Her clothes had also shifted, from everyday grunge to a brown, shapeless robe cinched in at the waist by a simple leather belt. Leather shoes with a little bell on the heel completed the look.

What in the hell? I looked at the door, just in case someone was coming in, but so far, no one. As for the librarian, she was still at the far end of the room, reshelving books.

I got up and pulled Glenda into a corner, away from any potential prying eyes. "You're staring," she said in the same voice as before. "Something different, right?"

Time stopped. My heart skipped a beat or three. And suddenly, everything fit together — Valerie flipping out and the person I'd seen disappearing in the ladies' room. "Uh...yeah. Are you what Valerie said she saw in the lady's washroom? You, um, transformed in front of her?"

"Yes. I used a spell to hide my true appearance. I didn't realize that my real form would freak someone out that much."

Is she serious? "Well, yeah, I mean, it's just... Don't take this the wrong way, but what are you, anyway?"

"We're called Tellkarians. You'd probably call us 'elves', but from reading your literature, elves are much shorter."

Uh, yeah...again. Maybe what she was saying was true but call this a total freakout moment for me. I didn't do drugs, so what was going on?

Glenda turned her attention to the wall and made a series of gestures while muttering something incomprehensible, and a window five feet across by three feet down appeared with no frame and two separate panes with a line down the middle. It didn't shimmer or move. It simply hung in the air a foot off the ground.

On the other side, blue grass and a forest with various flora waited. All it needed was the obligatory bunnies hopping around and maybe some cute, anthropomorphic butterflies.

No, no way! "Uh, what am I looking at?"

Glenda chuckled. It sounded like the tinkling of wind chimes. "What you're looking at is a forest on my world, Tellkar. It's prettier than a postcard, isn't it?"

"Yeah. Oh."

'Oh' was the only word I could really think of to sum up this situation. "And...what's the name of this world?"

"Tellkar. I just said so. The capital city is called Mattaca, and that's where I'm going. So, are you coming?"

Chapter Four

A Whole New World

There were times in a person's life when the words simply wouldn't come out. Up until that moment, I'd never experienced failure in saying anything.

Except for now. People didn't shape-shift, they didn't open portals and they didn't journey to other worlds.

There *were* no other worlds.

Or alternate universes.

Or dimensions, or any of the above.

Or were there?

Apparently so. Disbelief slowly gave way to acceptance, and with that acceptance came curiosity. What did her world really look like? Was it safe? Much as I wanted to follow her in, indecision made me stop.

Glenda uttered a soft grunt and pushed on the panes until they opened inward. She stepped halfway through but turned back to offer a friendly smile. "Listen… Think it over. I can't stay on Earth for a long time. I'll tell you why tomorrow. I'll come here at nine, and we'll talk. I promise. Deal?"

As if in a trance, I said, "Deal."

"Later."

Glenda stepped through the window. Transfixed by the sight, I watched as the window sealed itself up then disappeared in a burst of light. *Oh, holy crap.*

And what had I done? I'd turned down an offer to go somewhere that no one had ever seen. What was that saying about a window of opportunity opening and closing fast?

It had opened, and like a dumbass, I'd thrown away the chance to at least see what was on the other side.

Anguish hit. "Nick!"

Oh, hell, this was just too much. I ran to the door, tried opening it then realized that I'd locked it accidentally. *Crap!*

My hands fumbled with the lock, and I jerked it open, pushing my way past a few students who stared at me as though they'd seen a ghost.

Downstairs, I found Nick at his locker. As usual, he was sweating and patting his food case with a loving hand. He turned around at my request. "Yeah? What's wrong, Mark?"

"Come upstairs. Now!"

We went back to the library. Some students were there this time, deep in study mode, and I pulled Nick over to the spot where Glenda had vanished and pointed to it with a trembling arm. "There."

He looked at the spot then at me. "There…what?"

"Glenda's gone."

My best friend's face resembled vanilla pudding, bland and tasteless. "Oh, she went home. No problem. She's always running out on you, anyway, and—"

"Nick, shut up and listen, okay?"

A few of the students there glanced in our direction, so I lowered my voice and stabbed my finger at the vanishing point again. "She went through a window."

"Holy shit, she jumped?"

He seemed almost stoked at the prospect of someone offing themself. While I was trying to figure out how to explain things, Nick waddled over to the window, opened it and stood on tiptoes to crane his neck around.

Then he swung back to face me, and he looked disappointed at not seeing any roadkill. "Mark, I hate to break it to you, but no one's there."

It took everything I had in me not to scream, and I forced myself to stay calm. "Listen carefully," I whispered. "She didn't jump, Nick. She created a window and disappeared into it. Just like I told you the other day — it's all true. The green person, remember? That's who I saw. It was Glenda."

My best friend stared at me as though I'd been smoking something I should have stayed away from. Nick raised his chubby hands as if to send a wall of calm my way. It had the opposite effect. It pissed me off. "That's. Not. Helping."

A sympathetic look appeared in his eyes. "Mark, I know Glenda's sort of interesting and maybe you like her and that's cool, but she's not some kind of magician or anything, and —"

"I saw her do it!"

There it was. I was shouting, and more people turned around, so I yanked my best friend over to a quiet corner and promised myself not to freak out. *Take deep breaths. Think, speak calmly, stay frosty.*

Call this a mindbender of colossal proportions, and as unbelievable as it was, I just had to tell someone.

Perhaps Nick understood, or perhaps he thought that I was going to chuck him out of the window as his expression turned serious. With a wave of his hand, he indicated that I should start talking. "Mark, tell me everything."

So…I did. To his credit, Nick didn't laugh or make fun of my story. He listened, his mouth open, body unmoving, and he didn't say a word until I finished speaking. Finally, he blew out a deep breath and whispered, "So…she turned into an elf?"

Fantasy wasn't exactly my specialty—neither were fantastic creatures and where to find them. "Or something. I don't know what she is. I'm calling her an elf, even though she's taller. She said that she couldn't stay on Earth for very long."

A spark appeared in Nick's eyes, and a note of wonder coated his next words. "Maybe that's why she never hung around—atomic structural differences, incompatibility with our world, vibratory signatures… Man, this is something."

Vibratory signatures? Whatever. "You believe me?"

His expression read honest all the way. "If I can see it, yeah, I'll believe it. You're my best friend, Mark. You've never come up with anything this loony before. I mean, when you first told me, I thought you were joking, but you're not, are you?"

"No, I'm not."

He chewed on his lower lip before replying. "Okay, I believe you. Why not?"

Yeah, why not?

What else could we do except go back to class? That's what we did until noon, when an announcement came over the PA system saying that the school would be closing for maintenance purposes.

With nothing better to do, Nick and I walked home together. It usually took about twenty minutes, but since there was no pressing need to get back, we took our time. I was still freaked out about what I'd seen and needed time to process it all.

By the time we got home, it was just about twelve-thirty. We agreed that he could meet Glenda tomorrow to see her in her true form — that was, if she showed up and if she gave her permission.

"Cool, man," he said. "Later."

He moved on out to his house that lay on a double lot at the end of the block. As I watched him go, a case of the envies hit. His place was large and ultra-modern, with all the latest gadgets. If there was such a thing as a privileged upbringing, Nick was the poster child for it, but he never lorded his social status over anyone.

In contrast, my place had old furniture, cracks in the walls, a threadbare carpet, creaky stairs and was in a general state of disrepair.

I'd learned how to do home fix-'em-up jobs, mainly by reading books as a little kid and going online to watch how-to videos when I was older.

But no matter what I did, the sink still dribbled water when I turned it off, the floorboards creaked and there were drafts in the winter. Still, it was the only home I'd ever known, and it was my anchor to everything, even though my mother never thought about getting someone in to fix things up right.

It was all about saving money. I couldn't blame her, but other kids had parents to talk to. Me, I talked to my furniture.

"Hello," I said as I walked in. Naturally, silence greeted me — and how pathetic was that?

After I fixed myself a sandwich and cleaned up the place, I flopped on the couch and tried to reconcile what I'd seen. It was too amazing, too fantastic…but why had Glenda suddenly revealed herself to me?

Tomorrow… I'd ask her tomorrow.

If she came.

* * * *

School. Eight-fifty-eight a.m. the next day.

"You think she'll show?" Nick asked as we waited for the doors to open. The other students milled around in their groups, while my best friend and I stood a distance away. Crowds had never been my thing.

I'd been wondering that myself, but then a little voice in the back of my head told me to turn around. I did, and sure enough, Glenda strode up to us. "Hi," she said in the flattest of all voices. "Doors not open?"

"Not yet," I replied cautiously. "Uh, how are you?"

Her face didn't betray any expression, but her eyes were full of curiosity. "Fine. Why?"

"No reason…"

As luck would have it, the doors opened, we got our books then we went off to class. Things went smoothly until noon, when the powers-that-were told us that the day was over. Go home. Enjoy life. Have fun.

I couldn't do anything without wondering what would happen next, but Glenda met me at my locker and pointed up. "Library," she whispered.

Message received. Up we went, but instead of taking me to the library, she poked her head into the ladies' room then pulled me inside. "We have a little time," she said.

Once there, she leaned against the wall. "Yesterday, I promised to show you how I did things, and now, I'll show you again."

I put up my hand to stop her. "Before you do, tell me why you decided to show me and that I'm not crazy."

Glenda giggled. "Second part first—you're not crazy. First part—because I like you. Most of the other students here treat me like garbage. You never did."

Explanation provided, she got up, sauntered over to the center of the room and she transformed into the elf-like creature I'd seen yesterday. Then she did the same form-a-rectangle gesture as before, complete with the incantation.

In half a minute, a part in the air occurred and a window formed. It seemed tangible enough, although it shimmered. Glenda grunted and repeated the incantation, and this time, the window took on a more solid form.

A split appeared in the window, and the panes went inward to reveal the same green-and-blue tableau as I'd seen yesterday. The smells of what lay on the other side were real. Warm air drifted over. "This is… This is totally cool."

My guide to the other side walked over to it, turning back to extend her arm, then she tapped an imaginary watch on her wrist.

Is she serious? "What? Go with you? Now?"

Glenda placed her hands on her hips in the manner of a drill instructor. "Look… I made you an offer yesterday. I meant every word, so either you come along, or you stay here and lead a dull, uneventful life. Which is it to be?"

I'd wussed out yesterday. Not today. Don't let the window of opportunity go. "Let's motor."

In we stepped to the other side. As we passed through, I thought I heard Nick call my name. Too late now. My adventure had just begun.

Chapter Five

Welcome to Tellkar

For a second — which seemed more like an eternity — I didn't move. A smell not unlike cedar drifted over me. If this was an illusion, it was the best I'd ever seen, but then reason took over. Holograms didn't emit smells. Holograms were unreal. This was real.

Glenda asked softly, "Do you like what you see?"

I was too amazed at first to answer, then I pulled the words out. "Uh, yeah. Like I said, it's cool. I mean...this is...your world," I said, looking around, not actually believing I was here, not at first, anyway.

"Welcome to Tellkar and my home city of Mattaca."

The greenery of the trees, a rich and vibrant jade that matched my guide's skin, faced me, as did calf-high blue grass. A brook of red water babbled away five feet to my left, and trees, tall and thick-trunked with wide-spreading green branches and mushroom-shaped leaves gave the area shade.

As for the air, the cedar smell was stronger now, but all the same, that, along with a general sweetness in the air, calmed me down. "Wow, this is...amazing."

Glenda wore a warm smile. "Glad you think so. Just get used to the fact that this isn't Earth anymore. My world is more countryside and agrarian than anything. We can't stay long, but I wanted to show you that I was telling you the truth."

Oh, she'd told me, but at that time I hadn't listened to her talk about alternate realities and other worlds and beings and now I was here and what was she saying?

"We can't stay long," she repeated as she took my hand and guided me along a path at the edge of the forest. "My, uh, presence here isn't welcome — and the king won't like me returning. Not like this, anyway."

"King?"

"I'll explain."

Glenda led me down a well-worn path through the forest until we reached a small hut. Small and circular, made of wood, it had a thatched roof, and a smell of something akin to chocolate drifted out.

Numerous huts dotted the landscape like mushrooms that had sprouted among the trees. A few people were out front of their abodes, either picking at the grass or taking what looked like fruit from the bushes.

Upon closer examination, they were the same size and color as Glenda, and I wondered how everyone could tell each other apart, but that could wait for another time. When they saw us, they blanched and ran inside their houses.

"That was rude," I observed. "I guess you don't get many aliens here."

Glenda shrugged. "It wasn't only for you. It's mainly me. This is a farming community, and farmers keep to themselves."

"They're sort of like that on Earth, too."

At the front of the door, Glenda checked the surroundings, but the neighbors didn't reappear.

"I never talk to the people around here," she said as she continued to check out the immediate area. "They don't trust me, and yes, I'll explain that, too."

My guide opened the door and waved me in. "Visitors first," she said. "It's a custom. Oh, and take off your shoes, please."

Uh-huh. On my world, in any suspense or horror movie I'd seen, if someone went first and walked into an unfamiliar house or room, they were asking to get their head blown off.

Still, I'd come this far, so I went in, taking off my shoes as I did so. A small room colored entirely in green greeted me, with a jade-green rug, green wooden tables and leaf-green curtains that shut out the sunlight.

At the far end lay what looked to be a kitchen, although I didn't see anything electrical in nature, such as a fridge or a microwave oven.

As if reading my mind, Glenda said, "Our houses have fireplaces, and that's how we heat them in the winter. Our summer here is longer, maybe eight months. We're about halfway through it. Autumn lasts about a month."

While I digested those words, she continued to lay out the details, gesturing to the various objects when necessary. "We have kitchens, although we cook over fires. Our water comes from a freshwater supply near here. We don't refrigerate food. If we don't cook, we go to town to have a meal. If we don't do that, then we pick berries from nearby bushes and go to communal fields to find vegetables."

Well, that answered a few questions, but then the carpet moved, which raised even more. A pair of tiny ten-fingered hands reached up and cradled my running shoes. "Unusual material," the carpet said in a high-pitched voice. It sounded like a boy on the verge of puberty, and I froze.

"Uh, Glenda, this carpet is alive," I said, lowering my voice to a whisper.

"Of course he's alive," she said as she took off her shoes. "By the way, he can hear you."

More hands came out to cradle her shoes, then the carpet formed a boot tray that held our footwear a few inches off the ground. "His name is Fennimur, and he's in charge of the shoes."

"Nice to meet you," the carpet called Fennimur said. "What is your name?"

Talk about weird! Half in shock, I answered, "Mark?"

"You are sure?"

Okay, the rating on my Weird-O-Meter scale just shot past fifteen. It had been a solid ten coming here, but now I was talking to a friggin' carpet. "Yeah... Mark."

Glenda chimed in. "He is our guest, Fennimur. Now, hush, and let us talk."

"I am sorry. You have so few guests. I get lonely."

She reached down to pat the carpet. "I know. I apologize for my absences. But we are here now, and I must talk to my guest."

The hands withdrew and the carpet lay quiet. I looked around and pitched my voice low, just in case. "Is anything else alive in this place?"

For that, I got a brilliant smile from my guide. "Just us."

She led me to the beanbags and sat. It automatically adjusted itself to fit her body proportions. I did the same, and the bag seemed to caress me.

Weird—it was like getting a massage—and not. I half-expected the bag to speak to me, and sure enough, it did, in a motherly voice. "You're heavy."

"I'll go on a diet," I answered immediately, then I felt ridiculous for having answered a supposedly inanimate object. Then again, I'd just spoken to a carpet, and I prepared myself for more oddities.

Glenda laughed. "I forgot about the bags. I usually talk to Fennimur. He's a good sort. Anyway, like I said before, we don't have much time, but I'll tell you what I know. This is my parents' house, but they're dead, and now it's just me."

"I see."

No, I didn't, but all the same, I was here, and I couldn't get back to Earth without her help. "First off, my name isn't Glenda. It's Glynarra."

Glynarra. It came out Glee-na-ra, with the middle syllable slightly accented. "Our people have only one name. My father's name was Listral, and my mother's name was Astora."

"Okay. Uh, how is it that I can understand you and your, uh, carpet and beanbag friends?"

A gentle shake of her head told me that she wasn't sure. "I don't know, exactly. I think it has to do with the portal itself. Once you pass through, your mind becomes attuned to that of the world you're entering. That's all I know.

"When I first visited Earth a couple of months back, I landed in Portland by chance. I walked around and listened to your language. Understanding and using it are two different things, so I guess I made some mistakes at first."

"You're doing okay," I answered.

For that reply, I got a smile. "I had to blend in, so I assumed the shapes of various people, learned some of your customs by watching television and listening to others and I went to your school to meet people my age."

"How did you get your name?"

"From someone I met. My last name, I just made up. Anyway, I wanted to learn, and our people have the ability to process information very quickly. That's how I knew what to write on your tests."

And all this time I'd killed myself cramming for exams. If only I had her ability, school would be a snap, but then again, I was a long way from the halls of higher education.

Glynarra went on to explain that while there were multiple kingdoms on this world, two stood out. "The first is this one, the capital city of Mattaca in the kingdom of Worthington. The second is about a day from here on foot, although it's much faster if I open a portal. The kingdom is called Kott."

And, as it turned out, Kott and Worthington didn't like each other very much, even though they lived relatively close together.

"Both kingdoms are the most powerful on this world in terms of the magic they wield, as well as their armies," she said. "The other smaller kingdoms mind their own business and side with no one."

She shook her head in apparent dismay. "We're the same people. We have the same appearance, almost all of us are shape shifters and have various abilities, but there's one thing that Kott doesn't have."

"Uh, money?" I asked, trying to be helpful.

"No. On our world, we barter for things. If we have a meal, we give something back, usually spices or herbs to help the tavern owner. If we need clothes, then we give back what the tailor needs, such as needles or cloth or buttons."

Now I had to try again. "Okay, power or position?"

"Getting warmer," she said with an impish smile. "Here...let me give you a hint."

She mimed drawing a window, putting her hands up and together, then drawing a rectangular box in the air and opening it. What was she talking about? Oh, wait, Captain Obvious to the rescue.

"You're the only one who can open windows to other worlds?"

Glynarra's smile grew broader. "Hey, you catch on fast. And, yes, that's true, but there are others with great abilities, although no one has the same kind of ability that I have."

Jeez, I had so many questions. "So, let me guess. The kingdom of Kott wants you for your powers?"

There, riddle solved. Game over. All I had to do was a happy dance...then Glynarra's face fell, and she leaned over to rest her elbows on her knees and cup her chin in her hands. "No, *my* kingdom does," she whispered.

More history followed. Magic — what I thought of as magic and what she referred to as ability — abounded in this realm.

"But for convenience's sake, let's go with magic," Glynarra said in the manner of a professor imparting wisdom to a group of first-year students. "Those are the terms that you can best understand. There's ambient magic in inanimate objects — the carpet we talked to — and magic in the forests."

That included the trees, the grass, the insects — anything that lived and breathed in carbon dioxide and breathed out oxygen or vice-versa had their own particular brand of magic.

Glynarra's expression turned thoughtful. "My parents said that the magic was from the collective souls of our ancestors. We were and are connected to this world, and it to us. That's all I know, whether it's true or not. But you've seen that things here have a life of their own."

Yes, I'd most definitely seen that. Glynarra continued, her voice gone serious. "When it comes to people though, magic is one thing, but it's the innate ability of people to harness that power that's where we're all different.

"Our shape-shifting powers start when we're around three. Some can't shift at all or tap into the magic here. They have no powers. They're called 'lessers'."

Abilities also ran the gamut from A to Z. Some had the ability to heal, others had great strength or intellect or control over the elements, but very few people existed who could open windows.

At that point, Glynarra got up to do a series of graceful stretches. "Sorry... I'm a little stiff," she said while twisting her torso this way and that. "I need to stretch out. Anyway, like I said, we all have different abilities."

She shifted her position to doing a series of lunges and spoke between reps. "I'm the only one who can do what I can do."

Everything became clear…sort of. "Okay, why does your kingdom want to stop you from, uh, going anywhere?"

Her face set like cement and she blew out a deep breath. "It's all about control. King Lensa rules Worthington. His parents died last year, and he inherited the kingdom. He's greedy and powerful, and if he could, he'd rule all the other kingdoms. He doesn't want his people running off to any old world. If they did, then there'd be no one to farm his fields, take care of his stables and serve in his army. He employs only people who have no abilities."

"So, they're like slaves?"

A glower broke the cement. "Yes…slaves."

Things were starting to make sense, but why had she brought me along? I wasn't a knight of the realm. I had nothing to offer, except moral support. "I get it. But…but what can I do?"

In response to that question, she spread her hands wide in the classic I-don't-know gesture. "Confession time—I got lonely. You seem nice. I know you don't have any abilities, so I guess you can go back to your world, if you want."

Loneliness was something that I knew all too well. And she'd asked me to come. Maybe she liked me after all…

"Me, I have to handle Lensa," she was saying. "He killed my parents because they wouldn't allow me to transfer my powers to him. I didn't want that, either."

"Transfer?"

According to Glynarra, it involved a process of using a spell to literally wrench the power from individual A to individual B. The giver always ended up dead.

"Only one person has the transfer ability."

"Lensa?"

She began to pace back and forth. "Yes and no. It's his magicians who make that possible. He's an empty vessel. It was said that before he took power, he displayed only shape-shifting abilities. Others say that he consulted those who practiced the dark arts — you'd call it black magic — and honed his innate powers that made it possible for him to absorb powers from others. I honestly can't say."

Glynarra stopped pacing. "So, that's my story, and now you know the basics. The neighbors don't talk to me because they're afraid that if I associate with them, Lensa will find out. They're afraid of what he could do to them. Fear rules them, and I'm taking a chance that they might inform Lensa or one of his men that I've come back."

"Informers," I muttered.

She picked up on it. "Yes, we have informers here, too — people I've known since I was a child."

Glynarra went on to say that while the vast majority of people here were law-abiding and decent, Lensa's soldiers patrolled everywhere. Informers were everywhere. If the authorities couldn't catch her outside her home, they'd try elsewhere. They'd almost caught her on more than one occasion.

Bitterness coated every word. "So, now you know about the magic here. I brought you here to show you I wasn't joking about who and what I am. But there's also danger." Glynarra began to weave her arms in a window-creating gesture. "I'll send you back. It's too dangerous here for you."

Danger or not, I couldn't abandon a friend. And, admittedly, I was attracted to her, so I put my hand on her elbow to stop her. "I think I'd like to stay a while."

She turned to me, her expression hopeful. "Are you sure?"

I didn't have to think twice about it. After all, if I went back, I'd be reduced to living alone — as usual — doing stuff on my own and wondering 'what if'.

Oh, and I'd have to listen to my mother telling me that I owed her. No, this option was way better than simply riding out my time on Earth. "I'm sure."

A smile broke out on her elfin face. "Then you'll need a disguise. Hold still."

She turned to face me, muttered something in a language unknown then stepped back. "There. Now, you look like us."

That was fast. I'd expected a shifting of my atomic structure, pain, disorientation… But no. Nothing. The whole thing had taken only a few seconds, assuming Glynarra was telling the truth.

"Only I know your real appearance," she said. "My magic, my knowledge. Call it a simple spell of disguise. It'll last for a few hours."

She took my hand and guided me to the far part of the room where a full-length mirror was. I gasped. "I, uh, look like you."

The mirror revealed all. I now had jade-green skin and hair, gold sparkles instead of silver, and a lithe but muscular physique clad in the same shapeless brown robe. In short, I passed for a native.

"And you're quite good looking for a Tellkarian," she replied with a grin.

Since I had no frame of reference, I took it as a compliment. I decided to take a chance and asked, "Do you prefer me in this form or my human form?"

A faint bluish hue came to her cheeks, perhaps her version of blushing. "You're nice-looking either way. Anyway, we should get out of here. We need to walk while I recharge."

"Recharge?"

She pointed to the door. "My abilities are finite. Same with everyone else. Outside of using magic or our abilities, we all need food and rest. Right now, I need to get my mind ready, and I need to eat."

That made sense. "All right. Where to?"

"Just a moment."

Glynarra ran to the kitchen, checked in a cupboard, and took three small squares of something and tucked them into her robe. "Sorry," she said as she returned to my side. "I had to get something first."

I decided not to ask. We collected our shoes, our carpet friend said goodbye and offered us his best wishes then we went on our way. In keeping with the illusion, my shoes shifted to the same style Glynarra wore. As we exited, she closed the door but left it unlocked, so I asked her about it.

"Protected by a spell," she said. "My parents had that ability. Even though they're dead, their magic still protects my house. That's why I've never been attacked there, and why I stay there when I come back from Earth. Not even the king would try to force his way in. And I'm the only one who knows how to remove the spell."

"I, uh, don't suppose your magic will protect us outside," I said, hoping for the best.

"No. We'll have to be careful. That's why I use disguises."

So much for the protection of ambient magic. Our path took us through the forest, and while walking, I asked Glynarra if people shape-shifted often.

"No," she replied as she stopped at a bush to pick some leaves. Murmuring, "There, that should do it," she stowed them inside her robe. "We don't shape-shift unless there's a reason, like hiding, like what we're doing now."

Now, I knew. We continued walking, and ten minutes later, we ended up on a road that led into a city filled with one and two-story wooden buildings. It reminded me of pictures that I'd seen of early industrial revolution Great Britain, minus the steam engines and pollution.

Quaint-looking stores advertising robes and other simple goods dominated the area. Chief among the shops were taverns — The Duck Inn, The Food Shop and The Sated Stomach, among others.

Lamp posts dotted the cobblestone avenues, and creatures like horses — if horses had tusks, stood ten feet high and had eight legs — drew simple open-air carriages along the streets.

Pedestrians strolled along, all wearing the same shapeless type of robe. I wondered why no one recognized Glynarra, and, as if reading my mind once more, she whispered that she'd also altered her appearance.

"You see me as I really am, but for everyone else, they see someone much older. No one will know."

She still stole quick looks at the passersby, as if trying to detect who was an informer and who wasn't. While she was conducting her search-and-find mission,

I asked a more pertinent question. "Why can't you use your window powers to take us to Kott or somewhere else?"

Glynarra's answer came quickly. "First off, I can't open a portal to just anywhere. I can open a window near a location, within a couple of miles, but getting exactly to the place I want to go?" She shook her head. "I'm not that good, yet. Second, when I open a window, Lensa will know. He has someone who aids him, a person called a 'vertok'. You'd call it a seer. It's only one person, but he'll know when I open a window, and they'll track me down.

"Every time I leave here, and every time I come back, I'm taking a chance, like, right now. The thing is, they can't detect me right away, and it takes them time to travel to my location. No one here can fly, and some people like the vertok can only teleport for short distances. Teleport is the correct term, isn't it?"

"Yes."

She nodded. "Now you know why I'm always on the move."

"What about soldiers or civilians?"

Her eyebrows arched. "You mean informers or spies? Like I said, there are plenty. When the soldiers arrive, that means we've been found out, but I don't trust others. I never use my name, and I always change my appearance when I go outside."

Spy time—mum was the word. After a few more minutes of walking, with Glynarra still checking for spies and me taking in the clean smells of the city, we arrived outside a small, one-story wooden building.

It was another tavern. A wooden sign hung above the doorway, something straight out of Shakespearean England—The Bent Nose Tavern.

"Is this the place?" I asked.

Glynarra nodded and blanched. "Yes, and…oh no."

"What?"

She pointed to a group of eight soldiers harassing a young woman, poking at her shoulders and yelling at her. In a quick move, Glynarra grabbed my arm and pulled me around to the side of the tavern. There, she muttered something.

"What did you do?" I asked.

"Used another spell to make you look older."

I looked in a window, and now I had grayish green hair and a withered face. "It's temporary," Glynarra said as she leaned against me. "Sorry… Even that spell takes a lot out of me. It'll last just long enough until we go inside."

Sounds of angry male voices drifted over. "So, you say you do not know Glynarra?"

"I do not," the young woman, who couldn't have been more than sixteen, squeaked. "My name is Dianatta. Please, allow me to go on my way."

Formal speaking—the people here used few contractions. I wondered why, then I decided that it was a different culture and that was all there was to it.

A crowd stopped to watch the goings-on, but no one made a move. Fear permeated the air, and most likely, the people in the crowd didn't want to be on the king's hit-list.

The soldier shoved the girl hard, sending her sprawling. "Leave."

He then turned to his men. "Keep looking."

In unison, his men turned and marched away. The girl picked herself up, brushed her robe off and ran away, wiping her eyes as she went. Soon after, the crowd dispersed. No one bothered going after the girl to offer a kind word.

Glynarra breathed a sigh of relief. "They're gone."

"They were, uh, Lensa's men?"

"Yes. That's how it's been here the past year or so. Hurry, let's go inside."

Glynarra glanced around nervously, but the soldiers didn't return, and only the pedestrians and those strange horses clip-clopping their way along the cobblestones broke the silence. Still, no one gave us a second look. "I think we're okay for now," I said.

Glynarra wasn't reassured. "All the same, say nothing. We'll sit and eat, then I'll talk to a contact of mine."

Well, in every person's life, they had to act at least once. This was my time to shine, and I intended to give an Oscar-worthy performance.

Chapter Six

The Way Ahead

Inside, the décor seemed to have come straight out of a British movie from the late nineteen-thirties. A low-ceilinged wooden affair, it had candle-powered lamps strategically placed to throw light in the center of the room, but it also left the corners dark and shadowy. Privacy was clearly valued here.

Patrons sat in their booths, ate, drank and often put their foreheads against each other's, as if to impart the secrets of the universe. If they were worried about the king's men listening in, no one could fault their way of keeping things quiet.

While the décor was quaint enough, the odors must have come from a considerably older time. A heavy, nose-hair-wilting smell hung in the air, an odoriferous combo of unwashed bodies, food and wine.

And why did Glynarra want to meet her contact here? I figured that an open space such as the forest would be better, but it was her world, not mine.

Speaking of contacts, a quick head count netted me ten patrons, all of them with similar features. Once again, I wondered how everyone could tell A from B, but they had to know. Either it was the markings around their necks or else it was their voices—something.

Nothing much seemed to be happening. From what I heard, the patrons were discussing the weather and various happenings, so unless they were using code, I never heard any sales talk. Quiet was the mood. No one raised their voice above a low murmur.

Another sniff of the air revealed a smell, something heavy and redolent, that stood out from the usual odoriferous emanations of people when they drank too much. Rude though it was, I felt compelled to ask, "Is the smell here from the food or the people?"

I pitched my voice low once we found a table in an empty corner. As soon as the words came out of my mouth, I regretted speaking so quickly. Glynarra gave me a look that spoke of amusement coupled with anger.

Then she shrugged and her look of anger faded, as though it wasn't important enough to get mad over. "I suppose you're right. We usually don't have what you call body odor. You don't smell, do you?"

I took a quick sniff of my body. A little sweaty, but nothing horrid—yet. "No. Sorry for asking."

"That's okay. Our species usually doesn't suffer from body odor, but certain kinds of food cause us to stink. If they're eating what I think they're eating, then that's what's causing this smell."

Curiouser and curiouser. "Uh, and what is it? I'm human, remember? Is it safe?"

Glynarra shushed me as another male Tellkarian walked over with a wooden tablet in hand. He was somewhat taller than the average native, and wider, too, almost my height, and thicker in the chest and shoulders.

He asked us in a deep voice, "What is your order?"

"Two tankards of blett and an order of notsaku," Glynarra replied.

Our server noted our order on his tablet with a sharpened fingernail then walked away. Once he was out of earshot, she murmured, "That's a lesser."

"A what?"

She tossed me a glance as if to say *don't you remember?* "I told you before. They're people with no powers. They're usually larger than the rest of us, and the king uses them as slaves, farm workers and soldiers. They're bigger, so that's their function in our society, and no, I don't care for it."

News flash—apparently this world had its own form of discrimination. Still, I said nothing. Earth was still too messed up, so it wasn't right to hurl any accusations.

I had another question, though. "Uh, I hate to ask, but what did you just order?"

My question earned me a chuckle. "Blett is like ginger beer on your world, and notsaku is like a fried pork cutlet. The thing is, our worlds have similar tastes. Not only that, magical powers or not, I found out that our bodily systems are almost identical. A check on your internet showed me the internal layout of the human body. Pretty cool, really."

I didn't have time to think too deeply about it as our server walked over carrying two large tankards of our drinks in his hands while balancing an enormous plate of meat on his head. He set the drinks down then reached up to pull the plate off and gently lower it to the table.

Glynarra had already reached into her robe to bring out the leaves she'd picked. "This should be enough," she replied. "In exchange for the meal."

Leaves? We were having a meal and she was paying with leaves? Then I remembered that they didn't use money here.

Our server took the leaves to examine them. Small and pointed, with black and gold spots, they gave off an enticing honey-like fragrance. After he sniffed them, he nodded in appreciation.

"Yes, these will do nicely. Thank you, patron."

Someone else called for service, so our waiter bobbed his head again and politely excused himself. Glynarra pushed a tankard at me. "Drink up."

I put the tankard to my lips and cautiously took a sip. The blett had a slight bite to it, like ginger ale, but it also had the deeper, richer taste that ginger beer possessed.

My throat craved more, so I drained every drop, put the tankard down, thought of ordering another, but I decided not to be greedy. "Good."

Glynarra offered a shy smile. "Glad you liked it. You're my first human."

"'Scuse me?" I wiped my mouth and wondered what she was getting at.

"I mean, the first human I've ever really spoken to."

Oh, that. "And what do you think of humans?"

She cast a look around the tavern, but no one seemed to be interested in two ordinary elves talking. Scoping-out job over, she switched her gaze to me.

"When I arrived in Portland, I had to acclimate myself as fast as possible. The computers you use—we don't have such things here—were easy enough to figure out, once I saw someone use one. And, in my case, a little magic can change anything."

Magic? Change? Oh, wait. "You mean, you altered the school records?"

"It was easy," she replied with a smile. "My magic works on other worlds, too—not always as well, but it works. You see, it's all about using ambient energy. Every world has some kind, and on Earth, I found that I could attune myself to its rhythms.

"Anyway, a simple spell of alteration did what I wanted. Voilà, I was Glenda, from a high-toned private school in upstate New York. Ithaca, I think you call it. No one asked any questions."

Speaking of alterations, were we still in disguise? I whispered the question to her, and she replied in a low voice. "You are. I'm back to my default self. That way, my contact can recognize me."

"Cool."

Her story continued. On Earth, she had learned English quickly. Learning bits and pieces of our culture had taken longer, then she'd decided to hide out with people her age. Hiding out... "Uh, where did you stay?"

"Sometimes in hotels," she said. "I can change my form, remember? I simply followed people into hotels where they stayed, and when they went out, I copied their forms and took their place in their rooms. I can even sound like them, if necessary. I can also copy a person's powers if they have any, but that doesn't last long."

Glynarra went on to say that if she couldn't use a hotel, she used alleyways and abandoned buildings. Her clothes were castoffs that she found in an alley.

Changes in temperature didn't bother her as much as they did humans.

All right, so far, so good, but what about the shapeshifting? "Uh, how long can you look like someone else?"

Her answer came promptly. "About an hour at most. After that, I need rest, so I shift to my default self."

She excused herself to dig into the notsaku, slicing it up with a serrated knife and a long, extremely thin two-pronged fork that the server had brought over.

"Delicious," she said between bites. Slice—eat—slice—eat. Her meal went rapidly down her throat. "Not hungry?"

"Uh, not really, no."

Similarities in internal organ arrangement or not, if there was something in the food that didn't agree with me, winding up in a hospital wasn't on the menu. To keep the conversation going, I asked, "Um, so what do you think about humans?"

Glynarra chewed thoughtfully on a piece of meat and swallowed it. Then she put her knife and fork down and spoke in a frank manner.

"Well, I don't know everything. But from what I saw, you have a lot of problems—racial differences, religious differences, money difficulties...more than we do. We're all one race. We don't have religion, so that helps. We do invoke certain names when we cast spells, but those names are from people who originally cast those spells long ago."

A short laugh came from her. "Maybe I shouldn't judge. We're not perfect, either. We have our lessers here, and while they're not discriminated against, per se, they often end up doing menial jobs. Oh, and I'm on the run from Lensa, our wonderful king."

She practically spat out the last few words, but again, considering he'd killed her parents, no wonder she felt bitter…

"Hello, Glynarra, are you well?"

A voice to our right spoke up. I looked around and found a tiny and extremely obese version of us waddling over. He spread his arms wide in a friendly manner and greeted her with a loud and hearty, "Glynarra, how are you?"

In a swift move, her hand shot to grab him around his throat and place him on a chair. He was barely three feet in height, and she lifted him with ease. "Handlee, what did I tell you about using my name?"

He let out a strangled squeal. "Glynarra…sorry… This is a safe place. Trust me."

A few people looked our way, but just as quickly, they went back to their meals and private dealings.

"Trust you," she echoed. "You would barter your mother for a year's supply of villata."

He gurgled, "Only a half-year."

Villata meant nothing to me, but I'd already figured out that this Handlee guy wasn't trustworthy. With a throat clearing sound that indicated disgust, she let go of him. He sat back, rubbing the damaged area. "Still the angry girl? You need my help and my information."

"Yes, I do. But that does not mean yelling my name out in public. Understand?"

He bobbed his head. "Yes."

The waiter came over and took the fat little man's order. He ordered something called *mabutak*. Even the name sounded gross. We sat in silence until the order came, with me fidgeting and Glynarra fuming. Her clenched fists indicated major anger.

When the dwarf's order came, it wasn't anything I wanted to try. Mabutak was a charred brown mess in the shape of a meatloaf, but it had a noxious smell, like a potent and horribly pungent mix of rotten eggs and wood alcohol.

"Ah, this is a treat," Handlee said while sniffing the mess and licking it as well. "Hunting this animal is difficult enough, but when it is prepared well, it is heavenly."

I hoped that the animal had taken a few of its hunters with it before expiring. Handlee and his attitude turned me off, as did his manners.

Speaking of which, they were disgusting. Licking the food was bad enough, but then the little elf-man picked up the mass of meat with both hands and shoveled it in—all of it—and the juices of the roasted beast squirted out the sides of his mouth. He chomped and chewed and swallowed, and once done, he offered up a massive burp.

Immediately, a stink came from him. That was what I'd smelled when I'd first walked in here, and now I knew what caused it.

"Everything is ready," Handlee said, patting his belly after emitting another enormous belch. "Two bearers from Kott will meet you and escort you in safety to their kingdom. I have already sent word to the king there that you will visit him."

He beamed as though he'd just concluded the business deal of the century. Glynarra didn't appreciate his good humor, as she snapped, "Meeting point."

"The Bridge of Dying Sighs. Tomorrow morning. Early, before daybreak."

"Names of the handlers."

Handlee wiped his mouth by using his robe. "Morhoon and Wisster. You will know them by their markings. Stars around their necks in a V-pattern instead of blotches or sparkles. They are twins."

So that's how they knew each other. Interesting. Glynarra took in the information and nodded. "Thank you. We will leave, now."

We got up, but Handlee stopped us by saying, "Are you not forgetting something?"

Notably, he didn't use her name or ask me for mine. In fact, he didn't even bother looking at me. He was only concerned about getting paid.

Glynarra gave him a mean look. "You are talking about compensation, yes?"

"Yes. I will take a bag of fretish, and—"

Now, a savage grin emerged. "You will get the fretish once I get to safety in Kott. I have heard that you have often sold others out. I asked around. You are always after a better deal."

"But—"

"Do you not trust me?" Her voice was full of sarcasm.

Handlee looked as though he was about to cry. "You promised!"

Our server walked over, and Glynarra fished around in her pocket, this time bringing out the three squares that she'd swiped from her kitchen. They looked like chocolate but what they tasted like was anyone's guess.

"This is for my friend's meal," she said after handing them over and indicating the chubby little intermediary with a nod of her head.

"Acceptable, patron," the server said. "Our thanks."

Glynarra then nailed Handlee, who was quietly swearing, with a look that caused him to shut his mouth. "I just paid for your meal. Consider us even."

We left then, and my guide around this new world led the way, curtly stating that we had to leave the town and go through a forest. A few people stared at us as we walked by, but I didn't make eye contact. Glynarra stared straight ahead. Neither of us spoke, and while the sun overhead was hot, I didn't sweat much.

My guide's mood, though, had turned foul, and she kept up a constant muttering, mainly a series of expletives, comparing Handlee to a certain part of a person's anatomy, one that looked like a mouth but wasn't.

Finally, we left the confines of the town and entered the cooler climes of the forest. As we tramped along, her muttering reached a crescendo until she exploded with, "That little pig!"

"Handlee?"

She halted to do an angry dance, stomping her feet and waving her arms around wildly. "Who else? I heard that he had a good rep as an intermediary, so I contacted him, but what does he do? He says my name. And you know how popular I am among the people here. There are spies everywhere, and I'm sure that Lensa would love to capture me in any way possible."

A grunt like a wounded animal came from the pit of her stomach to paint the air. "In this realm, keeping silent is a virtue. All he is, is vice."

Handlee didn't seem like the type to be that decent. Opportunistic seemed to be the best way to describe him. "Then why use him?"

Glynarra offered a sigh of resignation and motioned for us to continue walking. "He knows people," she said after a fashion. "That's how it works here. You never go to the main person directly unless it's an emergency. It's always done through an intermediary, and Handlee is that intermediary."

That sort of explained why she didn't open a portal in or near the kingdom of Kott. Perhaps it was all about the introductions, but all the same, this situation was getting weirder and weirder.

I did have a question, though. "Why can't you go somewhere else? I mean, I know this is your world, but if this King Lensa guy is after you, then, I don't know…leave?"

Glynarra rubbed her chin, musing over my words. "It's not that easy," she said. "This is my world, yes. I want to stay here, and I swore to avenge my parents. But I can't go to Lensa and challenge him. He has a magical barrier around his castle, so I can't simply walk in there. That's one thing. The second thing is, even if I decided to move to another world, I'm not sure it would be habitable or friendly."

Oh. "You, uh, can't do a pre-search or anything like that?"

She grunted out her reply. "When I cast a spell to find a world, it's like you typing in a search for, say, 'action movies' on your internet system. A lot of sites will come up, right?"

"Right."

"So, when I input my command to open a window, it's like a generalized search. If I've been to that place before, then I keep the incantation in my head, like you'd save a file. Are you with me so far?"

Understood. "No problem."

She spread her arms in a gesture of helplessness. "But I can't know what a new world is like until I get there, if you know what I mean. And I have to get the incantation right. If I make a mistake with one word, I may end up in the wrong realm."

That wasn't an inviting prospect. "Yeah, okay."

What she said made sense. But there had to be a catch. And, sure enough, she told me. "And there's one more thing. I can only stay on a world for a short amount of time."

Surprise — not. She'd mentioned it when we were still on Earth. Nick had mentioned molecular instability, but that was scientific reasoning. Then the answer hit me between the eyes. This was a world of magic. "Let me guess. It's a curse, right?"

Glynarra stopped in her tracks and gave me a wide-eyed stare. "How'd you know?"

"Humans are geniuses. Remember?"

My answer provoked a chuckle from her, but then she explained how bad her situation was. "The king had his most powerful magicians — what you'd call magicians, and there are only two of them — curse me after he killed my parents. He said that I'd always be bound to this world. I found out the first time I left." She took in a deep breath. "I went to a world called Carna Seven. The people there looked something like us. They were friendly, but after about three days, I began to feel weak and sick. Once I returned here, I felt better. The same thing happened on the next two worlds I visited."

What a rotten deal! "Lensa's doing this to screw you over, right?"

By now, we'd reached a clearing. Glynarra nodded and took a seat on a fallen bough. "The only way I can gain my freedom is to bargain with Lensa or fight him. That's why I'm going to Kott. If they back me, I'll help them with my powers." With her elbows on her knees, she rested her chin in her hands and ruminated on things. "If they can't force Lensa to lift the curse, then I'll have to try another kingdom or get a few of them to support me. And if that doesn't work, I'll go somewhere else."

So, the task ahead of us was no less simple and no less binding. While I could get back to Earth pretty much any time I wanted, she couldn't live anywhere unless she managed to get the scumbag king to lift the curse.

"...go home?"

"What?" I'd been zoning out and didn't hear what she'd asked me. "Uh, can you repeat that?"

"Do you want to go home?"

Did I? Not really. Life on my world was an exercise in solitude, loneliness, boredom and being ignored by my mother. Answering Glynarra as tactfully as possible, I said, "No, but where could I go?"

She offered a shy smile. "Somewhere new...maybe with someone you like?"

Her smile then turned radiant, and a blast of heat went through me. Was she coming on to me? "Uh, Glynarra, are you trying to pick me up?"

Glynarra didn't have to answer as her radiance level intensified. Yep, she was trying to. Not that I didn't find her attractive—I did—but was this the right time? And was this magic, or was it my hormones running me? Probably both.

"Yes," she said softly. "You stuck up for me when I needed help. I can tell that you're interested in me."

Oh. "Uh, how?"

A coquettish smile came through, like a kitten that wanted its owner to pet it and feed it. "By how you look at me."

"Oh." I hadn't realized that I was doing it, but she had me on that one. "And how do I look at you?"

She quickly affected an expression of longing, with a moist-eyed puppy-dog stare and a slightly slack jaw. Was that how I appeared to her? Call that emo to the max.

"And while I'm not a mind-reader, I'm pretty sure you care," Glynarra continued with a confident attitude. "If you didn't like me, then you would have called the authorities when I first transformed, right?"

Good point. "Uh, well, yeah."

If that wasn't an 'aw-gee-shucks' moment, I didn't know what was. The sound of thuds pulled me back to reality. Heavy, rhythmical and metallic—they were soldiers.

Glynarra jerked her head around at the sound. "They're here. Lensa's men—they've found us out. We have to hide."

She pointed to the bushes, and we dove in. "I can open a window, but I have to have quiet so I can concentrate."

Handlee, that little rat. He'd sold us out. It couldn't have been anyone else, but at that point, it didn't matter. We stayed quiet and still, and a few seconds later, ten soldiers came into view. They had a prisoner, a young man, with them.

He struggled mightily to get free, but one guard clubbed him over the head and he fell to the ground, stunned. "Stay there," said one of the guards, and he planted his foot on the hapless man's neck, then turned and ordered one of his men to fetch the king.

Jesus, this wasn't good—at all. "Can we leave, yet?" I asked Glynarra.

"No, I can't open a window here," she replied, still watching the action. "I have to chant, and they'll hear me."

We waited, then the soldier returned with a man who wore a green robe edged in gold thread. The men bowed, and the lead guard said, "Sire, we have found a man with ability."

That was Lensa? He didn't look like anyone special. The king bent over and lifted the man's chin, grasping it tightly. "And what is this person's ability?"

"It is that of shadows," the lead soldier said.

Lensa nodded, closed his eyes, muttered something dark and evil, and out of nowhere, two men in gray robes appeared. "The king's magicians," Glynarra whispered in a shaky voice.

Without preamble, the magicians began chanting in unison while Lensa stood stock still. The prisoner began to writhe in pain, and a grayish but almost transparent essence—perhaps his spirit or soul—flew out of his body and into Lensa's.

Holy mother of God.

Mr. Prisoner screamed something incomprehensible then stopped. One of the guards bent over, put his hand in front of the now-shriveled husk's mouth and shook his head. "He is dead, sire."

Lensa didn't even bother looking at the body. He merely patted his body all over, grinning broadly. "I feel wonderful. Good job, captain. Well done. Let us return to our castle."

They marched off, leaving the victim behind. Who was he? Did he have a wife or children? Who would weep for him?

No one, it seemed. Glynarra stepped out of the bushes first. I followed her, staring at the body. "This is what our king does on a regular basis," she said grimly after eyeing the dead man. "Now you know."

Yes, now I knew. She got to work, but before she could start, the sounds of metal-clad feet returned. "Lensa knows," she said fearfully. "He knows I'm here."

"So, what now?"

"We leave."

Chapter Seven

Interlude, Part One

In a series of quick movements, Glynarra formed a window. It wasn't complete, though, as it shimmered in and out of reality. "Uh, anything wrong?" I asked, feeling my bowels quiver and hoping I wouldn't have an accident in front of her.

The tramping sounds got closer, and that couldn't have helped her confidence. It wasn't doing anything for mine. "We have to wait," she said, her voice shaking from nervousness and fear. "I invoked the proper incantation and the proper gestures for Earth."

"I thought they were all the same."

She shook her head. "No, like I said, they're all different, and I had to memorize every one of them. The gestures are different, too. So, now we're going back to your world. That's the only place I feel safe for now."

"Fine."

More thumps of metal-clad feet sounded. They grew louder by the second, and Glynarra's movements doubled in speed as she repeated the gestures. Left arm sweep at waist level. Right fist—punch forward. Then both her hands traced a heart shape. After that, she spread her arms as widely as possible.

"C'mon. C'mon," she muttered and pounded her fists on the ground. The window solidified. "Yes!"

Let's hear it for magic, as the window opened wide, almost beckoning us in. We scrambled through, and instead of ending up on some alien world, we landed in a small park. I recognized it as a park near my school.

I fell face-first onto the ground and came up spitting dirt. I looked around, but fortunately, it seemed as though no one had seen us come through. A blast of light signaled that the window had closed. We got up and brushed ourselves off.

Glynarra immediately shifted into her Earth form with the same hoodie-grunge outfit as before. She pointed to a small bench and we sat to grab some relaxation time. My heart wouldn't slow down. I leaned back, inhaling great gulps of air, and it seemed as though I'd never get enough.

Eventually I did, but the danger of that situation hit and hit hard. I looked at the sky. Judging from the position of the sun, it was about three in the afternoon, and it occurred to me that the timeline between my world and hers was roughly the same.

Neither of us said anything at first. We'd come that close to getting caught, and the thought of ending up in an alien prison didn't thrill me at all.

"Where to, now?" Glynarra asked with evident relief in her voice. "I've got about three days before we go back."

Good question. "Well, you can always come to my place."

She arched her eyebrows so high they almost met her hairline in an "Oh, you really think I'll go for that" expression.

My bad, so I hastily added, "Uh, I mean, no funny stuff. Like, it's not a hotel or anything luxurious, but we've got an extra room, and you need to sleep and get your strength back and so on, so — "

"I accept your offer. I trust you."

"Oh."

Well, at least she understood. Dorky explanation accepted, we set out. Along the way, I asked her if she'd ever thought this would happen. Glynarra offered a mirthless laugh.

"No, I was a dutiful daughter. My parents were workers in a local factory. We use magic for a lot of things, but we still manufacture our goods the old-fashioned way. We have machines, lathes and such, and working with gold and silver is a time-honored tradition on our world."

She told me about growing up in her city, playing with the other kids, studying at home, learning about magical spells that most people could do and resigning herself to a dull and unadventurous life. "Didn't you do anything for fun, like playing games?" I asked.

Glynarra tapped the side of her head as if to draw out memories. "Well, we didn't have movies like you do, but survival training was fun."

"Survival training?"

"Fight training, really. We all have to learn."

To demonstrate, Glynarra went through a series of strikes, kicks and punches. At first, it looked like a windmill style of boxing, all wild left crosses and right hooks and kicks, but within the chaos, there was order. The punches then came through. Like karate, they looked crisp and powerful. Call that beyond impressive.

In contrast, I wasn't that great a fighter, but although I didn't like confrontations, I also didn't like backing down.

"It's a just-in-case scenario," she said as she stopped her demo to catch her breath. "We rarely had fights growing up. But if someone challenged you, then you had to fight."

Peace, though, was prized in her society. All that changed when her powers came around. "Up until a few months ago, I could only shape-shift. My mother taught me a few spells, and I picked up that knowledge quickly, but most other people could do the same thing.

"It didn't matter to my parents. They loved me, and they were good to me. But I always thought that they were disappointed that I couldn't do what they could, outside of a few minor spells."

Hold on a second. "Uh, not to be dense or anything, but if you don't have the, um, gift inside you, how can you learn to do spells?"

Glynarra raised her hands in a gesture meant to indicate that the truth was self-evident. It wasn't evident, at least to me.

"Our world has ambient magic. It exists everywhere, and all a person needs to do is to utilize a certain combination of words in order to tap into that magic. That's what I learned from my mother. The only people who can't do that are the lessers." She blew out a deep breath and styled her hair behind her ears in a series of quick, deft movements. "But it isn't always that easy to tap into things. Abilities vary between people. Some need more practice, while others don't.

"Anyway, like I told you, my portal abilities came around one day. I simply knew what to say and what to do. It scared me at first. I mean, I opened a window to a world that I didn't have a clue about, walked in and found that the people there wanted to eat me. I couldn't leave there fast enough."

A self-deprecating laugh came from her. "I made a lot of mistakes. I did find a few places that I can hide out in, at least for seventy-two hours. Then I have to leave, but they understand, and it's all good."

Glynarra raised her hands, palms up, as if to say she was here, so I had to handle it. Handle it I would. "Well, you're here for at least three days, right? And in the future, you can, uh, you can always visit, you know."

She smiled. "I'd like that."

At my house, she seemed impressed by its size. "Are all houses like this? I've only stayed in hotels, but never for that long."

How could I tell her that my mother and I were on the lower end of the socio-economic earning scale? I couldn't, even though she'd probably understand. Instead, I settled for saying, "Some places are bigger. Some are smaller. This is sort of in the middle."

We walked inside and she took her time checking things out, running her hand over the dresser, poking her nose into the spaces between shelves and behind the couch, and picking out a few novels on the downstairs bookshelf and speedreading them.

Since she was occupied, I asked, "You mind if I take a shower? I, uh, got a little grotty over there."

Glynarra waved her hand as if to say she'd be fine. I pointed to the kitchen. "If you need something to drink, the fridge is there. You'll find cola on the second shelf."

"Thanks."

I went upstairs, hosed myself down, and donned fresh clothes. Being clean definitely improved my outlook on life.

My guest sat in the living room. She had a can of cola open and was sipping from it. "I usually don't have sugary drinks."

"No?"

"On my world, anything sweet is rare, but this is a nice change. Did you have a good shower?"

How to answer that? My hair was still damp, but the heat would dry me off soon, and I was thirsty. "Uh, yeah. You sure you don't want to take one?"

"Our species doesn't smell unless we eat certain kinds of food, remember? We're lucky that way."

I grabbed a can of cola from the fridge and joined her in the living room. We drank up, then I asked her if she could do her magic here.

"Yes…and no," she replied as she finished off her drink. "I told you before that I could, but the ambient energy here makes things a bit more difficult. I can open portals here and use simple spells to change information around, like on your computers. I can control nature to a certain degree, but not like back home. It's the same on other worlds, too. I don't know why. Perhaps that's part of Lensa's curse." A disturbed expression flashed across her face. "All I ever wanted was a normal life on Tellkar—I mean, normal for me. That's all. I didn't wish for power or fame, only to be like everyone else."

She looked at me. "I guess that's out of the question, isn't it?"

Glynarra sounded so forlorn, so lost, that I couldn't help but feel sorry for her. What could I say to assuage her grief? She'd lost her parents, she was somewhere and nowhere at the same time and she could never put down roots anywhere.

"I'm sorry." That was the extent of my words of comfort.

With anyone else, they may have screamed and cried and cursed the gods. In Glynarra's case, she shrugged off my apology as well as the notion of self-pity.

"It doesn't matter, only you said you were sorry. No one else ever did. Once my parents were killed, my friends, those I'd grown up with, weren't around anymore. They couldn't risk the king's wrath, so they shunned me. You saw how they acted on my world. That's how it was and is."

I finished my drink. "Could you use a friend?"

A tiny smile crossed her face, and she reverted to her default state. "Yes, I'd like that."

Time to take a chance. After all, she'd come on to me before...sort of. "And something more?"

Her smile broadened ever so slightly. "And something more...perhaps."

My stomach growled, which was my cue to get up and head for the kitchen. "Well, since you're here, we might as well eat something. How do you feel about tuna fish sandwiches?"

"Anything is fine."

Chapter Eight

Interlude, Part Two

The next day. Saturday. Noon.

Ah, the glorious weekend — no school and no worries, save for me acting as a tour guide for my guest. Although I'd skipped school for the past couple of days, it didn't matter. My score of eighty-four ensured that there would be no summer school. No one from the registrar's office called, and I had some freedom to do what I wanted.

Glynarra preferred to sleep on our couch and seemed most comfortable there, but since she didn't sleep more than five or six hours, she always needed something to do.

Boredom was something that didn't sit well with her. Watching television was fine at first, but she didn't care for the news shows. Our bookshelf was also no match for her reading skills. She absorbed the knowledge of each book in a matter of minutes.

Then she got the itch to move, as she put it. She'd shifted back to her default form, and assuming no one came over, we were safe from prying eyes. I drew the drapes anyway, just in case.

"I like your house," she said. "But I can always stay at home on my world. I want to experience life here."

Progress. "Feel like going for a walk?"

"Good idea."

She transformed into her human form, rocking the grunge look, and after we went outside and I locked up, she took my hand in hers.

That was nice. A touch of her warm flesh on mine, a certain kind of closeness…and she was just being kind. I didn't want to delude myself too much over the possibility of a relationship with her, and I wasn't really sure how she felt about me.

On the plus side, she'd said that she liked me, but on the negative side, there was that curse thing going on. And she could jump into a window anytime, with me being stuck here, so, again, this wasn't the time for self-delusion.

We strolled along the street, neither of us saying anything for a time. Glynarra had her own battles to fight, and as for me…

"Hey, Cornhole, what's up?"

Who the hell is that?

Oh, wait, I knew. It was Joel Catton, the self-proclaimed genius and wart on the butt of humanity. He also happened to live close by, so I sometimes saw him on the way to school, which guaranteed that he'd say something stupid. Catton was a jerk, but I was determined not to let him bother me. Not today.

He walked over with a smirk that widened with every step he took. "I still say you're lucky with your marks," he said, practically gloating. "Eighty-four isn't too shabby, but it rates low to someone like me."

What an asshat! "What's it to you, Joel?" I asked.

He ignored my question and posed another, all the while sneering at Glynarra, and what the hell was wrong with this picture? "Got your girlfriend with you?"

"She's my friend," I answered, feeling simultaneously protective of her — White Knight time — as well as pissed off at him. "So, I'm going to ask you again. What's it to you? Finishing in third place grades-wise sucks, doesn't it?"

Burn! He knew about getting beat by Nick in the grades department, not to mention losing out to my companion.

Joel's face reddened and he mumbled something about her getting lucky. Glynarra, though, wasn't in the mood to take crap from him or anyone else, and she let go of my hand to walk over and confront him.

"If you studied harder, you'd have a better chance of beating me," she said. Then she added, "In about a decade."

Oh, call that a double burn, but in an attempt at being an alpha male, Joel crossed his skinny arms over his even skinnier chest. "Who the hell would date you, anyway?" he asked. "I mean, seriously."

Enough of this crap. "I would," I put in. "And I don't see the ladies flocking around you. Flies, maybe, but not ladies."

Glynarra started laughing, and Joel's face turned even redder. His fists clenched and unclenched, but she murmured, "I got this."

Uh-oh, the train was coming down the tracks, and he simply didn't see it. Glynarra gave him a curiously evil smile. "Have you ever eaten a dirt pie?"

"What?"

"I haven't been at your school very long, but I know people there don't like me. That's fine, but you should know this. You're taller than I am. That's all."

She then shoved her face to within an inch of his and he flinched. "Don't insult me again. Either you apologize or get ready to eat a dirt pie. Which is it to be?"

Joel's smirk had disappeared, replaced by a look of fear. Apparently, discretion was the better part of valor, as he uncrossed his arms, mumbled, "Sorry," then moved on.

Once he was out of sight, Glynarra turned to me, her face calm and composed. "That's how you get rid of *nedak*."

"What does that mean?"

"Slime."

"Oh."

* * * *

Zelber's, the largest department store in downtown Portland, was crowded. Older couples who wanted to get out of the heat, younger couples who wanted to spend time in each other's company, the married-with-children crowd besieged by their offspring who whined for ice cream—it seemed that the entire population of my city was there.

As for Glynarra, she was delighted by the numerous shops and seemingly endless supply of food stores and kiosks. She made it a point to poke her head into each store, bakery and restaurant, all in the name of soaking up a different culture.

Naturally, a few people stared at her clothes, her features and especially, her hair. While that was rude, they would have done far worse if she'd shown them her true form.

"Don't worry about it," Glynarra said when I returned the gape of some punk. He outsized me by a few inches and about thirty pounds, but at that moment, I didn't feel like taking any crap. It was about time that I stopped standing by and stood up to people who couldn't keep their asshat behavior in check.

As for Mr. Tough Guy, we'd locked gazes, then he moved off at the urging of his girlfriend. He tossed us a glare that promised payback at some unspecified time, and I did the same. "It's okay," Glynarra said softly. "I'm fine."

"It's wrong, and you know it," I replied, still angry at how rotten some people could be.

"Of course it's wrong. But I'm used to it, and I can take care of myself. Let it go, and let's try some food."

We sampled the various culinary delights in the food court, and she took in the sights and smells with a sense of childlike wonder. Chocolate fudge ice cream became an immediate favorite of hers.

"I never thought the food of this world could taste so good," she said after devouring her fifth cone. She'd already eaten three slices of pizza and four egg sandwiches. Her appetite rivalled Nick's. "My home world's food is good, but it's nothing like this."

And she'd said that she didn't usually eat sweet food or drink sugary beverages. Good thing I'd taken out enough money from my account. Things on Earth cost. Here, we didn't barter for our meals. I made do with a slice of pizza and a can of cola.

We stood at the balustrade on the fifth floor, looking down at the other levels and the ceaseless flow of humanity. People shopping, talking, and eating—just another day in Portland for the everyday crowd, but Glynarra could hardly be considered an everyday sort in any way. "No?" I asked.

She shook her head. "No. Our factories are local. Our products are simple. The robe I had on? That's what most of our people wear. We don't believe in being ostentatious."

Speaking of which, Valerie Morton was coming in our direction. Two of her friends accompanied her. They were dressed to slay, with off-the-shoulder, brightly colored summer dresses, perfectly coiffed hair, just enough makeup to accentuate their eyes and cheekbones, and an attitude of 'you-can't-touch-this'.

Naturally, every guy over the age of fifteen turned to take in the sight of three pretty women. They worked the crowd, milked it for attention and soaked up the compliments of them being hot, hotter and hottest.

Glynarra wasn't moved at all. In fact, she turned to me with a bemused expression to ask, "Is their display of fashion supposed to impress me?"

"Are you impressed?"

"No."

"Well, that's the answer."

Valerie led the trio, and when she spotted us, she waved. But it was a short, nervous movement, accompanied by a tentative smile, and it was directed only at me, not my companion. "Hi, you guys. What are you doing here?"

"Just taking a walk," I answered, wondering what Valerie's goal was. "And you?"

"Shopping," one of Val's friends said. "We have to look good. At the beach and the pool, looking good is what it's all about."

Wonderful—more Val clones to deal with. I really wanted to like Valerie, but she was too shallow to ever think of forming a meaningful friendship with her.

And if I felt that way, chances were that Glynarra wasn't keen on making Valerie her bestie, either. At that moment, Valerie was eyeing Glynarra critically, and I had the feeling that she'd say something about my friend's so-called lack of fashion sense.

Sure enough, she did. "Glenda, you have to try something new. The grunge look is so thirty years ago."

Glynarra's response was to give her a dead-fish stare. "And what would that be?"

"I'll show you. Like I said, fashion makeovers are my business, and with the right hair and makeup, you'll be a lot more attractive than you are."

Some people never learned. Val happened to be one of them, but she was so set on imparting her unwanted advice that she didn't realize that she was offending someone—or maybe she did and didn't care. She took Glynarra's arm and steered her into a ladies' fashion store. "I'll make sure you look pretty."

Glynarra turned around and winked. Uh-oh, deja-vu was going to happen all over again. My suspicions were confirmed two minutes later when Val ran screaming from the store, yelling about sea monsters and magic and needing to find a police officer.

Her friends followed her, throwing accusatory glances in my direction, and what did I do? Nothing. I simply turned toward the store's entrance.

In a slow, almost insouciant manner, Glynarra sauntered over and gave me a look of mock innocence when I asked her if she'd shown my classmate an alternate version of life.

"Well, maybe it was a little different," she admitted with a rueful smile.

"How little?"

"I think you call it a Kraken."

* * * *

Forty-eight hours later.

Things went smoothly for the next two days. We slept separately, me in my bedroom and Glynarra on the couch, I got up early to make breakfast, we talked about various things and no one called.

After the incident at the department store, Glynarra and I stayed inside. I didn't want to be held responsible for someone else's mental breakdown.

My guest spent a lot of her time eating. Watching anime and western cartoons amused her for a time. "They're simple pictures," she said, "but they're kind of cute."

Cartoons had never been my thing, even as a kid. If she liked them, though, fine. She watched them, did her exercises and martial arts *katas* — anything to keep busy.

However, on the third morning, Glynarra said that she felt poorly. It had to be the curse. Curious and concerned, I asked her about the symptoms.

"Headache," she promptly replied. "I have a headache, and my body feels like something's crushing it."

"We'd better go then."

Time to go, but just before she did the window thing, the telephone rang. I picked up the receiver, and my mother's voice came through. "Mark? Are you all right?"

Something had to be wrong. She never called when she was on the job. "I'm fine, Mom. What's up?"

My guest wandered over, staring curiously at the receiver in my hand. We had an old-style rotary dial phone, something my mother liked for reasons unknown. Glynarra murmured, "Is that how you communicate with each other? I never used a pay telephone or smartphone here."

Oh, crap!

I cupped my hand over the receiver, but it was too late, as my mother asked, "Is someone there with you?"

Damn it, does this have to happen now? "Uh, yeah, I've got a friend over."

Immediately, my mother's tone shifted into suspicion mode, and what had I done to deserve this?

"Does your friend have a name?"

Fine, tell her. "It's Glynarra."

"What kind of name is that?"

Immediately, I got flustered. "It's Welsh. No, it's Irish…Gaelic…or something." *Aw, hell, this isn't working.* "Mom, I thought you were busy. You know, jobs and making money and all that." Flummoxed or not, it wasn't too early to get in a dig.

My mother's next words made me rue my wisecrack—a little. "Well, yes, but I thought about what you said…about us talking more, so I called."

All right, maybe she cared, but then those warm and fuzzy feelings I had disappeared when she added, "And you've got someone over, someone with a strange name."

Apparently, Glynarra overheard, as she made a face that indicated anger combined with disgust. Worse, now wasn't the time to talk. She mimed opening a window. Message received. We had to leave soon.

"Mom, she's a good friend. But I'm kind of busy, and —"

"Busy with what?" Anger and real suspicion coated those three little words.

Aw, man! She didn't get it. She never would. "We have to go," Glynarra said then clammed up as she realized that she'd made a mistake.

I waved her off, but it was too late. "Where are you going?" my mother asked. "Why is she answering for you?"

"We're, uh, going out, and she has a voice, too."

It wasn't the best answer around, but at that time, it was all I could think of, and while my mother sputtered out her responses, consisting of 'strange girls' and 'owing her' and 'being responsible', I couldn't wait any longer. "Mom, can you call me back in a couple of days? I should be free then."

"Mark, you're going to tell…"

I hung up. Glynarra began weaving her arms. "I'm sorry. When we return, I should get better."

She grunted out the incantation, and a window began to form. "Where are we going?" I asked.

"The Bridge of Dying Sighs," she replied after repeating the incantation. "Shh… I have to concentrate."

A moment later, a window opened. We stepped through, emerging at the edge of a forest. I saw only trees, no bridge. "I think you missed our target."

Glynarra grunted softly as she scanned the area. "I told you that my aim wasn't precise. I know where to go, though. C'mon."

She led the way through the forest, and after fifteen minutes of tramping over branches and through grass and bushes, we found ourselves a hundred feet from a small, unadorned wooden-arched bridge that spanned a babbling brook of crimson red water.

It was just us. Only a few insects buzzed around our heads. Thigh-high grass brushed against our legs. A hot sun shone overhead and immediately, I started to sweat. The forest had offered shade, but here, nothing.

"Any special reason we're here?" I asked.

Glynarra swept her hand around in a gesture that reminded me of a motion picture camera giving the audience a panoramic view.

"This probably means nothing to you, but to us, it's the halfway point to the kingdom of Kott. This bridge is supposed to be magical and protect those who journey to and from each kingdom."

"And the sighs?"

A wry smile suffused her lips. "It's been said that long ago, there were two lovers from both kingdoms. They couldn't get married for some reason, and their families decided to kill them to stop them from running away."

Wonderful, another riff on an old Shakespearean play. "And?"

She shrugged. "And they died on the bridge. Right here. If you put your head close to the water, it's said that you can hear their final breaths."

Pass on that, thanks. Glynarra didn't either, so she took my hand to lead me to the bridge. A few feet before we reached it, though, she stopped and said, "You hear that?"

"Hear what?"

"Metal boots. Soldiers."

Marvelous, like we really needed this now? Glynarra turned to me. "Hold still."

"Why?"

"You still look human."

She muttered something and a moment later, she stepped back. "Look at yourself in the water."

I did and found that I was once more in the guise of a Tellkarian native.

"We'd better go," she said, but in the space of a few seconds, no less than fifteen spears came out of nowhere and landed with thuds in a circle around us, penning us in.

I tried to pull one of the spears from the ground, but a shock hit me and put me down. I lay there, my body tingling all over. "What the hell?"

"Magic," Glynarra whispered. "Say nothing. I'll talk for you."

I wanted to protest, but the arrival of twenty men in armor dissuaded me from speaking. They had their swords out and ready, and I didn't dare move.

Two men stepped forward and removed their helmets to reveal identical features and stars around their necks. They must have been the twins that Handlee mentioned.

Glynarra snarled. "Morhoon, Wisster, I should have known that Handlee would sell me out!"

One twin smiled. "Glynarra, call it a better offer. Handlee merely mentioned that a payment of fretish could be received by capturing a dangerous criminal. You are a dangerous criminal. King Lensa, our lord, thinks so."

"You are a pig, Morhoon."

He bowed. "Guilty as charged."

His twin stepped forward. While they looked identical, Morhoon had a deep voice. Wisster did not. When he spoke, he reminded me of an old woman. "Who is your companion?"

"Not your affair," Glynarra replied. "Take us in, if you dare."

A high-pitched giggle came from twin number two. "That we will. You are fortunate that our lord requires you alive."

For some reason, I didn't feel fortunate—at all.

Chapter Nine

No Easy Way Out

Marching under a blazing sun wasn't my idea of fun, and for an all-too-brief moment of insanity, I thought that Glynarra and I would be treated civilly.

Stupid assumption on my part. Our captors pushed us to march at a brisk pace. They didn't handcuff us, but with their weapons, they didn't have to. Making a break for it didn't seem to be the best plan, as I had nowhere else to go, and Glynarra seemed to accept our fate.

After an hour, the inside of my mouth had gone dry, my eyes felt like they'd been fried by the sun, and my lips began to dry out and split. I'd stopped perspiring, mainly because my body didn't have any extra water to sweat out.

Oddly enough, the guards didn't notice my condition or Glynarra's lack of exhibiting one. She didn't perspire, and she never seemed to tire.

In my case, death would have been preferable. My muscles started to cramp before we cleared the forest's edge and turned left. They twisted in agony, and I stumbled numerous times until maybe forty minutes later when we arrived at a two-pronged road. One of the guards called out, "Halt! Rest break."

Very considerate of you guys.

I hit the ground hard, not caring if anyone thought me weak or not. Wearily, I looked around. From the position of the sun, as well as the direction we'd come from, the road seemed to split off into a north-south kind of deal.

Beyond that, there was nothing. No forest, no buildings…nothing. Had they brought us here to execute us or was this just another form of torture?

If marching under a hot sun was torture, sitting under it was overload. Tellkar's sun was way more intense than Earth's. It beat down mercilessly, and my skin itched. My joints also began to hurt—a lack of water could do that.

Glynarra sat beside me, saying nothing, but once we'd rested around ten minutes, a guard prodded me in the back with the butt end of his sword. "Get on your feet," he ordered.

"How about five more minutes?" I asked. "A drink of water would be nice, too."

For that, I got a smack to the back of the head. The guard who hit me took off his helmet to reveal a patch over his right eye. "Get up."

Another guard said, "Starra, do not abuse the prisoners."

"They are prisoners," Starra replied without a note of pity. "They should be treated as such."

"I am your superior. Do not make me cite you for insubordination."

Our more supportive guard's voice was sharp, and Starra growled his disagreement, but at least he didn't hit me again. I had one more dig to toss at him and said, "You know, you shouldn't hit anyone in the back of the head. It's dangerous."

"Up! Get up and march to your right."

Obviously, Mr. Eyepatch aka Starra didn't appreciate the need for rest. We got up and started marching again. The road was gravelly, the dust kicked up in my face and our journey continued until dusk fell.

Our guards were clever. They knew how much we could endure and when we needed water. Or, at least, they knew when Glynarra needed water.

As for me, they didn't seem to be overly concerned about my welfare, although they tossed in a few comments about me being weak. Fine, let them insult me. Perhaps they wanted me to fight back.

"Do not try to escape or retaliate," Glynarra whispered to me during a break. "They will kill you. Trust me on this."

"Okay."

What else could I say? The desire to kick butt appealed to me, though. We continued marching until it was too dark to see. "Halt," ordered Starra.

We collapsed by the side of the road. Starra said that we'd rest there for the night and reach the castle sometime tomorrow morning.

"You are too kind," I puffed out. The top of my head felt fried, and my face and neck were charred. A nasty degree of pain was building.

For that, I got the butt-end of a sword to the side of my head, accompanied by a harsh, "Be quiet, stranger."

After that, I didn't think about much else until someone kicked me in the side. I opened my eyes and blinked. It was morning. "Water," one of the guards said, and we got a small drink before setting off again.

Glynarra marched in time with the guards, her face set and proud. Her attitude inspired me, although once I saw the castle, it simultaneously impressed me while taking away some of my courage.

Impressive didn't halfway describe it. I'd seen pictures of British and other European castles on television and in the history textbooks. They were amazing.

Equally amazing were the three-dimensional walkaround tours I'd participated in online. I'd done them to earn brownie points for my history class. Admittedly, they were fun, but they couldn't compare to the real thing.

This castle was the real thing. Up close and personal there was no contest, Lensa's crib was more awe-inspiring — and much more intimidating.

The stone walls that lined the road looked solidly constructed and were over thirty feet in height. Once we reached the drawbridge, I checked out the walls. They were at least a hundred feet high, and there were four lookout turrets that stood another sixty feet up.

Men in armor patrolled every square foot of the premises. They carried nasty-looking swords as well as clubs, and they probably had other weapons as well.

"Halt," Starra said. "We must wait."

We stopped, as did the soldiers. Confusion hit. Wait for what? A public executioner? Perhaps the king would appear to pass sentence?

Whatever the case, I steeled myself for the worst. This was one place that a person walked into. It was a sure bet that those people didn't walk out.

If they didn't die by the sword inside, the stink of crap and other vile odors from the moat would certainly do major damage to someone outside.

I leaned over to whisper to Glynarra, "I hate to ask, but I'm assuming people chuck garbage from the castle, right?"

She confirmed my statement-slash-question by saying that people did just that as well as relieving themselves through a literal hole in the floor. "From what I know, there are such rooms with holes in them on every level."

Crapping in holes. That was a primitive sewage system at its best and worst. All the waste went through numerous tunnels and ended up in the water. "It stinks here," I muttered.

"I'm not overly thrilled with it, either," she replied, subsequently falling silent.

A man in a gray robe appeared out of thin air ten feet away. "A magician," Glynnara whispered. "He knows the spell."

"For what?"

"For the barrier that surrounds this castle."

Right, the magical barrier. I'd forgotten. The magician, small and slender like everyone else, chanted something in a language unknown. A few seconds later, the air shimmered and the magician nodded at Starra, then vanished.

"Move," the one-eyed soldier said. "The barrier is down."

We marched over the drawbridge and into the main hall. Lined with wood, it featured over forty paintings, all portraying an elegantly dressed elf-man with a crown on his head in various poses. In every portrait, his nose was turned up.

At first glance, I thought he looked like everyone else, but upon closer examination, one feature stood out—his mouth. The right corner was permanently upturned in a snarl. An injury, maybe—but if so, why advertise it?

I had no answers, only questions. At least it was somewhat cooler here, but the guards didn't let us linger. They shoved the butt-ends of their swords in our lower backs to hustle us through the hall and down a series of roughly hewn stone steps to the jail area.

Like all the other jail cells I'd seen on television and in the movies, it had stone walls, iron bars and no cots or benches upon which to sleep. It also had a small hole in the corner, presumably where one stood or sat and delivered.

Although it was hot, it had a two-by-two-foot window with bars on it that allowed light and fresh air to enter. "Halt," said Starra. "Bind them."

What?

Too late, as a guard twisted my arms behind me and bound my wrists together. Once he finished, he said in surprise, "This one is not like us."

Glynarra's spell had worn off, and I stood there in my Earth clothes, a relative giant, even though I was only a few inches taller than the average Tellkarian. "That is because he is not," Glynarra replied. "Apparently, your eyesight is as dull as that thing you call a mind."

For her answer, she got a slap across the face. The blow echoed throughout the room and stunned her, then the guard tied her up. She struggled while they did it, and Starra came over to club her over the head with his fist, stunning her.

After that, with a moan of pain, she sagged to her knees, and they continued their job. "You bastards!" I yelled.

They paid no attention to me. Once they finished, they sat her up and another guard gently patted her face until she came around. Then our jailers left us alone.

"Are you all right?" I asked, sotto voce.

Glynarra shook her head slowly and groaned. "I will be, but I need to have both arms free in order to perform the spell properly," she whispered. "Just saying it won't work. That's how things are around here. They know that, and that's why they tied me up, the slime."

I struggled to my feet, pacing around and trying to keep the blood flowing while working my arms and shoulders against my bonds, all the while cursing myself out for having gotten into this situation. It wasn't easy, considering my sunburn, but I kept at it and tried to formulate a plan of action.

While the people from this realm were small, they were as strong as I was. Moreover, they were armed. I wasn't.

Swords were the mainstay of the guards' weaponry, but then I noticed that they also had a one-yard wooden stick strapped to their sides. It didn't look overly offensive, and I mentioned that fact to Glynarra.

"It's called an extender," she murmured after they'd closed the cell door on us and ran to inform their master.

"An extender?"

She grunted and shifted her weight until she'd found a more comfortable position. "It shoots out to five times its length. The weapon has two options. One is that it has a blade on it that emerges when it's extended, and it's sharp. I've seen it run through metal and wood—and people. The other end is blunt, but it's strong enough to cause a bruise and even break bones. Be careful you're not on the receiving end."

Uh-huh, point taken. "Sounds like a telescopic spear. Uh, do they believe in torture on this world?"

"Always, at least in this kingdom. From what I know, Kott, the place we wish to go, their king is more benevolent. Not here. King Lensa is beyond cruel. You've seen what he can do."

I remembered the black magic exhibition and the shriveled husk of his victim. "Yeah," I replied and hoped that my voice didn't shake. "I saw."

Glynnara's answer came out with sadness. "Outside of his magic, he's also a skilled fighter and doesn't mind killing. Officially, his parents died of old age, but the rumors are that he killed his parents—just as he killed mine."

Now, anger tinged the sadness, and her temper soon rose to a boiling point. "I think I already told you. Three months ago, my powers came around. We're the same age, eighteen."

I just remembered that I'd be eighteen soon. In all the confusion, it had slipped my mind. "Yeah, you did. I've got a couple more days to go. And?"

She shifted her position against the wall. "Well, while I was learning to harness my abilities, I also learned more about what my parents could do. My father had the ability to cast certain spells, while my mother used to talk to the ground."

"'Scuse me?"

Glynarra's mouth twisted in thought. "She knew how to make cures for fever, injuries and various minor ailments, such as an upset stomach, all from roots. She'd talk to the ground, and the flowers and plants would tell her what to do and how to do it." She gave a self-conscious laugh. "Then I could do what no one else could. It was as if the wind whispered it to me. Anyway, my parents found me walking through a window one time and they got scared. They told me to hide what I could do and never tell anyone."

"Because of Lensa?"

Glynarra nodded. "Because of him. Like I told you, he seeks power and gets it any way he can. If someone has an ability he doesn't possess, he finds them and has his faithful magicians transfer the powers to him."

All that power—and what could he do with it? "If he's that powerful, why doesn't he just march on Kott and take it over?"

"They have a mighty army, the equal of his. And they also have magicians who are as powerful as his are. Furthermore, the other kingdoms are split over who they support. If a war ever comes, it would be one of attrition—and Lensa seeks an overwhelming advantage. Having my power would make him unstoppable."

Well, call that the ultimate buzzkill, and if she had to die in order for the king to receive her powers, totally not worth it.

My friend hung her head down and sighed. "When Lensa found out about my abilities, he came with a group of his soldiers to my parent's house with an ultimatum—hand me over or suffer the consequences.

"My parents refused. Upon his order, his men killed them, right in front of me. Only one soldier protested, but his wishes were ignored."

Tears began to flow down her face. "I was inside at the time. I watched them die. Before my father went to the great darkness, he cast a spell to protect my house, one so strong that it couldn't be broken by anyone."

She fell silent then, weeping, and not knowing what else to do, I wiggled my way over to her and gently nudged her shoulder. "You, uh, can lean on me. It's okay. Things in life…they don't always work out."

Hollow words — they'd have sounded hollow to her. But I meant what I'd said and hoped that she'd understand.

Her body stiffened, but then she leaned against me, silver tears soaking my shirt. She cried, yelling out in anguish that she wanted her parents back and that she also wanted revenge. Her wails of inner torment continued, and I couldn't do a damn thing to help her, even though I wanted to.

A man wearing the common robe here came in and identified himself as an off-duty guard. At first, his manner was most polite. "Your king is presently occupied. He has a hunting party to attend to. When he is ready, he will visit you. I suggest you prepare yourselves accordingly."

Maggot. "How do you expect us to do anything, you moron?" I asked. "You have us tied up. We can't move. Got that? And we need water. You got *that*?"

"You are a troublesome beast," the guard responded. With a face filled with scars and a practiced sneer, it only increased the ugliness. "You should show better manners to your superiors."

My anger boiled over. "Find one, and maybe I'll be nice. Until then, either give us some water or else get lost. You're nothing but the king's go-fer, just a little weasel."

The guard snarled something that I didn't catch. Apparently, saying weasel in English translated to something far worse over here. "Do you wish to fight me?"

"Let me out, and I'll kick your ass, tied up arms and all."

As tired and lousy as I felt, I meant every word. Comment delivered, I waited, and the guard took a key from his belt and opened the door. "Then let us see what you can do, beast."

I didn't give him a chance to get set and kicked him in the side of his leg, at the knee. It twisted, and he went down, howling in pain.

"Like that? I got more, shorty."

I kept kicking him and yelling that he'd better let us go. "Get up and fight, punk," I yelled. "Get up!"

In retrospect, yelling wasn't the best idea, as another armored guard came in and took the extender from his belt. He pressed the side of the weapon and the stick shot out a good five feet, catching me in the stomach and sending me tumbling into the cell. The extender...

I fell, gasping for breath. When Glynarra came over to my side to help me, Mr. Guard used the device on her, knocking her down and out.

That did it. Pain or no, I got up and charged him. Once again though, Mark Cornish failed to learn. Mr. Extender shot out again, I felt the impact as it hit me right between the eyes, stars exploded in my field of vision, then...nothing.

* * * *

Some minutes or hours later.

"Ah, are our visitors...awake?"

A voice, somewhat high-pitched and oily, sounded in my ears. I blinked my eyes, focused...oh yeah, the events of the previous few hours came back in a rush.

Glynarra and I had been captured. We were in a jail cell in Lensa's castle.

A Tellkarian stood on the other side of the bars. Lensa. Up close, he seemed much older than we were, perhaps in his late forties. The star pattern around his neck was somewhat faded, indicating age. He wore a bright blue robe this time, studded with jewels.

A gold crown completed the picture of royal arrogance as he looked up-down his nose at us. And, yes, the snarl was there—a long, jagged scar that pulled the skin up on the right side of his mouth.

In a slow, almost affected gesture, he brushed some imaginary dirt from his robe and reached up to take his crown off and examine it closely. Then he flicked off another infinitesimally tiny mote of dirt on its side before replacing the crown on his head.

If the situation hadn't been so dire, I would have laughed at his ostentatious display of vanity. I didn't. Instead, I glanced at Glynarra to catch the expression on her face, but she was still asleep.

"What are you?" the little man asked.

Dickhead—not a 'who-are-you' question, but a 'what-are-you' one. It was his realm and his cell, but I'd be damned if I'd bow to this shrimp. "My name's Mark. I'm from Earth. And you are?"

He arched his eyebrows. Haughty—yes, that was the word. He personified it. "You are most impudent."

"Says the scar-faced midget."

A huff of disappointment came from him. "Although you should show manners to your betters, this one time I shall forgive it. I am the ruler of this kingdom and the sole person that holds your fate in the palm of his hand. That is who I am. As your tiny mind must know by now, I am royalty."

He said it with such—and here came the word 'haughty' again—arrogance, that I almost laughed. Almost…but not. It wasn't worth it.

"I am Lensa," he said. "Lensa, king of Worthington, and soon to be ruler of this world. You are to address me as 'sire' or 'your lordship'."

Glynarra chose that moment to wake up. Immediately, she focused her gaze of hatred on Lensa. "You," she growled. "You."

"Yeah, El Shrimp decided to swing by and greet us," I said in an attempt to rile the king up. "Tiny guys have to compensate for something."

Apparently, Lensa caught the inference as he scowled and gestured for his soldiers to open the cell door. One man did, and he hauled me and Glynarra out. Lensa took his time checking me over, and when he was done, he backhanded me across the face.

It stung, but I decided not to give in. I couldn't. "Got any more than that?"

Glynarra let out a harsh chuckle, and the king raised his hand again to strike. "You have some courage, Mark of Earth. I will grant you that. But you are no match for me or the magic I wield."

Speaking of magic, he twisted his raised hand. Immediately, an invisible force gripped my throat, and it began to close, choking me. The force was strong with this one.

"This is but one example of what I can do," he said. "Do you feel that, Mark of Earth? I could crush your throat in an instant, but I wish you to live a little longer."

I'd been on the verge of blacking out, but then the grip eased off. I gasped out, "Well, isn't that special of you? Thanks."

Lensa laughed. On anyone else, it would have sounded merry. On him, it sounded like the cackle of someone supremely rotten to the core.

He then swung his gaze over to my companion, who was by now glaring daggers, missiles and plasma bombs in his direction. "Glynarra, my vertok guided me to your presence, and your acquaintance, Handlee, was most helpful in guiding us as well."

Her mouth twisted in a snarl. "If I catch him, I will make sure that his next few days will not be pleasant."

Lensa smiled thinly. "His life is over. Consider that the lone favor I shall ever do for you."

The way he said it, so casually, made me want to heave. Death for that little traitor seemed extreme, even though he'd sold me and Glynarra out.

But what Lensa had done? It showed me exactly what kind of person he was—someone arrogant, vain, greedy and evil, not to mention dangerous.

Once more, Glynarra struggled to get free, but she wasn't going anywhere. "What do you want, Lensa?"

He sighed. "You still have not learned to address your betters in the proper manner, Glynarra. You shall learn, though."

"You are not my better," she replied through gritted teeth. "You murdered my parents in cold blood, and now, you want to take my life as well."

"Not your life," he countered with a smile that would have frightened a serial killer. He took a step forward, pointing at her. "Only that ability which you possess. Once you are relieved of that ability, you are free to live your life as you see fit."

She spit on his boots. They were purple, with little bells attached to the ankle part, like Glynarra's were. Perhaps that was a common thing here.

"Only my ability," she echoed. "Then why is it that none of the people you take abilities from ever survive? Is it because the process drains them to the point of killing them? I have seen your handiwork before. Do not lie to me."

Being spit on wasn't the king's style, but to his credit, he refused to get angry. He merely shrugged as he took out a handkerchief to wipe away the spittle. With a flick of his wrist, he then tossed the soiled material into the air, snapped his fingers and it vanished.

"That matter must be taken up with my magicians. They are the ones who know the proper spells and incantations. I am merely the vessel for the powers and nothing more. If those who contribute to my, er, well-being, lose their lives, is it not better that their powers be put to good use through me? I am, after all, the ruler of this domain, and what better way to use those abilities than to employ them as, shall we say, tools to rule?"

There was cold-hearted, and there was inhumane. Lensa fell into the latter category. Glynarra eyed him coldly and matched him word for word.

"Yes, you rule through intimidation and murder. You rule through brute force and magic and terror. You are not a king, only a spoiled child with no wife, no heir and no one who truly cares for you."

"Hmmph."

That was the extent of Lensa's response. His guard then asked if we should be spoken to first. "It would be my honor to perform such a duty for you, sire."

Right. By spoken to, he meant tortured. Lensa observed us both, looking down his nose, as it were, then waved his hand in dismissal. "For now, no."

He then leaned down to cup Glynarra's chin roughly and squeeze her jaw. "But know this, Glynarra. I will not torture you, for that might damage the magic that lies inside your body."

"How kind of you."

Lensa's laugh was hollow. "I am that, yes. As of this moment, my magicians are practicing the incantation. It must be delivered by both in perfect unison. If it is not, then the spell will not work."

"Let us hope it takes them a long time," she ground out.

Lensa released her and slapped her hard across the face. "Even if it does, you will not leave here. That, I can promise you."

He waved one of his guards over. "Put them back into their cell. Give them no food but give them water. As for the one called Mark, do not torture him — yet. I am indifferent to his existence, but the girl must be protected and well cared for. Is that understood?"

His man bowed. "Yes, sire."

Lensa departed, and the guards went with him. And Glynarra and I were alone, she with her rage, and me with a sense of growing despair at how to get out of our confines.

Chapter Ten

Escape

Jail well and truly sucked. While the window supplied light and fresh air, it also allowed the heat in. The stone seemed to retain every bit of power that the sun emitted during this infernal season.

Call it medieval to the max. On Earth, medieval didn't mean being well educated or being a good citizen. It was all about survival against filth, plagues, famine, accusations of sorcery and other things that could get a person killed before they turned sixteen.

And, more telling in that somewhat primitive era, the rulers back then knew how to use what they had at hand to get their way. They knew how to break people's wills down. Lack of sleep, lack of water, and light deprivation—they all took their toll.

Of course, they practiced various forms of torture. Confining prisoners to the stocks was one way, but worse forms existed. The Iron Maiden, the Spanish Donkey, whippings, the rack, and even more horrible methods of physical abuse could break the will of anyone.

If the jailers didn't use torture, they would simply let Mother Nature do her thing. And the heat got to me. Combined with the dehydration from before, along with a lack of food, I must have passed out, because the next thing I knew, someone was pulling me up. "Huh...what?"

Those were the first words out of my mouth, and another male voice said in a nasal tone, "Do not talk."

It was a guard. Despite the temperature, he wore a helmet that only allowed me to see his eyes. Oddly enough, they were full of concern. "I called for someone," Glynarra said weakly. "You fainted."

The guard carried two water skins with him. "I am not supposed to give you water," he whispered while looking around to make sure no one else was coming. "But to torture you like this is cruel."

Did I pass out? I wasn't even aware of it. Glynarra wavered on her knees. "Her first," I said.

The guard helped Glynarra drink, then he helped me. "Are you feeling better?" he asked, once I'd drained the water skin.

I nodded. Even though I wanted more, what I'd been given was enough to keep me going. "Thank you."

Glynarra also gave her thanks. The guard then stole out and we were alone again with the heat of the day. My sunburn began to itch, and at the same time, sweat ran from my pores, my mouth got drier than dry and the air seemed to shimmer.

However, there was no point in complaining, and if my companion didn't say anything, then I decided not to, either.

Respect was something that had to be earned. I'd heard that a long time ago, and my respect for Glynarra grew exponentially as she maintained her stoic attitude in the face of certain death. I only hoped that when it was my turn, I'd meet my Maker the same way.

I asked her, though, how Lensa had gotten his scar. A thin smile came from her. "I did it. It was the only chance I ever had to hit back. After he killed my parents, I was incapable of speaking. I never thought I'd see something like that, and the shock was great." Her voice grew soft. "There was so much blood. One minute, my parents were alive, and the next, they were not. Their bodies had been violated by swords, hacked apart, and they lay in pieces. Lensa stood over their bodies, grinning and well pleased with his filthy act."

Transfixed by her narrative, I asked what happened next. "What would you do?" she retorted. "I did the only thing possible—I slashed him with a knife. He wasn't prepared for it, and before he could do anything, I locked myself inside. The magic of my father protected me."

She bit her lip, bit it so hard that blood ran from it. "My only regret is that I didn't slice any lower. If I have another chance, I won't waste it."

Glynarra ducked her head then, shaking it back and forth slowly as if regretting her lack of fighting skill. She didn't offer any additional details and stayed silent.

Not moving seemed to be the smartest thing to do. I stayed as still as possible, listening to my breath hitch in my lungs and feeling the water drain from my body.

There was no clock here, so I watched as the sun gradually traversed the sky to dip behind the horizon. As it did, the cell grew cooler, which came as a distinct relief.

It was a beautiful world, beautiful and magical, but it also held tyranny and terror. It seemed as though the people from this world weren't that different from those on Earth.

Glynarra had mentioned our shortcomings — racism, inequality, biases — all true. I wanted to think that humanity would grow up one day and leave all of that behind, but that was a naïve thought. Fear was hardwired into our psyches, and it took only a gentle push to turn that fear into hatred.

Cogitating over the differences took my mind off my personal problems for only a short time, though. Whatever water the guard had given me was soon taken away by the heat.

My stomach pleaded for food, but more than that, my tissues begged for water. That consumed my thoughts, and just when I was about to scream my guilt of being human and frail to the heavens, a guard came downstairs with a torch to provide some light, sticking it in a holder opposite the cell door.

He didn't look at us, not once. After he left, another guard entered and came down the stairs, carefully holding a small wooden barrel to his chest.

The guard stopped at the edge of the cell but didn't open the door. What was he up to? Initially, I was suspicious. "Thanks," I said. "I thought all condemned prisoners got a last meal."

Mr. Guard also wore armor, but he had no helmet, and it revealed abnormally tiny ears and a nonexistent nose. In the dim light, scars covered the space where his nose should have been. It must have been some fight he was in.

He seemed taken aback and answered in a horribly nasal tone, one that radiated pain. "I am not familiar with the ways of your world, stranger, but if you make light of a gift of water, then there is nothing more I can do for you."

The voice...was familiar. I searched my memory. Yes...it was the guard who'd given us water earlier.

"He does not know of our ways, Vasso," Glynarra said. "He is ignorant, so please forgive him."

The guard seemed to find that amusing, as he let out a mild hiccup of a chuckle, which, considering our situation, was so not needed. "Glynarra, that is most kind of you."

"You guys know each other?" I asked, surprised at their banter.

Glynarra frowned. "We've met before. He was one of the guards present at my parents' death."

Oh, I'd messed up. She really didn't need anyone to bring on past trauma. "Sorry," I murmured to her.

Her eyes had held anger, but it dissipated. "That's okay. You didn't know."

Vasso popped the lid and said with a surprising amount of gravitas, "It is good that you remember me, Glynarra. If you recall, I did protest the king's wishes and stayed behind to help you bury your parents' remains. Once I returned here, I was sorely beaten by the king's men for making my views known."

He pointed at his nonexistent nose, and I winced. That was the price he'd paid for being decent. It was too much, and internally, I raged at Lensa's brutality.

Glynarra's voice caught when she spoke. "I did not know that. You did only what was right. It was beastly of Lensa to treat you that way. I am truly sorry that you had to suffer such a grievous injury."

Vasso bowed his head. "Even though you shall meet your doom, you still have consideration for others, for this stranger to our realm and to me. It is a true shame that our king does not recognize your worth."

At the mention of the word 'doom', my bowels twisted, but Glynarra didn't show a trace of fear. Instead, she offered up defiance, asking with a tinge of anger and sarcasm, "And when shall I meet my doom?"

Vasso indicated me with a wave. When he spoke, it was with a deep measure of regret. "It is not just you, but your companion as well. I have heard from others that it will be tomorrow morning, at dawn. King Lensa's magicians have been practicing most diligently, and they have assured the king that they will be ready."

He then beckoned us over to the bars. "Please, allow me to give you water. It is only right."

Glynarra went first, and he reached into the barrel, took out a ladle, and gave her the precious liquid, slowly pouring it into her mouth. He then did the same for me. The water was cold and refreshing, and once I'd had my fill, the guard closed the barrel and made to leave.

At the stairs, though, he paused to ask, "Stranger, do you have gods on your world? If so, do you pray to them?"

Odd thing to ask, but why not answer him? "We have a lot of religions. Some people pray and some don't."

He pursed his lips as if considering the validity of my answer. "Then if you believe in one or more of those gods, I suggest that you use these last hours to pray to yours."

The door closed quietly behind him, and Glynarra muttered something that sounded like a swear word, although I couldn't be sure.

She then growled, "This is my world, and that pile of offal that calls himself a king wants to take me out of it. He's given us nothing but death and despair."

"Well, he gave us water," I said, attempting to tone things down a bit, although the concept of losing my life made me quiver with fear inside.

Glynarra laughed, a sharp, brittle sound. "Yeah, he did."

Funny, she used formal language with her own people, but with me, she spoke like anyone else from my neck of the woods would — mostly.

Alone now, my thirst gone for the moment, I attempted to find a comfortable position. It wasn't possible, as the bindings were too confining.

Additionally, my shoulders had long gone numb from the cramped position, and I could barely feel my hands. Our captors were smart. They knew how to bind and where, not to totally incapacitate, but to hamper movement to a great degree.

Still, by wriggling around, I managed to get some blood flowing in my extremities, and the pins-and-needles effect was welcome, even though it made me want to scream.

What wasn't welcome was the stink of the makeshift toilet. The stench that emanated from it still permeated the immediate area, but at least we had some fresh air coming through the window.

To take my mind off our impending execution as well as the stink, I asked Glynarra why she'd chosen Earth. She stared at me for asking what seemed like the dumbest question around. "Do you have to know?"

"Well, since it's our last night here, I'd like to educate myself." It was easy to be flip, but I did it to calm myself down as well as to try and take the tension away.

It had its effect as she laughed again, but without humor. "Traveling around, once I got the hang of it, was fun. Trial and error. That's how I found out where to live. Then I found your world. I thought it interesting."

As she related her story, she said that she was fond of Portland. In her walks around the city, she'd found my school.

"We don't have formal schools on my world. We learn at home from our parents and friends, and we have the facility to pick up new information quickly. I told you that, right?"

"Yeah, you did."

Glynarra wrinkled her nose as if it had an itch and she couldn't scratch it. "Well, anyway, it was simple for me to impersonate people there—mix and match features—learn the language. Then I met you and your friend Nick, and after that, we came here."

It sounded like an adventure, and I reminded myself that I was already hip-deep in hers. Glynarra wrinkled her nose again. "My nose itches."

I'd been right. "Uh, and you want me to scratch it?"

"Hold still."

With a slight grunt, she moved onto her knees and sidled over to me, rubbing her face on my shoulder. "The rough cloth helps," she said. "Thank you."

"Fine."

She sat back, observing me closely, and after a while, it got to be a little unnerving. "Something wrong?"

Glynarra shrugged. "No. I'm just curious about you. Like I said, you're my first human—I mean, the first Earth person I've ever spoken to at length. I don't know much about your people, even though I've been on and off your world many times. You're nice. So is Nick, your friend."

How to take that? What else could I say? "Thank you."

My cellmate seemed to find that funny, as she chuckled. Once her good humor died, she asked, "Are you united with another Earth person?"

"What?"

"United."

It took me a few seconds to figure out what she meant. "You mean, married?"

"Yes. Sorry…I used the wrong word."

It wasn't exactly wrong, but… "Uh, no, I'm going to be eighteen in a couple of days, June fifteenth. We usually don't get married that early, at least in North America."

Nevertheless, her question got me curious. "Are you?"

Glynarra shook her head and winced. "Sorry, my arms hurt. My neck does, too. Anyway, the answer's no. We're usually united by this age, but I chose not to."

"Why?"

Dimness of the cell or not, the purple in her eyes shone out and seemed to illuminate the space between us. "I never found anyone I liked. Some of the other men in my city thought me attractive, but they didn't like it when my powers were different. Others, I didn't find them attractive." She then stared at me. "Do you find me attractive?"

A direct question—that's what I liked about her, although I had almost zero experience in dating. I'd had one date in my life about six months ago…Barbara Morris.

Barbara was tall, blonde and pretty, with a snubby nose and a sunny smile. It should have been a no-brainer that I'd go out with her again. She wanted to, but I wanted something more.

Something more in my case meant getting the proper feeling. As dumb and as old-fashioned as it sounded, that was how I rolled. If I didn't feel any connection to a girl, why be hypocritical and go out with her?

In contrast, Glynarra was on the short side, but the fact that she had green skin, sharply pointed ears, pretty, pixie-ish features and practically glowed in the dark meant she was different.

Her attitude was one of defiance, not of compliance — one that I respected. That was also different. And different could be good.

Moreover, she made me feel as though I could do anything, even though I had to depend on her to get me from here to there, interdimensionally speaking.

"Well?"

Glynarra's question brought me back to reality. "Uh, yes."

A faint smile adorned her lips. "Well, I find you attractive, too."

That point settled, she asked me about my future plans. Considering our future would end tomorrow morning, why make plans? On the other hand, humor her. "Oh, uh, finish school, get a job, get out of the house, something like that."

"Are you comfortable there?"

Could she read minds? We were going to die anyway. "Honestly, no. My mother's never around. After my father died, she got into her job. So, we never talk."

Glynarra arched her eyebrows. "Never?"

It felt somewhat embarrassing, but whatever. Say it now. "Almost never. I mean, most kids my age don't really talk to their parents that much, but I'm weird, I guess. I wanted parents to talk to, along with friends, if that makes any sense."

"Anything else?"

"She always forgets my birthday."

Glynarra nodded. "You already told me, so I'll remember. Anyway, I was fortunate. I could always discuss things with my parents. At least you have a mother."

A mother in name only, I thought sourly. I wondered what else to say, but then Glynarra's head sagged. She was tired, and I found myself spiraling into the land of darkness as well.

Before sleep found me, I thought I heard her whisper, "I promise to remember your birthday," but I couldn't be sure...

* * * *

"It is time."

A voice spoke, deep and harsh, cutting into my sleep time. The voice then repeated itself, more forcefully this time. "It is the day and the hour. Wake up."

A slap to my cheek accompanied the command. I looked up, blinked and focused on the slapper. It was the guard from yesterday—not Vasso but the mean one...Starra. He held a torch in his right hand.

"Your presence is requested in the courtyard. It is time for you to meet the eternal darkness."

Was it dawn already? I didn't remember passing out, but if Mr. Eyepatch was here, then it meant our time had come. I struggled to my knees. With a grunt, I got to my feet and looked through the window. The sky was still dark, but faint fingers of light were poking their way through the dimness.

Glynarra had already woken up and was on her feet. Her face was set, and her eyes radiated hatred. "Uh, I have a last request," I said, acting as humbly as possible. We had one chance and one chance only. "If it's okay."

The guard had pulled his sword halfway out of its scabbard, but he pushed it in again. "What is it?"

"Could you untie my arms, please? I have to go to the bathroom."

Sure, it was an old ploy, but the guard didn't have to know that. With a grunt of impatience, he ordered, "Turn around. I shall untie you."

"Thank you."

I did as he requested, and once the bonds were free, I went to the hole in the corner to let fly, shaking my arms out. "Hurry it up," the guard said, sounding as though he simply wanted to get this over and done with.

"Just getting the blood flowing," I answered as I turned my head to wink at Glynarra and mouthed, "Get ready."

I got an almost imperceptible nod in return. It was now or never, and she crouched, tensing her muscles.

"Have you finished, stranger?" the guard asked. "I do not have all day, and you will not have tomorrow. Hurry."

Once I finished, I turned and charged. Glynarra did the same thing. Starra wasn't expecting an attack, and armor or not, our combined impact sent him into the bars, headfirst. Bone met metal, and guess which one won? After a distressing crack sounded, he slid down, unconscious, and I picked up the torch and put it in one of the holders on the wall.

"Nice job," Glynarra murmured. "Get me out of these ropes."

"Your wish is my command." I grinned as I untied her. Call it a cliché, but it fit.

Once free, she shook her arms out and closed her eyes. "Be quiet. I have to concentrate."

Concentration was everything. A series of grunts came from her, indicating that she was getting into the mood. However, outside, someone yelled, "Starra, where are the prisoners?"

Hurry.

"Starra!"

The sound of thudding feet came our way. *Aw, hell, this isn't good.* "Glynarra, hurry," I muttered.

"Almost there," she said softly. "Almost…yes!"

A window formed and she pointed to Starra. "Get his extender."

Get what? *Oh, wait, the weapon.* I went to the guard and yanked it off his belt. It wasn't overly heavy, perhaps half a pound, and I joined her at the window. Yells and cries for our deaths grew louder.

"Where are we going?" I asked as she jumped in and extended her hand to haul me through.

"Anywhere but here."

Chapter Eleven

Horror World, Part One

We landed on a shelf of jagged rock, entering a world shrouded in dusk and shadows, wind and swirling sand. Marvelous, more darkness. Dust clouded my vision, and I couldn't see more than a few feet in front of me. This...wasn't what I'd expected at all. "Glynarra, what is this place?"

"I don't know," she answered with a great deal of uncertainty as she scanned the area. "I had to hurry...didn't have enough time to get a fix. Maybe I made a mistake in the incantation to open the window. I only know that I've never been here before."

She didn't know. We'd gone from certain death to...what? I had no idea, but this place could only be described as foreboding, and I didn't want to lose it in front of her.

Wind or not, it was hot here, at least a hundred degrees, and I started sweating right away. At the very least, it didn't have a hot sun overhead, so perhaps my sunburn would go away soon, but why couldn't we have landed somewhere nice?

While that wasn't Glynarra's fault, our situation wasn't optimal in the least. The air was heavy and filled with dust, and it made us cough. In waving it away, some of it got into my lungs, and I began to choke.

I managed to hack it out, but Glynarra fell to her knees, wheezing. "Got…in my chest…" she managed to rasp.

A whack on her back from me loosened things, and she spat out a wad of mucus. It landed on a rock, drying immediately. *What kind of a world is this?*

Not only was the environment forbidding, but also the darkness began to get to me. It wasn't so much the darkness itself, but because of what lay inside it. In a rush, my childhood phobia hit. *Damn it, I'm supposed to be over this!*

Obviously not. To take my mind off the fear of things going bump in the night, I asked, "Um, can you see around us?"

Glynarra was breathing better now. She'd gotten to her feet and peered into the gloom. Then she pointed straight ahead. "Our species has good night vision. We're on a hill, on a large section of rock. There are… I see many holes in the distance, on a flat plain."

Flat plain…holes…we could be anywhere. I muttered, "I wonder what this place is called."

"Horror World," a voice said from behind us. "You're the new fish, right?"

We whirled around. A man faced us, holding a torch that illuminated his body and features. He wore a soiled and torn jumpsuit that, in the flickering firelight, looked as though it might have been green once. With the swirling wind and dirt, it was almost impossible to tell.

Wind or not, a fetid smell came from him, like he hadn't showered in a few months. On this world, though, I wondered if they had water. If they did, then they didn't believe in the concept of proper hygiene.

He gave us a reassuring smile that was totally out of place here. "Welcome to hell."

While I digested his statement, he took a step closer. About five-ten, he wore no shoes and had something around his neck. Long, plastic, lenses — binoculars, maybe. Whoever this guy was, he was roughly humanoid.

On second thought, not really. When he turned partially around to check out the area, his features shone through, gloom or no. He had a square head with a face on the front. That was human enough.

When he twisted around a bit more, I saw another face on the back of his head — with three eyes instead of two. Call that decidedly not human. Now, I'd seen it all.

His hands were oversized, with four stubby fingers each, each one double the size of mine. Thick and powerful, they seemed capable of tearing through just about anything. He was also totally bald. As for his age, perhaps he was in his mid-forties, but it was only a guess.

"Prisoners?" Glynarra guessed. "You're a prisoner?"

He nodded. "My name's Naxos. I'm the leader here."

"I'm Mark," I said and pointed at my friend. "That's Glynarra. We, uh, just got in. Our, um, ship landed us here a while ago then they took off."

Glynarra shot me a look of why-are-you-lying-about-the-transportation, but I shook my head slightly.

I couldn't say why, but telling a stranger that we had portal ability didn't seem wise. "Uh, Naxos, how long have you been—?"

"Six months ago," he cut in while waving the dust away, then he spit on the ground. "I've been here six months, fourteen days and maybe seven hours. I try to keep track of things because the time difference is confusing. I'm used to days and nights. Here, there's only dusk. This is a penal colony. No guards here. They aren't needed."

"Stupid question," I said, waving my hand for attention. "Why not?"

Like an owl, his head revolved around, and face number two nailed me with a glare. His third eye lay in the middle of his forehead, and it was a bright blue, in contrast to the brown of his other eyes. "Because the Underworlders make sure we don't leave. If they catch us, they eat us. That's why."

He turned away, both his faces frowning. "Underworlders," I repeated, not quite getting the concept. "What are they?"

A horrid screeching sound like the combination of squealing brakes combined with the dying cry of a pig split the semi-darkness.

Naxos got a look of alarm on his faces and jerked his thumb behind him. "That's their cry. We have to get out of here, go somewhere safe."

We turned to leave, but movement on the plain fifty feet away caught my eye and I tapped Naxos on the shoulder. "Hey, someone's out there. Look."

He and Glynarra turned around. A short, fat individual with multiple legs and arms was hurriedly skirting the holes on the plain. Even from that distance, I heard its pleas for help.

A blast of wind blew out the torch, and with a curse, our guide tossed the burned-out stick away. He then unslung the device around his neck and handed it to me.

"Look and learn, kid," he said in the coldest manner possible. "This is what happens when you don't obey the rules of this world."

I did as he said and looked through the device. As I'd suspected, they were binoculars. The running man was more like a centipede, although it had an oddly human face. I passed the binoculars back. "You know him?"

He squinted through the lenses and nodded. "Yeah, I know who it is, poor bastard. But I can't do a damn thing. He was hunting for food. Now, he'll *be* food in a few seconds."

It was a heartless statement, but if this world were as bad as he'd said, then it was a good warning. That warning came true, as what looked like a long, bone-white tentacle emerged from a hole to snatch the hapless runner and haul him below.

The centipede guy screamed—once. Then, silence, only broken by the horrid screeching sounds the monsters made. I shuddered at the thought of what was happening to the victim, and with an effort, I put that thought out of my mind. It wouldn't help thinking about him, not now.

"That was Flinnatta," Naxos said as he let the binoculars dangle around his neck. "Nice guy. Bum rap. Let's go. I'll fill you guys in on the details."

Harsh words for a harsh world. We turned around and started walking.

* * * *

Five minutes later

Despite the dimness of our surroundings, Naxos' footing was sure, and he led us to a cave not far away. Located on a hill, it was deep and dark. He said it had only one way in and one way out. It was large enough to stand upright and move around freely in, and it had a few strategically placed torches that provided light.

At the entrance, I gazed at around forty or so spears that leaned against the wall in a neat row. Naxos asked me about my weapon. "It does this," I said and pressed the trigger. The sharp end shot out, then I retracted it.

"Handy," Naxos said in an admiring tone. "Very handy. C'mon."

He led us deeper into the cave. About fifty people made up the population. Some of them were sleeping or staring off into the distance. Although their clothes were filthy and torn, they looked to be the same as what Naxos wore. All of them were barefoot.

Immediately, the smell of unwashed bodies came through. No water source here. My nose hairs wilted under the stench, and from Glynarra's expression of disgust, she wasn't overly keen on the smell, either.

As for the people here, those that weren't asleep or resting patrolled the entrance and the space just below it. All of them were armed with spears.

A few other members were sequestered deeper in the cave. I wondered why until I got a look at them. They were asleep, and humanoid or not, they all thrashed around fitfully.

"Monster shock," Naxos said as we observed a creature that resembled a cactus wave its branches and mutter something about the Underworlders coming.

"That's Eddra. It's a guy, by the way. He came here with his mate, and she got killed the first day by one of those things. He's had nightmares ever since. That was about sixteen days back, if my math is right."

PTSD had to be terrible. My fear of the dark was bad enough, but after seeing that monster snatch someone, everything else seemed miniscule. Naxos beckoned us over to a quiet spot where a great number of X's had been etched into the wall in ragged horizontal lines.

"Like I said, I got here six months ago," Naxos said, pointing at the X's. "I'm still alive because I listened to those who knew more and stayed away from the holes. That's key."

"What's the name of this place?" Glynarra wanted to know.

He made a sweeping gesture that included the residents of the cave. "We call it Horror World, but it really has no name. Like I said, it's a penal colony. We're all here because of crimes the authorities said that we committed on our home worlds. You might be wondering why we can understand each other."

It had crossed my mind. He pointed to his left wrist. In the firelight, a tiny bulge stuck out and a faint red glow pulsed from under the skin. "Translation chip," he said offhandedly. "It makes communication easier."

Yes, it did, then the word 'crimes' echoed in my head. "Crimes," I echoed, wondering what in the hell they'd done to merit this kind of sentence.

Naxos laughed. It sounded like a rusty saw mating with a wet wooden fence. "Yeah, we're criminals, at least in the eyes of the law. We all look different, but we have one thing in common—the laws on our worlds have outlawed the death penalty."

He called for water, and someone brought us four small plastic jugs. Naxos hefted his. "We have a well dug behind this cave. But we only use the water for drinking. Bathing's once every ten days. Sorry for the stink."

Well, that explained the body odor. He drained his jug right away, and we followed suit. He then took the fourth jug and poured it over his head. "Ah that was good," he muttered. "Like I said, we don't get a chance to clean up too often. Uh, where was I?"

"No death penalty on your world," I prompted, marveling at the extra water he got. Rank had its privileges.

He nodded and wiped the excess water from his front face. "Oh, yeah, right. Like I was saying, the authorities didn't want to kill us, so they sent us here. Minimum sentence is ten years. Most people die in the first forty-eight to ninety-six hours. Easy way to cut down on prison costs, eh?"

I wondered what crime he'd committed, but it wasn't the time to ask, not yet.

Naxos told us that the Underworlders would only come out at a certain point during the eternal dusk. They'd timed it to the second, it seemed. "Like I said, it's always dusk here. No storms, no sunlight, just dust and wind and sand and heat. That's it. As for the critters, one of their weaknesses is that they don't like bright light, hence the torches. Pretty neat, right?"

"Yeah," I said, striving to say something useful.

Another screeching cry echoed from the valley plains. "The Underworlders," Naxos said, his expression grim. "That's the cry they make to their other buddies when it's time to feed. They come out at this time to forage for food, just like we do at other times. That's why we don't go near the holes. Sometimes, they stay just below the surface, waiting to ambush us."

A sudden gust of wind entered, spewing dust around. Naxos waved the dust away and scratched his jaw with a filthy thumb. "Those critters don't like climbing through sand and brush, but we still keep on the alert at all times."

He pointed at the guards for emphasis. "During the other hours, the critters sleep or screw or something. Nobody's ever done a study on them, but we know this much. For about two hours, they haul their asses around the valley floor, searching for food."

"Are there other animals here?" I asked.

"Some," Naxos replied, checking his dirt-encrusted nails. He nibbled on his thick pinky then spit something out.

"They're small, multi-legged things. Problem is, we can't eat 'em. We found out the hard way that they're poisonous. We eat other things instead."

This was getting worse and worse by the second, and Naxos compounded it by adding, "After they feed, the Underworlders go below, but like I said, some lie in wait near the entrance to their holes."

He tapped the side of his head as if to draw out more information. "Oh, yeah, this is important. They hunt by sound. That's why you go barefoot. We all do. Walk softly, no talking, just pick up the food and go. From what we know, they don't see very well, but they have great hearing. They focus on the vibrations and sounds. They feel them. Anything that makes a vibration or a noise and comes within range of their tentacles, they grab."

"Anything?" Glynarra asked. She looked uneasy. I couldn't blame her.

His head revolved around to nail her with a stare from his blue eye. "Yeah, anything. Doesn't matter what kind of species they snatch. To them, anything's food."

He shuddered and twisted his head around to face front again. "It's terrifying. That's all I can say. I ain't afraid of much, but those things scare me. Once they latch on, they drag you below and that's it. Got the picture?"

I nodded. Glynarra did the same thing. A mental image of a monster reaching out to snatch me hit, ran rampant through my mind and it wouldn't leave.

"Second thing," Naxos said, interrupting my day-mare. "Since you're now part of our happy clan, when you go out to forage for food — and you will — you go out in a group. No questions on that, no debate. Safety in numbers. Got it?"

We nodded again, too scared of the possibility of getting snatched. "If those beasts attack, then light up a flare. When I got sent here, I got a huge supply of them. One of the judges showed mercy."

He took something from a pocket in his uniform. A sliver of plastic the size of my pinky finger, he turned it over, then he dug into his pocket and brought out a handful of them.

"Here... Take these." He handed them over. I pocketed half and gave the other half to Glynarra.

"They act like mini solar flares," he continued. "Just snap one of them in half and turn your face away. They're beyond bright. The flash lasts for about ten seconds, and it'll blind them."

To demonstrate, he told everyone to shield their eyes. "Ready…here we go," he said, twisting the stick.

I closed my eyes, but even so, a mini solar flare burned through my eyelids, and when I opened them again, spots clouded my vision, and I frantically waved them away. They soon disappeared.

Naxos chuckled grimly at my reaction. "Don't worry about flinching. I did the same thing when I first used these babies. Nothing to fear. Just remember that once you light one up, you can either run away or attack. I suggest running away."

"Why?" Glynarra asked.

He ran his stubby fingers over his front face, while using his other hand to scratch his rear face, a gesture that was more than a little disturbing. "Let me describe them to you. They've got six tentacles, and the tentacles are about twelve feet long and sticky. That's their trap. Their bodies are around five feet squared. That means they're a lot bigger than we are. Their skin is tough, like trying to cut through leather with a small knife. It's also fireproof."

From the description, it sounded as though they'd been facing off against giant starfish. I had another question. "Besides light, do they have any other weaknesses?"

Naxos bobbed his head in respect. "Hey, you're a pretty smart guy. To answer your question, they have one weakness, but it means getting close to their mouth. Just above their mouth is a slit. I don't know what it's for. Maybe breathing or maybe for something else, but if you can shove something sharp inside it, that'll make it let go. If you jam Mr. Sharp Object way down, you might be able to kill it."

He got up to take a torch from its holder and beckoned us over. He then waved it at the far wall where a skin from one of the Underworlders hung. Yeah, it was a starfish, white all over and large.

"I killed that one," Naxos said, not without undue pride. "It almost got me, but I found the slit and shoved a spear that I'd made as far down the hole as I could. It died soon after, and some of us hauled the carcass up here and skinned it. But like I told you, just like the other critters here, we can't eat them — poisonous."

A closer look revealed what we were up against. While the creature itself was ugly, the mouth was especially horrid, filled with six-inch long, irregularly spaced and extremely sharp-looking teeth. I also saw the slit, but what its function was, was anyone's guess.

Naxos snorted and spat from both faces. "They'll cut you into sections and chew you up good," he said as he returned the torch to its holder. So, that's how they operate. They're mean, hard to kill and they don't give up. Stay safe, stay smart, stick with those who know more and you might just make it."

With that, he went over to the entrance, grabbed a spear and stood on duty. The face on the back of his head closed its eyes, but I knew that he was watching the tableau below with his front face.

Glynarra and I found a spot away from the others. "Are we going to leave soon?" I asked, sotto voce. Naxos had been helpful, but something was bothering me, and I couldn't figure out what it was.

She shook her head. "I'm still tired, and I can't use my powers in the dark."

At her pronouncement, I wanted to scream in frustration, but I managed to rein my emotions in. "Say what?" My voice came out like someone was strangling me from the inside.

"I'm sorry I didn't tell you before," she said in a remorseful tone. "I can only form a window if it's bright out, like daylight. Here, I'm just like everyone else."

Naxos stood a few feet away, conversing quietly with one of the other cave-dwellers. He walked backward to face us, and that was weird in and of itself. It was even weirder when his back face opened its eyes. "Listen… You guys must be beat. Sack out. We'll wake you when it's time to forage."

"Thanks," I said. "Appreciate it."

Glynarra snuggled next to me. I was hungry but also too tired to eat. We had only seventy hours left for her to get something going or else she'd die. If that happened, I'd be stuck here for the rest of my life…for however long I lived.

Chapter Twelve

Horror World, Part Two

I must have fallen asleep, as someone's hand shook my shoulder. My sunburn itched and I woke up, scratching the back of my neck absentmindedly. "What? Where…"

"It's me, Naxos," a voice said.

I blinked my eyes. Naxos stood over me with a torch in his hand. "You've been out for a long time."

"How long?" I mumbled after yawning.

"About seven hours. You must have been whipped. C'mon. Get your friend up. We're going down to the plains. We have to gather food."

He turned around and made his way to the entrance where the other inmates joined him. I was still tired, but I shook off the fatigue. It was time to go. We had to earn our keep.

Glynarra was still asleep but woke up instantly at my touch, blinked, then muttered something about needing another ten minutes of rest.

"Sorry," I said as I got up. "We have to go. And I thought your species didn't need to sleep much."

"We don't, but if we're really exhausted, we take a few hours longer," she reminded me as she rose and stretched out.

Uh-huh.

Fifteen of us emerged from the cave. Everyone carried a basket and a spear, and I took my extender. No torches. The wind had increased in intensity and wouldn't allow the torches to stay lit. We all went barefoot and slowly made our way down the hill to the edge of the plains.

The back of my neck itched from the sunburn, but then the hair on it stood up. This was not good. I'd seen someone die here not that long ago.

With each step I took, my heart rate increased about five beats. By the time we got to our destination, it was slamming against my chest wall and threatening to jump out.

"Are you okay?" Glynarra asked. "Is something wrong?"

Fear of the dark, thanks ever so much. I hadn't even realized that my breathing was that rapid. "Whatever gave you that idea?"

"You're panting as though you'd run a long-distance race in five minutes."

Glynarra was nothing if not perceptive. *Fine, tell her.* "If you must know, I'm afraid of the dark and those damn holes. It's a phobia I have, okay? I thought I was over it, but I guess I'm not. Aren't you scared?"

She nodded. "I am, but I've been through worse. I can get through this. Focus on me. That'll help."

Her confidence gave me confidence, and I took in a series of deep breaths and focused on the task at hand. It had its effect, and I gained control. Horror ahead or not, it was fight or die, and I wasn't ready to die, not yet.

Mission—go out, gather food, get back safely. I could do that. Naxos led the way, and we moved as soundlessly as possible through the sand and brush until we reached the plain and started walking. All I heard was my breathing and thundering heart. *Do this… You can do this…*

"Stop," Naxos said quietly and pointed to two small lumps the size of tennis balls. He kneeled and gently worked them from the ground. They came out, the soil sifting from their roots and being blown away by the wind.

"It's a tuber," he murmured. "This is what we're collecting. We don't have a name for them, yet. They taste bitter, but they're edible. Near as we can figure, they've got a good balance of carbs, fat and protein."

He brushed the dirt off and handed them to us. "Eat. You'll need your strength."

They were hard and bitter, but hunger overruled taste buds. After I finished, I asked, keeping my voice low, "Um, don't you eat anything else?"

Naxos didn't get upset. He knew we were the rookies here. "This is it. Trust me. If we could find something else to eat, we would've found it by now."

"Yeah, but—"

"Fill a basket, get back to the cave," he ordered, all trace of supportive mentorship gone. "For now, no questions. Just do your jobs. We'll talk later."

He then directed everyone to hurry and make as little noise as possible, whispering over the wind that we had to move out in groups of three. "Mark, you, Glynarra and Unkoo go together. Use your flash sticks if you have to, but if you see those critters, run."

Naxos waved for another inmate to join us. When he came over, Naxos introduced us. "This is Unkoo."

Unkoo was a tree-like creature, not much taller than Glynarra. He had a wide mouth, irregularly shaped wooden teeth and he rolled along soundlessly on tubular roots. Multiple branches made up his arms. His head was completely flat, as if someone had ironed it that way.

He also had at least fifty eyes, and it was disconcerting to see them move in fifty different directions at once. He was pleasant enough, though. "What are you two in for?" he asked as we carefully made our way along the plains.

Think fast. "Robbery," I said.

The eyebrows, thin slabs of wood, arched on every eye. "Did you get away with a lot? Manage to stash some money or goods somewhere safe? If you did, it was worth it."

To my way of thinking, stealing was totally wrong, even if a person was hungry, but then again, I'd never been in that situation. Poor, yes. Starving and desperate, no, but I'd soon get there.

"Yeah, a lot," I decided to reply, and Glynarra shot me an arched eyebrows look, meaning she was either impressed or just trolling me. I couldn't tell which.

"Me, I got sent here for beating up my so-called friend," Unkoo replied after a fashion. "He made a move on my lady-mate, so I tore his branches off. Didn't kill him, though."

That was a new one, and while I should have been surprised, I wasn't. Maybe on his world that was akin to assault and battery or attempted murder. "And you got sent here for that?"

"On my world—it's called Gheerusa—the law is harsh but fair. We got all types where I come from. Our kind, and people sorta like yours, Mark."

He looked at Glynarra. "We don't got your type over there... What's your name again, girl?"

"It's Glynarra," she replied. "Call me Glyn. It's a nickname."

Surprised at her admission, I asked, "It is? You never told me."

"You never asked."

Unkoo laughed harshly. "Some couple you are. Don't even know each other's names. That's funny."

He kept chuckling as he used his branches to snatch the lumps we were supposed to gather. Glyn and I did our best to keep up, but against a being that had as many branches as he had, we didn't stand a chance.

Moreover, the idea of being in the near-dark close to some monsters that wouldn't think twice about eating me didn't increase my confidence level at all.

"Basket's full," Unkoo said. He came over and showed us his takings. In contrast, ours were only half full. "What's wrong, Mark? Afraid of a few holes?"

"Actually, yes. And the darkness."

Unkoo chuckled. "It ain't the hole, buddy. It's what comes out of it."

He started laughing harder, amused by his own joke. The sound level increased, and didn't Naxos say something about shutting one's mouth and making as little noise as possible?

This had to stop. I was paranoid enough. I shook one of his branches. "Hey, Unkoo, shut it. Those things are probably still listening."

Perhaps shaking Mr. Tree-Thing's arm wasn't the smartest thing to do as his mouth twisted in an ugly display of anger and every single eye glared at me. "Boy, don't you go around telling me what to do. I've been here for over four months. I'm a survivor, and…augh!"

A tentacle had snaked out of a hole and wrapped itself with lightning speed around his waist. It lifted him off the ground and began to squeeze. "Help me," he cried. "Help me!"

Help given, as Glyn and I ran over to do what we could. I used the extender and ran it through the creature's tentacle, but it didn't do much.

Instead, it started to squeeze Unkoo even harder. He continued to scream for help, and where was the rest of the hunting party?

They were nowhere to be found. Unkoo's pleas for help split the air, along with the wailing of the creatures. It was a horrible moment, a situation where I wanted to look away but dared not to.

"Help me," Unkoo gurgled. Brownish-black sap trickled out of the corners of his mouth, and it soon became a torrent. He was being crushed by an inhuman vise, a giant arm, and that arm did not want to let go. "Nooooo!"

Unkoo let out a horrid scream just before the monster then squished his midsection and separated his upper body from his lower body, the latter twitching. Glyn made a gagging sound and bent over, dry heaving. I thought I'd hurl, too, but I managed to control my stomach — barely.

There was nothing we could do. Unkoo's eyes stared sightlessly at the sky, and it was only then that I heard Naxos yell for us to retreat. "Back off," he called out. "Back off. It isn't worth it."

"You heard him," Glyn said as she inhaled and exhaled shallowly, her body quivering in fear. "Time to go."

I yanked my weapon out. We turned to leave, but another tentacle came out of nowhere and wrapped itself around Glyn's ankles, pulling her legs out from under her. She fell on her stomach but lifted her head long enough for me to see the terror on her face and in her eyes. "Mark!"

Oh, shit! The monster then began to drag her below. "Glyn!"

I started over to the hole, but Naxos sprinted in my direction, yelling that she was their dinner and that it wouldn't do any good to try to save her. Frantic now, I cried, "She's my friend. I can't let her die."

Naxos shook his head. "Mark, I get that you're with her, but don't go. I've seen others try rescue missions. They never came back."

I'd hesitated once before, when Glyn had first invited me to Tellkar, but not now. Hesitation meant her death, and her death meant mine. "Watch me."

Another cry for help from Glyn sounded. Heedless of the danger, knowing that my life would more than likely be over in the next twenty seconds, I dove in after her.

Chapter Thirteen

Horror World, Part Three

The surface of the hole was smooth and acted like a water slide, bringing me down at a tremendously high speed toward a fate that I didn't want to contemplate.

Darkness enveloped me like a blanket, and I shook off the fear that came with it. A flash stick lit things up as I sped along. Light exploded all around me. Marks were on the wall, nicks and gouges in the stone where the monsters had used their limbs to haul themselves up.

After the light faded, another image hit, that of one of the starfish killers waiting for me with its tentacles outstretched and mouth open wide. If those teeth ever latched onto me, I could kiss my ass goodbye.

I had only one weapon, the extender. Gripping it firmly, finger on the trigger, I grimly waited for the ride to finish. If I had to die, then I'd take as many of them with me as I could — and free Glyn in the process.

Sure, it was a dream. Sure, it sounded like an Alpha Male's vision of a truly heroic deed, but I had to pump myself up somehow. Fear competed with anger, and this time, anger won out.

By that time, the hole had shifted to a steeper angle. I was moving even faster and muttering, "Bring it on, you bastards. Bring it on."

My ride ended a few seconds later when I landed in a chamber, slamming into the hard ground. I came up spitting dirt, nerves on edge, feeling danger all around me. It was dark here, but no darker than outside, and my eyes soon adjusted.

A heavy, cloying stink, one of copper and shit and ammonia, attacked my nostrils, worming then shoving its way into my nasal passages and subsequently assaulting my sense of smell. If I survived this, I'd never complain about taking out the garbage again.

Along with the smell was an unearthly quiet. I listened carefully for the sound of slithering limbs and torsos, or the wailing cries of the monsters that hungered for flesh, but I didn't hear a sound.

Taking a chance, I pulled out another flash stick and twisted it, holding my face away from the blast of brilliance. After the stick lit things up, I was sorry that I did it. I'd landed in a chamber filled with bones and half-to-mostly devoured beings from every race imaginable.

Skeletons, some intact but most not, lay strewn around the chamber. Smashed organs, some of which looked semi-human, littered the floor, sending up a horrid smell of death and decay. Blood painted every section of the walls, every rock, and almost every square inch of the ground.

This was where the creatures took their prey.

This was where the hapless victims spent their last few seconds of life.

This was where they died.

The flash burned out, and I lit another, hopeful that I'd at least keep the monsters at bay if they entered. I had to find Glyn, if she was still alive. If she wasn't, then what was the use of it all?

An entrance to another chamber lay ahead. Heart thudding in my chest, I advanced on the opening and found fifteen-plus Underworlders lying prone on the hard ground. A faint sound of whistling breath came from them, and while they occasionally stirred, they didn't get up.

Were they sleeping? Right, eat a heavy meal, sleep it off.

"Glyn," I whispered. "Glyn?"

I got no answer, but then I saw another chamber, stepped lightly over to it and entered. There, I found more bones and rotting flesh, and the smell was even more horrible than before. Then I found another chamber then one more.

I'd entered a vast underground chain of carefully constructed rooms, large enough to house the bodies of hundreds of people. It was an alien anthill, only much deeper, bloodier and far more horrifying. No telling how far this alien anthill went, but I'd keep searching until I found Glyn.

"Hey, are you here?" I asked as loudly as I dared. "Glyn?"

I kept searching, going ever farther into this maze of death. I soon became disoriented, as all the chambers seemed the same, either filled with sleeping Under-worlders or rooms used as waste disposal areas.

"Glyn?"

I'd entered perhaps my twentieth chamber. No answer, and my heart sank. If she was dead, then I hoped that her end had been mercifully quick.

Anger filled me, ire at being stuck in this situation, rage at the unfairness of it all and fury at having to deal with a situation that I wasn't sure that I could deal with. If only Glyn were here, it would make all the difference in the world...

Something heavy fell on my left shoulder and spun me around. It was one of them. It had to be. Dimness of the cavern or not, I made out the features of one of the Underworlders.

My heart thudded in my chest. Panic seized me, but then the survival instinct took over. The slit, get the slit above their mouth! My finger fumbled for the button on the extender...

"Mark, it's me," the creature whispered.

Could monsters speak? Wait a second. *Glyn? She's alive?* "What—"

"Don't talk. Follow me."

As she led me through the chamber, my nerves on fire and my mind whirling, it came to me. She was a shapeshifter. She'd simply transformed into one of the monsters and they'd thought she was one of them.

Clever.

One of the real monsters stirred and made a move in our direction. For the first time, I saw its eyes. It had four of them, right above its mouth, bright reddish gold orbs. Perhaps it had more, but this was not Biology 101, and this wasn't another frog to be dissected.

Glyn picked me up with her tentacle and hissed at the other creature. It slumped back against a rock, gnashing its teeth, but it didn't make a move toward us.

Neither did the other Underworlders, who were sound asleep.

Odd, when they slept, their eyes folded up under a flap of skin near their mouth. I wondered why they needed eyes when they hunted by sound.

It was something to think about. Also, as strong as they were, they weren't overly intelligent. After all, they'd been fooled quite easily.

Glyn hauled me to the end of the cavern where a hole led up to the surface. In a flash, she shrank to her default form and what else could we do but grab each other and kiss and—oh my God, she was perfect!

Her tongue tickled mine, and I'd never been kissed this way before. Apparently, neither had she, as she pressed against my body in a most urgent manner. "Hey," I said as we broke the clinch to come up for air. "That was…amazing."

"Yes, the same for me, too," she answered and darkness or not, her face seemed flushed. "It was my first time to kiss someone. Was it okay?"

"More than okay."

Let's hear it for being alive. That counted for everything. "I think first kisses should be done in a safer environment," I said. "Don't you?"

A tiny smile came to her face. "Agreed. Let's go."

"How?" The tunnel was as smooth as glass.

"Give me a second." Glyn took in a deep breath, her arms and legs shook…then she whooshed out air and said with disappointment, "I can't shift."

"You can't?"

"No. Changing into one of those creatures took a lot out of me. I need to rest."

Oh, wonderful, what now?

I looked around and glory be, there was a crack in the rock to our right. We went over to examine it. "It looks large enough for two people to fit inside," she whispered.

"You go first."

Our refuge was a tiny cave with just enough room for us to sit, although I kept my extender handy. My back itched, so I rubbed it against the wall. It helped, but only a little.

Then we waited—and waited…and waited some more. I began to nod off, so Glyn said she'd take the first watch. "Thanks," I said, and I settled back against the uneven stone.

Minutes or hours later, someone shook my shoulder. I woke up immediately, only to find Glyn's purple eyes staring at me from out of the gloom. "Hey, you've been out a long time."

"How long?" My head hurt, so maybe it was due to the heat or the stress—or both.

"Not sure," she murmured, her mouth close to my ear. "At least eight hours. But our hosts are awake."

Oh, hell. I checked outside. Sure enough, the Underworlders were moving around, screeching their unholy cries. So, we kept silent and dared not move while they slithered by. Glyn sacked out, and I waited, my heart thudding in my chest, until they were gone.

Silence. They must have gone up top to hunt for food. We could leave, and I hoped that someone in the cave had medicine. My headache hadn't abated. "Hey, wake up," I whispered.

Glyn stirred and opened her eyes. "I was asleep?"

"About five or six hours, I guess," I said, rubbing my temples.

My guide observed me closely. "Headache?"

"Yeah, how'd you know?"

Her eyes widened. "How long have we been here?" *Like I'm supposed to know?* "Not sure. Why?"

"The curse," she muttered. "It's the curse. My head hurts, too. How's your stomach?"

Come to think of it, it felt like someone was pressing on it. It didn't hurt, not really, but I felt the pressure, all the same. "So-so. What's this about the curse?"

"I just remembered. Lensa cursed not only me, but also the first person who came with me. He wanted me to suffer loneliness."

And she'd just decided to tell me now. While I should have been angry, I couldn't dredge up the emotion. It wasn't worth it, but still, I had to know. "So...the curse is on me, too? I mean, only to alien worlds?"

Glyn's eyes filled with remorse. "I'm sorry. I should have told you before, but in all the confusion, I forgot. You're safe on my world or yours, but here..."

It wasn't necessary for her to say anything else. While I should have been angry, I couldn't dredge up the emotion. We had to get out of here and soon. "Let's go."

We emerged from the cleft and cautiously looked around. Nothing. At one of the holes, Glyn stopped. "I feel better now. I can shift. Wait."

She took in a deep breath and the transformation to one of the monsters began once more. After that, she wrapped a tentacle around me and started up the hole, but then another creature happened to slither by twenty feet away. It had obviously seen her shift, as it sent out a cry of alarm.

That cry alone was enough to send my heart racing, and I practically dropped a load, but then I remembered the extender. "Glyn, throw me at the monster."

"What?"

Fear combined with anger at our situation were prime motivators. "Just do it!"

Glyn hurled me in an arc toward the creature, and I descended right in front of it. Its mouth was open, and its eyes were hungry.

Too bad its brain was turned off. I had the extender out and ready. At the right moment, I pressed the button and the blade shot out. It went into the slit and right down a passage in the monster's body, killing it instantly. It didn't even have time to screech.

Earth and Tellkar one, Underworlders nothing.

I pulled the extender out and ran back to Glyn. It wouldn't take long for our starfish attackers to gather for round two. She grabbed me around the waist with a tentacle and we went up through the tunnel. Once we got to the surface, she shook herself all over and reverted to her default state.

"Let's get back to the cave," she said. "I need to eat and rest up. We still have to get out of here. I think we have about a day left—maybe less."

We started walking, but a horrid screech combined with the slippery, slithering sound the creatures made caused us to reconsider taking a leisurely stroll back to our shelter.

No less than six Underworlders emerged from below and charged, their tentacles causing their bodies to whip back and forth, hurling clouds of dirt into the air. Their cries of anger and hunger split the eternal night. Oh, crap, they'd caught on to us. "Run," I cried. "Run!"

Glyn didn't have to be told twice, and she grabbed my hand and hauled me forward. For a small person, she was incredibly fast, and while I was no snail, I felt like one beside her.

There...the hill came into view, and I risked a look behind me. Five of the creatures were hot on our tail. "Keep running," Glyn yelled. "Keep running!"

We ran for our lives, and soon, we outdistanced the enemy and went up the hill, back to the cave. I stole another look behind me. The creatures had given up the chase and had disappeared into their holes.

We'd made it, and a feeling of exultation almost made me scream in triumph. Almost—but not quite, as I was too exhausted from the narrow escape and my head still pounded from the magical curse.

Naxos and two other men were waiting at the entrance, the main man with his binoculars slung around neck. All of them were armed and ready, but we were safe—for the moment.

Puffing and panting, Glyn and I dragged ourselves through the entrance and fell to the floor, gasping for air. Naxos' front face broke into a grin. "Mark, Glynnara, you made it back."

"How long have we been gone?" I asked, still tired and confused and relieved at getting out of that lair.

"About half a day." Half a day? Naxos' grin grew broader. "Come in. You need to eat and rest up."

Well, call that right neighborly. "Thank you," Glyn said. "I need food."

Naxos ushered us in. Someone had been cooking over a small fire, and we got served a few boiled tubers, those vegetables we'd picked up not so long ago. I was so hungry, I'd have eaten rocks and called that a six-course meal.

"Some escape," Naxos said, his good humor suddenly gone. Now, he sounded like a businessman laying out his plan for a hostile takeover. "Yes, that was some escape. Very interesting how you pulled it off."

Another cave dweller said that he'd never seen anyone move so fast. He scratched his hand and it hit me. All of them had a universal translator in them, but how was that possible? Did they come from the same galaxy? It was possible, but highly unlikely.

What was it? Think, think, nagged that little voice in the back of my head. Think...and...oh, a terrible thought popped into my head. Everyone here was a different race, but everyone who wore clothes all wore the same color jumpsuit.

More than likely, they'd come from the same kind of supermax prison. It was probably the prison's way of getting rid of inmates that it didn't need or couldn't accommodate. The translation chip also made sense. Different species needed to understand one another.

Oh, we'd fallen in with some very bad company, but for now, I decided to play it cool. Naxos knew about Glyn. He must have been watching us through his binoculars. "We got lucky," I said carefully. "And?"

"And, we're wondering what other special attributes you have that might help us."

Oh, there it was. He knew. Naxos turned to the rest of the group that was now standing and watching us with a mix of hunger and anger and hope in their eyes. "Yeah, you might be able to help us, after all."

Another being—a cucumber-like individual who said his name was Brotta—mentioned that he'd like to get back to his world. "I been here almost as long as Naxos has. See, I was framed. If I could get back, I could clear my name."

Uh-huh, everyone here was innocent. Sure, they were. Glyn had grown decidedly quiet, so perhaps she'd caught on to them at the same time I had.

"What's everyone here for?" I asked.

At first, no one said anything, but they looked to Naxos for guidance. He shrugged and waved his hand as if to tell them to start talking. "Stealing," one person answered.

"Assault and battery," said another.

Still more said they'd been tossed in jail for not paying rent, littering and the last one was a praying mantis type that scratched its head almost bashfully. "I got intoxicated in public. It wasn't one of my better moments."

That was strange. "Seriously?"

"I drank a lot and shot up a few stores and businesses. Didn't kill anyone," he muttered.

"All right, enough of the true confessions," Naxos said as he put up his hand for quiet. His followers immediately moved back while he leaned forward, his eyes narrowed and his mouth a grim slit. All pretense of friendliness had gone.

"I just got one question. How did you get here? We came in by transport ship and got dumped here with a minimum of supplies, but when you two arrived, I didn't hear or see no ship. None of us did, and we watch the sky every day, just in case, so be a good guy and tell us. Sharing information here gets you extra privileges, like stayin' alive."

Damn it, this isn't good! All the same, I put on an aggrieved act. "Hey, we got here same as you did. Don't blame us if you didn't hear a ship come in. We had silent running. I don't know, maybe you were sleeping, and —"

And that's when I clammed up, as the tip of his spear went to my throat. I didn't dare make a move. Naxos kneeled beside me, and his front face was taut with anger.

But more than that, it was filled with purpose. Purpose in his case meant killing me, if necessary. "Listen very carefully, Mark. I'm going to make one suggestion. Tell us the truth. I know you're lying to me."

"Tell me how."

A mean smile adorned his front face. "Your face and neck are sunburned. Where we're from, ain't no hot sun. It's hard to see in this semi-darkness, but under the torch lights, yeah, I see it all."

The tip of his spear pressed harder against my skin. "Unless the world you're from has a tropical climate, then I know you're lying. You're also not wearing a suit like we are, and prison ships don't have sunrooms. We didn't hear any ship's engines, and that means no one's come here recently."

A shudder of fear ran through me. Was this the end? Not yet, as Naxos said, "Let me reiterate. If I have to kill you, I will. I've done it before, and I'll do it again. It would just be another notch on my belt. So, start talking, or — "

"It was me."

Glyn spoke up. Everybody looked at her, and the sharp edge of death withdrew from my throat. A few of the residents started murmuring amongst themselves, then someone asked, "How?"

"I can make windows to other planets," she said, staring at everyone in turn. "Call them portals if you like. That's my ability. But I can't do it now. I need to sleep, and if you want to get home, then I need coordinates for your worlds."

En-masse, the group started talking, but Naxos yelled for quiet. "All right, you need rest, so let's let you rest."

In a quick move, he lashed out and caught her with a shot to her jaw that knocked her cold. I started to protest, but someone bashed me on the head from behind, and as I toppled over, I saw the grinning faces of the mob.

Then…darkness.

Chapter Fourteen

Flight

Minutes or maybe hours later, I woke up, my head splitting from the pain, pain from being bashed as well as the curse's unholy magic.

Assessing our situation wouldn't really help, as it was a simple matter to figure things out. We were caught between the proverbial rocks and an extremely hard place. After all, how could being in the company of a gang of cutthroats be considered any better than the monsters they ran from?

Still, the prisoners here had been tossed into a kill-or-be-killed situation, so perhaps it was too harsh to judge them. All the same, we were their prisoners, and there didn't seem to be any way out.

My thoughts turned in a different direction. What was up with Glyn's idea of coordinates? Her powers didn't work that way, not that I knew of...

Wait. A blast of realization hit me, followed by the obvious 'duh' moment. My girlfriend had been stalling for time.

The only thing was, we didn't have that much time in which to get out of here. I looked around. No one seemed to be around, save the PTSD sufferers, and they never moved from their positions. Perhaps the able-bodied had gone out to forage for food. I saw my extender near the wall, next to the spears.

Beside me, Glyn stirred, opened her eyes and asked in an angry, shaky voice, "What happened?"

"You got punched in the jaw by their fearless leader," I replied while shaking my head to get rid of the fuzziness. "Someone knocked me out, too. I have no idea how long we've been asleep."

"Marvelous," she muttered. "My jaw hurts. So does my head."

"Bad?"

"Have you ever known a headache to be good?"

She had a point. While she moaned in pain and shifted her weight around, I went through the negatives. There were a lot. We were up against almost fifty people here. They were armed with spears, they could probably fight and they were as desperate to get out of this place as we were.

I tried getting up but found that my hands had been tied behind my back. Glyn's arms were also bound behind her. We'd come from one kind of prison only to enter another...

"Hey, you're awake."

I picked up my head to look at the speaker. Another inmate, a crablike being no more than two feet high with a curiously humanoid face, scuttled through the entrance, gazed at us through beady black eyes, then it made its way over, holding a small bucket and ladle in one of its claws.

"I got you something to drink," it said in a high-pitched voice. It sounded male, but who really knew? "This is water. I got it just a few minutes ago from our source. Trust me. It's clean."

At that moment, trusting anyone wasn't the smartest thing to do, but we had no choice in the matter. The crab-being served Glyn first then it served me, all the while clucking about the heat. It said its name was Kanyaka.

"Prisoner number eight-hundred-eighty-one-thousand at your service. I am one of the unfortunately incarcerated."

Finally, I'd gotten some information. "I heard before that you're all prisoners. Naxos and the others said so. Are you?"

"Were," it corrected me with a short laugh. It looked around as if expecting an attack. Even though no attack came, it lowered its voice. "I'm not supposed to tell you, but we were once part of the largest prison in the Valurian galaxy. Now, we're free — sort of."

"Sort of," I echoed and decided to go with the male designation. "Mister, you're stuck on a world filled with creatures that ingest you and spit out your bones. I've seen their death chambers. They're not pleasant."

Kanyaka nodded his head. "No, they're probably not. I've never been there, and I don't want to find out, thank you very much. You were out a long time, by the way."

"How long?" Glyn asked.

"About six hours. Naxos hits hard. I've been here as long as he has. He took over from the other guy."

"Other guy," I echoed. "I guess they had a difference of opinion?"

Kanyaka raised his claws as if to say that's how it is. "Yeah, pecking order and all that. See? When we came in, there were about twenty other people here. A guy named Zill ran things, but him and Naxos had a set-to, and now, Naxos is running the show."

Uh-huh…it didn't take much imagination to figure out what had happened. "Anyway, Naxos hits really hard," the little crab-guy said while making a brief journey to the entrance then turning back to us.

"At first, we thought you were dead, but you were still breathing, so we left you alone and figured you'd come out of it."

We'd been out that long? I stole a glance at my girlfriend. Her face seemed more drawn than usual. My headache had intensified, and it felt like someone was doing their best to mash my organs from the inside.

Getting out of here was imperative, but since Kanyaka was so chatty, maybe we could get some information from him first. "What were you in prison for?"

Our water-bearer friend shook his head. "Stole a few items on my world and a couple of others that I wanted to fence on the black market. Small parts, you understand. They would have netted me good money, but I got caught, so…"

He lifted his claws in a what-can-you-do gesture. "And the others?" Glyn asked. "Did they tell you what they're here for?"

"You obviously don't know prison life," Kanyaka countered. "If a prisoner doesn't want to tell you anything, they don't have to. Me, I don't mind." He mused on his almost-successful mission. "I'd always gotten away with my heists. I was good at what I did, and I would have gotten away with this heist, too, but another guy in my gang decided to sell me out. I trusted him, and he went straight to the police on my world. The little rat got off scot-free. The authorities gave me ten years."

Curious now, I asked him what parts he dealt. "Oh, they were fuses to a kind of bomb," he said with pride. "Not a huge bomb, but it would have done damage, I can tell you that."

"How much?"

"Enough to blow up a city."

He excused himself then, leaving us to contemplate what kind of psychotic group we'd gotten captured by. Time passed, and thoughts of prison and freedom and death filled my head.

After about an hour had passed — and in that hour, I started to feel worse and worse — my thoughts of being kept hostage and possible freedom got interrupted by the sound of tramping feet and harsh voices.

Figures filled the entrance, with Naxos leading them. He had a spear in one hand, and he held a basket of tubers in the other. He put his basket down to stare at us, and a faint grin flashed across his face.

"Hey, our stars are awake," he said in a surprised tone. "More than wonderful. I apologize for smacking you, Glynarra. Sometimes I hit too hard for my own good. Glad your brains still work. That means we have time to talk."

"I gave them some water," Kanyaka said. "I figured they needed to keep their strength up."

Naxos offered him a lazy smile. "Good thinking, buddy," he said.

While his words sounded friendly enough, in a flash, his faces changed from mild to twisted killer mode. In a lightning-fast move, he rammed his spear through the crab guy's head.

Kanyaka uttered a shrill cry of agony and sank into death. Glyn gasped, and I tried my best to keep the contents of my stomach under control. It wasn't easy, but I managed.

Naxos pulled his spear out and shook the blood off it, speaking in a quiet, sing-song tone to the now-dead Kanyaka. "Orders are orders. I told you not to talk to them, but you did, didn't you, you moron? Now, I had to kill you."

He picked up the crab-man's body and tossed it to one of his friends. "Cook up our friend here for dinner. Seafood's on the menu."

Oh, that was beyond sick! Different species or not, that was cannibalism, and it made me want to heave. Naxos leaned his spear against the wall, walked over to check on our bonds then he took a seat across from us. He seemed unperturbed by his most recent act of violence and gave us an oddly reassuring smile.

"I suppose our now-dead shelled friend told you where we came from," he said. "Supermax prison?"

Glyn nodded. "Yes. That, and about your rise to the top here. Did you have to kill him?"

Naxos sighed and spoke to us as though we were six-year-old children who needed to have everything explained twice. "Weren't you listening? I gave him orders not to speak to you, but he disobeyed them. Everyone here has the same order — say nothing until I give the A-okay on it. If my soldiers are going to live here, then they have to follow orders."

Mad, this man was beyond insane. First, he was a prisoner, and now, he thought of himself as a major or an army general. "So, how many people did you kill?"

I asked. "I mean, you had to have killed a lot to be sent to jail."

Naxos chuckled. "You're right about that. Well, let's see." He scratched his jaw. "Around a hundred, I guess. Maybe more. I lost count after eighty."

Oh, man, Naxos was beyond cold. "You were a mercenary?"

He shrugged. "Yes, and no. I did a lot of jobs. Where I grew up, being poor was for losers, so I got into doing what I did at an early age."

Naxos chuckled again. For a murderous mercenary, he also had a sense of humor, warped though it was. "I got good at it, too. What I want you to understand is this. I did what I did for money…period."

Change being captured by a murderous mercenary to being captured by a psychopath…no remorse, no conscience and no soul. He continued with, "I had no problem getting rid of anyone if they didn't go along with what I said. That's all I have to say about that."

Naxos paused to scratch his faces. His regular face was unshaven, but the rear one was as smooth as a baby's butt. Weird, but then again, look where we'd arrived.

"And the prison you were in?" Glyn asked. "Are you going to tell us about that?"

A rusty laugh clawed its way out of his throat. "You're pretty inquisitive, aren't you? Okay, I will. Why not? We've got time."

No, we didn't, but no sense in telling him about our predicament. He probably wouldn't have cared. "Yeah, time," I echoed. "I'd like to learn something."

A laugh came from the big man as he proceeded to tell us that he and the other members of this fine crew had been on a floating rock in space. Named

Pentatarrus, it was a manmade asteroid, and it housed some of the Valurian galaxy's worst examples of humanity.

"Murderers, rapists, thieves, politicians, mercenaries… You name it, that prison had it."

"Politicians?" I asked.

Naxos offered a throaty chuckle. "Tell me one politician who doesn't deserve to be in jail. Just one. I'll wait."

Since I had no answer, I shrugged. Naxos took my gesture as confirmation. "Yeah, I figured as much. Anyway, we were captured on our own worlds in a distant galaxy. After that, the authorities sent us there. Being chained up in a ship's brig for two weeks was bad enough, but it never hit me how tough a supermax jail could be."

Naxos shook his head at the memory. "On our worlds, we had some standing, no matter what we did. On the ship, we were less than nothing."

His lips tightened. "Maybe you heard that things can only get better, right? In our case, they got worse. Once we arrived, the guards penned us up in stone cells six days out of seven. There were no rules, really, because we were shut inside our cells most of the time. They were just big enough to walk around in, do some calisthenics and that was it."

Naxos stopped to rub his brow, narrowing his eyes, and his voice growing colder and angrier. "On the seventh day, we had to work, mainly gathering up the bodies of fellow inmates who'd died from exhaustion or sickness or something else. That wasn't fun, but we did it.

"Fights, we had them. Why not? What were the guards going to do, kill us? It was entertainment for them, and I honed my skills there. So did everyone else."

His concept of entertainment was far different than mine, but whatever. "I hope they fed you," Glyn said.

Naxos snorted at her statement. "If you call pellets food, yeah, we got fed. Forty pellets the size of my thumbnail—that's what we got two times a day. We had a hole in the ground to crap in. Nothing to wipe ourselves with."

His mouth twisted like a mutated pretzel. "No showers, no way to keep clean. Didn't matter what race. We all stank. High heat, armed guards, prison animals genetically designed to eat anything the guards ordered them to... It was hell." He shrugged. "Still, we lived if we toed the line. Then the prison got overcrowded. The planets in our galaxy have some sort of collective peace pact among them. One of their laws is that they don't believe in capital punishment, so I was telling you the truth about that before."

A grim look came over his face. "They don't believe in the death penalty, but lemme tell you, life in that prison is worse than death. A lot of prisoners bugged out, went insane. They tried escaping, just so the guards would kill them. For them, death was preferable."

Naxos chewed on his lower lip. "Still, things kept getting more crowded, so they came up with the idea of shooting us off to this place. The authorities gave us two choices. Choice one—stay in prison and maybe survive. Choice number two—build a new life here for as long as our sentence ran."

"Did most of you take the deal?" I asked.

His friends chuckled at the question, and he swiveled around to address them. "Well, you heard the man. Did you take the deal?"

As one, the group answered, "Yes."

After some general grim laughter, he turned back to us. "Yeah, we did. Ten years — that's the sentence for everyone. They transported us here in cargo ships and dropped us off on this planet at various points."

Glyn asked, "You never searched for the others?"

Naxos stared at her as though she'd lost it. "Why? We're cons, and a lot of us are killers, like me. Trust me, honey. Getting together with our own kind would have caused more problems.

"Anyway, what's the point? There's no way off this rock, and it would just bring more conflict. Believe it or not, that's what we don't need. If we make it to ten years, then we get parole. That's why we have these language chips in us."

He pointed at his wrist. "But they're not just language chips. They're also tracking devices, geared to our hearts. We can't dig them out. If we try, they explode. I've seen that happen, and it isn't pretty. On the flip side, if our hearts stop, the chip deactivates. Problem solved, at least for those who make the rules."

I wondered if someone had come up with the idea of cutting a hand off, and Naxos seemed to read my mind.

"Deactivating the chip by chopping off a hand or limb doesn't work," he said. "The moment the signal is interrupted, it explodes, so that's out. So, we're at the mercy of these chips. If we make it, the authorities know where to find us."

"How do you know they'll pick you up?" Glyn asked.

A mean smile came over Naxos' face. "I don't. Get it now? In my line of work, you can't trust anyone, but sometimes you have to if you want the job to go through smoothly. Right?"

He looked at us for confirmation, so I nodded. Then he cleared his throat. "Anyway, with the lawmakers there, they don't care. They really don't, so why should we?"

Naxos sounded almost reasonable. "And the thing you have to understand is that the authorities are just as corrupt as we are. So, why trust them? If we go elsewhere, we can deactivate the chip and start over. We don't have the tools here to do that, but on another world, they might have what we want."

He shoved his face close to Glyn's. "That's where you come in. I want you to open a gateway for us. To anywhere is fine. Once we're safely somewhere else, we go our separate ways and good luck to us all. No hard feelings."

Would he keep his promise? He hadn't, at least in Kanyaka's case. I doubted he'd keep it in ours. Killing meant nothing to him, and he'd kill Glyn—and me—if we didn't go along with his plan. He had to be stopped, here and now. The only question was how.

Naxos rose, dusting his jumpsuit off. "Rest up. I'm going to get the group together. There are forty-eight of us here plus me, and we all want out."

Glyn let out a faint moan of pain, and I felt a faint ripple of hurt run through me. Either the timeline here moved faster than we thought or else I'd miscalculated the number of hours we'd been out. Our seventy-two hours had almost run out.

Her head sagged, but she lifted it long enough to nail him with a glare. "Untie me, then. I can't open a window unless my arms are free to move. That's how my magic works."

Naxos shook his head. "Uh-uh, sweetheart, you'll have to do better than that."

She flared, practically spitting in his face. "You idiot, I *am* doing better than that. If you don't cut me free, you'll stay here for the rest of your life, which is guaranteed to be nasty, brutal and short. The choice is yours."

My girlfriend continued to stare at him. A few of the other inmates started yelling at Naxos, and after much catcalling and insults and challenges to his leadership as well as his manhood, he gave in. "All right, but no funny stuff."

He reached into his suit, took out a knife with a curved blade and cut her bonds free. Then he cut mine. "Okay, you're free. Now, do that magic that you do."

Glyn rotated her shoulders in and out, shook her arms, and rubbed her wrists to get the blood flowing. "I need something to drink, first. And Mark needs water, too."

Naxos grimaced, but he snapped his fingers. Someone walked over with two small jugs of water. I drank my water down right away, feeling more pain and pressure—and wondering what would happen next.

My girlfriend took her time drinking, so perhaps she had a plan and was going over everything in her mind. Finally, after she drained the jug. "That was good."

"Glad you liked it," Naxos said in an even voice. "Now, get on with it."

"I need light."

"We have torches."

Glyn shook her head. "Not enough."

She then faced him, her manner defiant. "I can only do this when it's bright out, like daytime."

Uh-huh, the glimmer of a plan had started to come together. Naxos looked around then twisted his back face toward her. "This is the best we got. What do you suggest?"

I chimed in with, "How about those flash sticks? I saw how bright they were. They last ten seconds, right?"

Naxos turned his front face to me, and his mouth split into a smile. "I like that idea."

He then swiveled his neck around to face Glyn. "How long will it take to open a portal and keep it open?"

"Around thirty seconds," Glyn replied as she reached inside her robe and handed me her stash of flash sticks. "There are forty-eight people here besides you. Do the math."

It seemed easy enough. Three groups of sixteen. I'd give the signal for each group to fire away in turn. Naxos seemed excited and told everyone to get their flash sticks ready. Glyn breathed in and out deeply. "I'll need to do this out in the open. This place is too confining."

Yes, I was beginning to get the gist of her plan, but while it sounded good to me, our head jailer immediately became suspicious, shaking his massive head. "Sorry, honey. That's asking more than I can give."

Immediately, more catcalls came his way, so finally, he yelled for everyone to shut up. His people quieted down, and he put his sweating, ugly front mug close to ours, his voice filled with menace.

"All right, but if you try and screw us over, you'll regret it. You need thirty seconds to open a gateway. I'll only need two to cut your throat."

Threat delivered, he motioned for everyone to join him. We walked out en-masse to the edge of the plain. Everyone took a spear, while Naxos settled on my extender. I got nothing.

Glyn repeated her breathing ritual, while I got everyone lined up in groups of sixteen each. Then she nodded to me.

"Okay," I said, pointing at group one and concentrating hard. The pain of the curse made it hard to think. We were cutting this way too close. "When I point at you, fire away. Same deal with groups two and three. You all got that?"

"Get on with it," Naxos said, looking around nervously. "I don't like our position."

"You don't have to hold it for long," Glyn said then turned to me with a ghost of a smile on her face. "Let's do this."

You go, Glyn. I'm ready. I pointed at group one and said, "Now."

Everyone set off their flash sticks and a brilliant glare filled the gloom. Glyn's arms worked furiously, and she grunted a few times, but nothing yet.

My finger went to group two. En-masse, they set off their flashes. While doing so, the horrid screeching began. Feeding time at the zoo would be starting soon. "Almost there," Glyn said as the outline of a window formed. "Get ready."

I aimed my finger at the third group as the screeching from the creatures and the scraping sound of their limbs grew louder. The light charges caused everyone to flinch, so intense was the flare.

At its peak, the shape of the window solidified, and as the light faded, I asked Glyn, "Do you really need the light?"

"Yes, and I have just enough," she replied with a grin as she grabbed my hand. "Mark, *now*!"

Naxos realized that he'd been duped and roared for everyone to kill us. His arm shot out and latched onto mine. "You're coming with me!"

No, he wouldn't. As Glyn brought out one flash stick that she'd kept in reserve and set it off, I shielded my eyes, but Naxos didn't, and the bright light temporarily blinded him. He screamed and released me, holding his hands over his eyes on both faces.

A nanosecond later, a long white tentacle came out of nowhere to snatch a female prisoner next to him and haul her into a hole. She went kicking and scratching all the way, shrilly begging for help.

Her cries set off a mass surge of the monsters, and they scurried toward us, screeching their unholy cry. More and more prisoners got hauled away to their doom.

"Mark, you bastard," Naxos yelled, feeling the air around him. "I'll get you for this!"

Sure, you will.

Now, the agony began in earnest. The curse was at full power and my time had run out. I tapped him on the shoulder. He turned around and I let fly with the hardest left hook to his unshaved face that I'd ever thrown in my life.

Naxos fell, and immediately, a creature slid over to latch onto his waist. It began to squeeze, and he reached for his flash sticks, bellowing pain and rage. "Mark, I'll find you — find you, kill you…you and that girl!"

"Maybe next time," I said as I grabbed the extender from him.

Naxos triggered his flash stick and the creature flinched, but it didn't let go. I doubted that it ever would.

"Now, Mark," Glyn yelled. "I can't hold this any longer."

She and I dove in. My last image of the prisoners was of them fighting off the monsters that wouldn't be denied the pleasure of a good meal.

Chapter Fifteen

Downtime

The portal took us back to a forest. We fell through the gateway, it vanished and Glyn stared up at the trees. "Home," she muttered and let out a sigh of immense relief.

"Here? Why here?" I asked.

She wiped her forehead. "The curse, remember? I can't stay away from my world for more than three days. I have to return here. You're feeling better, right?"

In fact, I was. The awful pressure and pain had gone. And while I hated the concept of being linked with someone who had a curse hanging over their heads, I'd chosen this path. If Glyn could stand it, I could, too. "Yeah."

"Good. Me, too. Let's rest up and figure out what to do."

We got up and staggered our way over to a clearing. There, Glyn checked a few bushes and came back with some berries in her hands. "These aren't much, but they'll do."

Small, lumpy and red, they tasted like raspberries, but with much more tartness to them. Food was food, though, and it helped.

Glyn rested her body against mine. "I never thought we'd get out of there. Thank you."

What was she thanking me for? She'd done all the work. "Good old portal to the rescue," I answered, still marveling at our escape.

I wondered if Naxos had gotten free. Even if he had, he would never be truly free...then I decided not to think about that anymore. "What now?"

With a rub of her palms against each other and a small inhalation and exhalation of breath, she began her portal-opening routine. It was only interrupted by the sound of voices.

"Soldiers?" I asked.

Glyn shook her head. "No, they sound young. Shh...let me finish."

She began to work. A few seconds later, the familiar window pattern began to form. I caught a glimpse of a blue spot—an ocean, perhaps—then voices from behind us startled me.

I turned around to see a young couple in their late teens or early twenties standing four yards away. Their mouths dropped open when they saw Glyn.

"It's her," the woman said with alarm. "Glynarra, the one our ruler seeks."

Uh-oh, this isn't good. Glyn...hurry!

"It *is* her," the man said. "Alert the guards. King Lensa should be told."

Finks, they would rat us out.

The girl ran off, and the man came over to grab my forearm in a viselike grip. "Hold, stranger. You cannot escape from justice."

The portal faded. Glyn shook her head. "I need to concentrate."

We couldn't do that, not with Mr. Righteous grabbing me. Although I wasn't a violent sort, this situation called for it. Without another word, I slugged the man in the jaw. It gave me a certain sense of satisfaction to watch him hit the ground.

"Let's go," Glyn said, and we ran off into the forest. There, we hid among the trees until she felt rested enough to try opening a window again.

"Be quiet," she said and began to weave her hands around. As she did so, the sound of clanking metal came through. It was the guards.

"Glyn?"

"Almost there," she murmured, "almost there... yes!"

The portal opened, and the same blue tableau greeted us. The clanking grew louder, but Glyn pulled me inside the window at the same time I snatched the extender and the portal slammed shut behind us.

For some reason, this time we fell from a great height. It was daytime when we entered, a clear blue sky was above us, and below us was...

"Water!"

I shouted my warning just before we plunged into an ocean. I came up spitting out thin, clear fluid. It was fresh water, it smelled clean and it was cold and cleared my head in an instant.

The flash sticks that I hadn't used floated on the surface briefly before sinking. They'd saved our lives, but now, they weren't needed.

Part of me wanted to yell at my girlfriend for dropping us into the water. The other part said, 'who cares?' We'd escaped, and that was all that mattered.

Glyn bobbed to the surface, glanced around, then gasped and pointed to a spot off to the right. "It's land!"

"Can you swim?" I asked.

Despite our situation, she grinned. "Yes. Chase me."

Chase her. I followed her finger to where she'd pointed. It was a beach of whitish-pink sand, and land had never looked so good. My extender floated nearby, so I grabbed it and started swimming after her.

Glyn cut through the water, her robe notwithstanding. In contrast, my clothes weighed me down, but the beach was in sight. I wasn't going to drown, not after all we'd been through.

After about fifteen minutes, we reached the shoreline and collapsed there. I tossed my extender on the sand. Safe—perhaps we'd be safe here. It was quiet enough, and that made all the difference. I lay face down, while the water lapped gently around me.

It was only then that I realized I'd left my shoes behind on Horror World. It didn't matter. We'd been that close to dying, and now, maybe we had a chance to live. Losing our shoes was a small price to pay.

Glyn lazily lifted her arms and waved them at the sky briefly before letting them fall into the surf again. "Well, we're here. Piece of pie."

"Uh, piece of cake," I said, gently correcting her.

"Cake?"

She began laughing and turned over to face me. "I'll have to study English more. You'll have to teach me."

"Promise."

With that, we pushed ourselves out of the surf and onto the beach. An old saying ran through my head. Terra firma—the more firma, the less terra. I thought about telling Glyn the joke, but then I realized she probably wouldn't understand. Instead, in a lame attempt at conversation, I said, "You're a good swimmer."

If it sounded lame, Glyn didn't think so, as she pulled herself over to lie next to me. "When I was a little girl, my parents would take me swimming in a river near our house. Once this is over, I'll show it to you."

"Deal." I wondered, though, if it ever would be over.

Still, a person had to have hope. I sat up to survey the area, craning my neck first to the left then to the right. The beach stretched for miles around in either direction.

A forest lay roughly five hundred feet away to our right, but as I looked behind me, I saw no houses or buildings, nothing but endless sand.

Well, if nothing else, call this place an island paradise. Come to think of it, any place away from that hellish planet we'd come from was a paradise.

"Have you been here before?" I asked.

Glyn sat up with me. "No, but when my powers came around and I began practicing, I opened a portal and saw this. I remembered the incantation, so I took us here." She gave her hands a rueful look. "I wish I'd thought of this incantation before we went to that hellhole. Sorry. I was nervous at the idea of being recaptured."

"It doesn't matter," I said. "We're here."

Since I felt better, hot sun and sopping clothes notwithstanding, I got up and started trudging toward the trees.

"Where are we going?" Glyn asked.

"Maybe there's fruit on the trees or the bushes," I said, pointing to yellowish fruit. "I think I see bananas."

"They are not what you call bananas," a voice said.

Deep and sonorous, it came from everywhere and nowhere, and suddenly, I felt totally insignificant — an ant before a person, a lab smear under the lens of a microscope. I stopped in my tracks and asked, "Who are you?"

"The question is, who are *you*?"

Uh-oh, there was overstepping and there was stepping in it. I'd done both. The voice had come mainly from the sky, so facing upward, I pointed to myself first then my girlfriend. If this thing was a god, we were toast. "Um, my name's Mark, and this is Glyn."

"From where do you come?"

"Earth, for me, and Tellkar, for her."

The air was still, the weather continued to be hot and fine, then the being spoke again. "My name is Xithantus. I am the ruler of this world. It is called Suidara."

Xithantus — it came out as 'Sithantoos', with the accent on the second syllable. Well, meet another alien, learn another name.

"We are honored to be here," Glyn said, bowing her head in a gesture of humility. Being humble was necessary in this situation. We were the foreigners, the visitors — the aliens.

For the first time in my life, even more so than on Tellkar and Horror World, I understood what being a foreigner and an alien meant.

My girlfriend raised her arms, almost in supplication. "We only ask that we be allowed to rest here for a while. Then, we shall leave."

"Step forward, Glyn of Tellkar. I must look into your mind and heart."

Could this Xithantus actually do that? Oh, wait, he was the ruler of this world. He could do anything. This was his crib, and we were his guests—or intruders, depending on his mood.

Glyn stepped forward and bowed her head. Nothing much happened at first, but then a narrow beam of blue light came from the heavens and played itself up and down her body.

She stood stock still until the light switched positions to me. Although I felt no pain, it was an odd sensation, as though every atom of mine was being examined, catalogued and filed away.

The light then faded away as suddenly as it had come, and our host spoke. "I have looked into both of your essences. Glyn of Tellkar, and your physiology is such that you have only a march of days before your being becomes incompatible with this world. I do not know why, but it is part of you. Mark of Earth, I detect the same abnormality."

Xithantus knew everything. He may not have been a god, but he came very close. "If you wish to eat," he said, "I will point out what is edible for your species and what is not. If you wish to swim in my ocean, I shall guide you. I only ask that you bring no others here without my permission."

"Agreed," Glyn said, sounding most humble as well as elated. "We thank you for your generosity."

"Go into the forest. You must eat first."

Well, when an all-powerful being said go, it meant go. The forest itself wasn't overly large, but the trees were tall, in the realm of two hundred feet or more. With broad green leaves and only a few branches, we walked unimpeded.

The yellow fruit I'd thought was bananas turned out to be a worm. Xithantus' voice surrounded us. "It protects the tree."

Protect was an understatement. The worm wound itself around the trunk. It had a very large head the same size as mine, and it also possessed razor-sharp teeth…a lot of them.

Worms that had teeth. By now, I was used to the strange and different. It snapped at us as we walked by, but it didn't do much more than that except growl. No problem. We could eat elsewhere.

Up ahead, Glyn pointed to a small green bush that held a variety of berries. Xithantus' voice came again. "The blue ones are fit to eat. The green and red ones are purgatives to your kind."

Purging myself wasn't on the menu. I tentatively bit into a blue berry, found it sweet and wolfed down a handful. "Good," Glyn mumbled, her mouth full of the sweet stuff. "This is a wonderful thing."

It was, and once we'd had our fill, we wandered out of the forest and back onto the beach. "Xithantus, may we swim here?" Glyn asked.

"You may," the deep voice came.

That was all Glyn needed to hear. She quickly stripped, laying her robe on the sand. I froze. She had a hot body, slender hips and…this wasn't appropriate, was it? "Uh, Glyn, you're, uh, naked."

"Yes?" she asked, arching her eyebrows. "Male and female, we all bathe together on our world when we want to. There is no shame in the body, is there?"

Of course not. Go with it.

I stripped off my sodden, smelly duds and we ran into the surf. A wall of water rose, and a face appeared. It was human, but with abnormally long ears and earlobes, and a prognathous brow and jaw. It had to be Xithantus, and it was. His voice came from the water, a deep, thrumming sound.

"This is but one image of me that I wish to convey. My ocean is open to you, but you must be careful not to go beyond a point that I shall show you. The pull of the water is perhaps too strong for your bodies. I am bound not to interfere with whatever transpires on my shores and waters."

Bound not to interfere — by whom? Whoever it was, that didn't matter. Once he delivered his warning, I called out, "Thank you. We'll obey the rules."

In a sudden burst of power, the wall lifted itself into the air and flew to a spot perhaps five hundred feet away. It then disappeared in a shower of spray. Glyn's eyes lit up. "You heard our host. Be careful. Let's go!"

Glyn and I swam slowly at first, tiny fish nipping at our feet. Then we picked up the pace and raced each other to the edge of the safe zone, accompanied by what could only be described as water pixies, tiny creatures of foam and spray that playfully splashed us as we swam along.

They reminded me of dolphins, but with curiously human faces. They leaped effortlessly through the air, pushing us to swim faster but also urging us to be careful.

"They're cute," Glyn called out between strokes.

"Yeah."

I couldn't say much else because I was running out of breath. She was a great swimmer, and even though I was on the swim team at school, her ability to plow through the water made me feel less than adequate.

In fact, Glyn pulled ahead of me as though I was treading water, but then, without so much as a sound, she sank beneath the surface. No sound, no bubbles. Confused, I treaded water, turning in every direction while calling out her name. "Glyn?"

I got no answer, and now, I was beginning to get scared. "Glyn?"

A tap on my shoulder made me turn to my left. A water pixie pointed with a foamy finger to a spot a few feet ahead. It then made the gesture of diving.

Oh, Jesus, the undertow! "Glyn!"

I swam to the spot and dove. Sure enough, Glyn was below me, motionless, her body borne along by the powerful current. The same monstrously strong current seized me, whipping me through the water in her direction. It was so strong that it threatened to pull me even deeper.

With everything I had, I swam to her and put my arm around her chest. The current continued to carry us along, but I swam crosswise, all the while kicking toward the surface.

My lungs burned, and black spots appeared in front of my eyes as we made our way up. In a last-ditch effort, I kicked as hard as possible. We broke the surface, and I inhaled great gasps of air. Using a cross-chest carry, I hauled her back to land.

It seemed to take forever. My strength soon maxed out, but a tiny miracle helped us. The pixies provided support by creating a strong wave that washed us back onto the beach.

Glyn wasn't breathing. Crap...I opened her mouth, did the breathing thing for her, then gently applied CPR. Nothing. "Glyn, c'mon," I implored.

The hot sun beat down while I worked feverishly to restore her life. "Glyn!"

In desperation, I pounded on her chest and that caused her to cough out a lungful of water onto me. She then turned on her side to retch out more water. I rubbed her back gently until she stopped spewing.

"Thanks," she said weakly.

"What happened?"

She pointed to her right hamstring. "I got a cramp. Then the pull...pull of the water dragged me under."

The muscle was pulsing as though it had a knot tied in it. "Hang on, Glyn. I'll massage it out."

I got to work, kneading the muscle. Glyn let out a few faint moans of pain, but she didn't move. It struck me then that we were both bare-ass naked, but this couldn't be considered an erotic moment by any means.

"She will be well?"

Xithantus' voice came from the sky and the sea. "I think so," I answered. "Just a bad cramp."

"I am sorry that I could not do more," the god of this world intoned in a somber manner. "Long ago, the one who created me issued such a proclamation. Since then, I have promised never to interfere in whatever transpires on my shores."

Another clue to his secret origin, and while I could have popped off an angry response, this was his world, after all. He had warned us about the undertow, and his vow was a binding one. I was simply grateful that Glyn was alive, and after all, one water pixie had alerted me to the danger, so...

"It is all right," Glyn responded, her voice stronger now. "You warned us. I hold no rancor toward you."

"It is good to know," Xithantus said. "Avail yourself of my hospitality."

A moment later, a structure made of sand emerged two yards away. I helped Glyn to her feet, and we made our way into our hut.

Xithantus was a good host. He'd hardened ground inside our abode to the consistency of glass. It was a total miracle, another in the long list of miracles we'd experienced as of late.

A large bed of somewhat softer consistency had also been fashioned. Glyn staggered her way over to it and lay down. "Thank you," she said. "I can feel the cramp going away. You...you saved me."

While it sounded corny, the way she said it, it came across as totally genuine. "Well, I'm a decent swimmer, and a water pixie pointed out where you were," I replied, suddenly feeling embarrassed.

Glyn slowly drew me down to her. Our eyes met. "I have to ask you something."

Romance? Maybe. I was ready. "Yes?"

"Could you wash my robe, please?"

Well, it had to happen. After that kiss on Horror World, I'd now been friend-zoned. "Yeah, sure thing. I'll be back. Relax."

Now that my get up and go had got up and gone, I trudged outside and down the beach, picked up her robe, then went to the water's edge to wash the sand out of it.

It took a while to wash it, but I managed. After that, I wrung it out, and when I got back to the hut I found Glyn fast asleep. Curled up, her hands under her head, she looked like an innocent child.

"Marvelous," I muttered.

A couple of sharp pegs protruded from the wall. I hung her clothes up on one peg, then went back and washed out my togs, hanging them up next to Glyn's. The sun would dry them faster that way.

A quick dip would do, and I ran into the surf, enjoying the cold water. As I walked out of the ocean, something flashed at the water's edge.

Two seashells sat side by side. They were conically shaped and with a cobalt blue sheen. Very pretty. An old saying ran through my head—listen to a seashell and you could hear waves crashing upon the shore. Why not?

I put one of them to my ear, but instead of waves crashing, I heard a song, something soft and lilting and timeless, the song of the sea itself.

It sounded like a combination of all the children's songs and catchy tunes I'd heard when I was young, only more entrancing. In a lovely melody, it related the beginnings of this world until now.

"A gift."

That was Xithantus again. "Thank you," I replied, looking heavenward.

"A history of this world. Please, take them."

"Thank you."

What a beautiful present. Glyn would most definitely love hers. I turned away after thanking our host again and went back to the hut. Glyn stirred but didn't wake up. With nothing better to do, I sat on the edge of the bed, waiting for my clothes to dry.

* * * *

Three hours later

The sun had begun to set, and a cool breeze blew in through the open windows. I got dressed outside, and when I walked into our sand hut with her robe in hand,

Glyn had woken up and pronounced herself fit as well as hungry.

"Here you go," I said and handed her the seashell and her robe. "The shell's a present from Xithantus. Put it to your ear."

She did as I asked, an expectant look on her face, then she put it down and clapped her hands like a little girl. "This is beautiful. I shall thank our host."

Glyn quickly donned her robe and ran outside, tossing an "I'll be back soon" comment over her shoulder.

I lay back on the bed, content for the first time in a long time. If we could only stay a couple of months...

"I'm back," Glyn announced as she handed over a mini mountain of berries that she'd put on a leaf. "Eat up."

We devoured our dinner, but once she finished, she shivered. "I guess I need warmth."

"I could hold you," I suggested.

Glyn bit her lip. "I have to tell you something."

Now what? Oh, wait, she was promised to someone else. People in magic kingdoms—that happened all the time. Or she was already married, even though she said that she wasn't. Or she wasn't interested...or something.

"Yes," I prompted, hoping for the best but fearing the worst.

"I, uh, have never done what I think we both wish to do."

Oh, she's talking about... "I haven't, either, if you want to know the truth. That's okay."

While I should have felt embarrassed over my admission, I wasn't. Sex was part of life and relationships—well, most of them anyway. For her part, Glyn said, "It's not that. On our world, being united is usually a business transaction."

And I'd had the dumbass romantic notion that people would find true love, something straight out of the movies, only more realistic.

She continued with, "People marry for position or wealth or power. Love isn't usually mentioned as a reason for two people who wish to be united."

Reality bit, but then I asked, "How do you feel about me?"

Glyn put her lips to mine. We kissed and it was just as sweet as before. "Does that answer your question?"

Up to a point, it did. "Yes."

Glyn settled against me. "I just wish to be around you and hold you and talk with you. Is that wrong?"

I tilted her chin up to kiss her again. "No, it isn't…but since you're not ready, how about we sleep—just sleep—on it."

My girlfriend's smile lit up the night. "I'd like that."

We lay down, then, and I held her close to me, feeling her warmth and strength. My eyes began to close, and I thought that I heard her whisper, "Happy birthday."

In all the confusion, I'd forgotten. Eighteen today. I felt a smile spread across my face, and soon after, darkness swallowed me up.

And it didn't bother me at all. Here, there was nothing in the dark to be afraid of.

* * * *

Forty-eight hours later

It was time to go. The sun shone overhead, hot and full. Glyn and I had gotten up early and gone for swims both days, taking walks, eating berries, and while I wanted to get closer to her, I had the feeling that she wanted to wait.

Fine, it was her choice, after all. Being close to each other was enough, along with us having our races.

The little water sprites stayed with us, perhaps mindful of the mishap on our first day here. During our race, a couple of them latched onto my feet, propelling me forward and helping me win the race back to land.

As we ran out of the surf, Glyn started laughing. "You had help. Those water creatures assisted you!"

"I'll take any edge I can get."

Her mouth opened and closed rapidly, but she said nothing save, "We have to go. Let's get dressed."

And now, it was time for us to leave. The headaches had begun only a few hours ago, accompanied by the internal pressure. Although it wasn't what we wanted, we had no choice in the matter, and even our host couldn't fix what was wrong with us.

Xithantus had promised that he'd provide us with a place to stay in the future. He — it — whatever — seemed decent, and we hadn't had a lot of decency as of late.

"My world is yours to enjoy," he said. "The one who created me did so before time began. I have been here ever since, but very few visitors come my way. The last ones were over three centuries ago."

Even gods got lonely, I mused. That was a mindbender in and of itself. "Thank you for the hut and for the seashells," I answered, staring into the blue sky. "We had a great time here."

Glyn then performed her incantation and got the window ready. "Goodbye, Xithantus," she said before we stepped in. "You have been most kind. If we succeed, then we shall see you soon."

As always, his voice came from every part of our surroundings. "Goodbye, Glyn of Tellkar. Goodbye, Mark of Earth. You will always be welcome here."

"Thank you," we said together, and stepped through the portal, only to emerge on Glyn's world. We waited a half hour, then we walked through another portal to a park near my house. Glyn's aim was getting better.

Better still, the pressure in my head and torso had faded. I was safe here, although Glyn still had her three-day parole thing going on. All the same, home had never looked so good.

Chapter Sixteen

Conflict

Naturally, my house was empty. My mother, for all her so-called worry about my well-being and who I was hanging out with, was still on her business trip. No one would come between her, her job and the paycheck.

Still, she'd called me before, and at that time, she'd also sounded concerned. That was a first, so maybe I shouldn't have judged her too harshly.

Another 'maybe' occurred to me, that being she might have been considerate enough to leave a message. I leaned the extender next to the door and checked the recorder, just in case.

Sure enough, six messages were on the recorder, all from her, all questioning my attitude, my friendship with some unknown girl and my commitment to my school life.

Talk about negative. While those were bad enough — as well as wrong — the last one was especially telling.

Mark, you won't solve any of your problems by running away. And I don't know who that girl you brought over is, but I can tell you right now that she's no good. She sounds like trouble, and I hope you show a little common sense.

Judgmental, wasn't she? And what was up with the 'you're-running-away-from-something'   garbage? There was no reason for that, no reason at all.

Glyn listened carefully but said nothing. Her face was expressionless, but her mouth set in a faint line that indicated disapproval—or what I took to be disapproval.

Once I hung up, she offered her opinion. "I don't know why she's blaming you. From what you told me, she's the one who's been running from everything."

More to the point, Glyn said nothing about my mother calling her no good, as if my mother really knew. She didn't. Embarrassed by my mother's attitude, I said, "I'm sorry for what my mother… I mean, she's wrong. You're the best person I know."

In fact, she was the only woman I knew who made me want to be around her twenty-four-seven. I'd never felt that way about anyone before, and it was a sure bet that I'd never feel that way about anyone else again.

"Thank you."

Sadness flowed from her eyes, but she shut it down. "I know you as well. Your mother simply doesn't understand."

What could I say? If ever there was a Danny Downer moment, that was it. I couldn't let it get to me, though. I had other, more important things to do.

I gestured to the living room. "Listen… I need a shower. Relax and get something from the fridge if you want. I'll be back soon."

Glyn flopped on the couch while I went upstairs to hose myself down. Inside the bathroom, I shucked my clothes and let the hot water run.

It was a glorious feeling, but as I dried off, I caught sight of my reflection in the mirror. My skin was still red in spots, and it was also peeling in others, revealing new pink flesh underneath, but that was nothing in the long-term scheme of things.

My eyes, though, told a different story. Ordinarily a deep brown, they had a smudge of black in the center, the color of death. And I'd seen it, up close and personal. The soldiers on Tellkar were one thing, but my experiences on Horror World had brought everything into perspective.

I'd witnessed my girlfriend drown, and it was only by sheer luck and a water pixie's help, plus Glyn's tough constitution, that she'd survived.

At that moment, I hated death, hated the concept and hated the eventuality of it all. Reason crept in, though. For all the emotion surrounding death, for all the wailing and gnashing of teeth about it, death remained impersonal, something no one could escape.

When I was little, I'd had the general idea that death was some bony dude in a black cape and hood. He carried a scythe, he never spoke and he only crooked a skeletal finger at his next victim.

As I grew up, though, my viewpoint changed. Death wasn't a person but an amorphous it-creature. It didn't carry a scythe. It didn't warn a person beforehand.

No, it came and took everyone it could simply because that was what it did. No hard feelings—no feelings at all. We were all just another name and number on its eternally and infernally endless list.

Could a person cheat death? We had, several times. And, if possible, we'd cheat it again. There were only two options available — live or die. I wanted the former in the worst way. Although I'd eventually succumb to the ravages of old age and disease, I wanted to get to that old age stage first.

Back in my room, while getting dressed, I wondered where we'd go to next. While cogitating the possibilities, another thought intruded. Was my mother right, though? Was I running from something?

After thinking it over, I concluded that she was wrong. I'd made the choice to help Glyn out. I'd made the choice to step through that window. And my mother had her priorities. Whatever, I'd talk it over with her when she came back.

After I'd thrown on some new duds and taken my ear shell, I went downstairs to find Glyn sleeping. I'd been hoping to talk with her more, maybe share another kiss, but it was not to be.

With a sigh, I covered her with a light blanket then took the other couch. Fatigue washed over me and soon it was lights out.

* * * *

Two-plus days later

Glyn was quiet at breakfast, although she complimented me on my culinary skills. They were better than my mother's. I'd honed them over time, due to my being left alone so often and learning to do things on my own.

My girlfriend ate quickly and waited for me to finish washing up. She leaned on her elbows, her hands propping up her chin. "We're going back today, aren't we?" I asked.

"Mm-hmm."

That was all she volunteered. It had been a quiet seventy-two hours. We hadn't set foot outside once, my mother hadn't called, and Nick had been our only visitor. He'd made a surprise visit on the second morning.

"I, uh, thought you might be here," he said when I opened the door. He poked his head inside, searching for my houseguest and trying not to appear too eager, which amused me, somehow.

"At school, you just disappeared. I came here four days ago, but there was no answer."

Dressed in a pair of pants that didn't quite reach his shins and a checkered shirt, he reminded me of Tweedledum. Or was it Tweedledee?

"Uh, yeah," I answered. "It's a long story."

Glyn had gone into the kitchen to get a drink of water, and I wondered if he would freak out when she came in as she truly was. We'd find out soon enough.

He carried three cardboard boxes, and I pointed to them. "What's in there?"

"Donuts. I got Bortoni's. They're prime," he said while tapping the boxes. "When did you, uh, get back?"

Bortoni's were the cream of the crop when it came to donuts. They made every other brand taste positively lousy in comparison.

"About three days ago," I replied, smelling the freshness of the deep-fried goodies that lay just a few inches away. "We wanted to keep, uh, keep a low profile."

Nick ran his tongue around his lips. "Yeah, that figures. I mean, did you really go somewhere? You were talking about green elves, and…"

Glyn chose that moment to return. She was in her default form, and Nick's mouth dropped open. The moment of truth had arrived. Would he scream, run from my house or contact the authorities?

As it happened, he did none of those things, save to ask incredulously, "Glenda?"

She chuckled. "It's Glynarra, actually. Call me Glyn."

Nick's body began to quiver. The old saying of "it must be jelly 'cuz jam don't shake like that" ran through my mind.

If that wasn't a sign of an impending fainting spell, I didn't know what was. "Uh, yeah, sure thing," he managed to get out.

Maybe I'd been wrong. I hurriedly took the donuts from him. If he dropped the boxes and some got smooshed, he'd never forgive himself.

On shaky legs, he sought the safety of the couch. His body now quivered violently like a person afflicted with palsy, and his voice shook as well. "Is that, uh, what you really look like?"

Glyn offered a kind smile. "I can look like anyone."

In a flash, she transformed into a copy of her old Earth-self, hoodie and all, a beagle, a mini dragon and more. Nick's jaw practically hit the ground. "Yeah, yeah, I get it."

My girlfriend then reverted to her elfin self. "So?"

Nick sat bolt upright now, his eyes fixed on her, and his mouth went in ten different directions before he said, "Uh, you're pretty."

For that, Glyn walked over and kissed him on the cheek. "Thank you."

He seemed a bit surer of himself after the love-peck, and three monstrous chocolate-fudge donuts later, he'd fully recovered. "So, tell me everything. School's out and I have to know."

Why not? Glyn gave him the basics and I added a few details here and there. By the time we'd finished, Nick's eyes were more glazed than the donuts.

"I never figured it was real," he said after downing his fifth cruller from box number two.

"It is," Glyn said. "I'm proof of that."

She reached for another donut. While they were beyond delicious, at that point, I couldn't take any joy in the pleasures of food. We had to decide what to do.

Nick bobbed his head. "Oh, for sure. I mean, Mark told me, but I never saw it or you or anything. This is just too wild."

Call that enthusiasm to the max, but we warned him to keep quiet. "Don't sweat it," he said. "I mean, who's going to believe me? I don't have any proof."

No, he didn't, then he added, "You guys leaving soon?"

"Soon," Glyn said. "I can't stay on any one world for more than three days."

Nick blew out his breath and gave me the I-told-you-so look. "Atomic structural inconsistencies," he mumbled.

After snatching another cruller, he got up to leave. "You guys coming back again?"

I accompanied him to the door. "If we can. Thanks for dropping in. I appreciate it. We both do."

My best bud suddenly got all weepy as a big, fat tear traced its way from his right eye down his fat cheek and his voice shook. "Man, I've known you for a long time…and now, this. I wish I could go with you."

Nick had always been a great supporter, ally and more. "Bud, I wish I could take you, too. But where we're going, it's not going to be fun. I'd like to say it will be, but it won't."

Call that a semi-lie, but Nick bought it. "Just promise you'll come around again."

"Deal."

I gave him a bro-hug, then he was gone. Glyn had been watching, and when I closed the door, she came over to say quietly, "You're a good friend, Mark Cornish. You know that?"

"I try to be."

I gathered up the dishes in one hand, the donut boxes in the other, and I went into the kitchen, while Glyn moseyed on over to the living room. Once I'd finished, I grabbed the extender and joined her. A window hung in the air. "Where are we going, exactly?"

Glyn climbed in. "Are you sure? I can handle things on my own."

Oh, come on! What's with the lone-wolf attitude? "Did I do something wrong?"

She shrugged. "No, but I was thinking. It's a matter of safety. The curse is still on, and I blame myself for not telling you sooner. It was wrong of me, but if you stay here, you'll be safe. And you should fix things with your mother first. That's all. You've been great, I care for you, but you have a mother. You have a family."

Glyn's attitude got me angry, although she happened to be half-right. "Where's my mother? She's not here. She's *never* here. It's always another business trip, another city and another job to do. Her work comes first. Everything else, including me, comes last."

My girlfriend seemed undecided after my mini rant. "If you're sure —"

"I am." I cupped her chin with my free hand. "Glyn, listen. I've been with you from the start. I did my best to help, even though I can't do magic like you can. I know about the curse. I'm prepared to face whatever happens. If you care for me, then take me along. Please. I want to help."

A grateful smile crossed her face, and she squeezed my hands in return. "Fine. We're going to the kingdom of Kott. Maybe if I can get an audience with the king, I'll be able to make a deal, maybe live there."

"Can you trust him?"

"I don't have a choice."

We stepped through and emerged a hundred yards away from a small castle. The gardeners hadn't been around for a few years. Overgrown weeds dotted the lawn area, the wood on the drawbridge was rotting and only five guards were on duty.

"Halt," one of them said to Glyn when we approached. He put up his hand as a warning, although his voice remained level. "I do not know your name, but I see a stranger with you, one that is not of this world."

When confronted by a guard who was armed with a spear and sword, a person had two choices. One, try to take on Mr. Armed Guard. Two, run.

Honestly speaking, at that moment in time, running would have been the best idea, but ten soldiers appeared out of nowhere and surrounded us. They sure knew how to blend in with the scenery.

"What is your business here?" the head guard asked.

"To see your king on a most urgent matter," Glyn replied and indicated me with a gentle wave of her hand. "This is Mark. He comes from Earth and is my companion. I am Glynarra. Your ruler knows of me. I wish to speak with him as soon as possible."

A look of recognition appeared in the guard's eyes. "Yes...I have heard of you. Your parents were Astora and Listral, were they not?"

She nodded. "They were."

"They were slain by King Lensa of Worthington's soldiers, were they not?"

Glyn's lips tightened. "Yes. How do you know of that?"

The guard said that two days after her parents had been killed, he'd been on patrol near the Bridge of Dying Sighs. A guard from Worthington was there, and even though they were on opposite sides, they'd had a civil conversation. The guard from Worthington had mentioned that he'd participated in a recent killing of two villagers.

"His name was Vasso," Kott's guard said. "It was not something he enjoyed. For him, it was duty."

Vasso was a lot more decent than I'd initially given him credit for. Glyn bit her lip. "It is as you say. I am here, now, to see your king—if he is agreeable to it."

The lead guard then snapped his fingers and another guard hustled over. "Alert King Kott at once."

"Yes, sir."

The other guard saluted and left. We waited as the sun beat down and I sweated and wished that someone would do us a favor and bring us water, but that probably wouldn't happen.

On the other hand, if I had magical powers, I could simply snap my fingers or wiggle my nose or ears and anything I wanted would simply appear. That latter thought almost made me laugh—almost.

A few minutes later, the guard returned and whispered something to his commander, who, in turn, gestured for us to follow him. "The king will grant you an audience."

Inside the castle, it was cool and quiet, and our footsteps echoed softly as we walked. We went past several rooms. Many had their doors open to reveal sloppily piled furniture and other goods. The floors creaked, and a faint smell of mildew hung in the air. Perhaps Kott didn't believe in living high.

After fifteen more steps, the lead guard stopped at a wooden door with a picture of an eight-legged deer creature carved on it. "This is where our king holds counsel," he said with great reverence. "Pay him obeisance, and he may aid you in your quest."

He knocked on the door twice, and a deep voice answered, "Enter."

The guard pushed open the door and we entered a hall where the king sat on a simple wooden throne. "Sire, these are the two visitors," the guard said. "Glynarra of Mattaca, and, er…"

"Mark…from Earth," I put in.

The king, larger than the other people here and fleshy, wore a faded gold-colored robe and no crown. It sat beside him on another throne. He seemed to be in his late fifties, although it was impossible for me to tell.

Although he was royalty, he reminded me of an athlete past his prime. And his kingdom made me think of something that belonged to a past age—worn down, shabby, and unneeded.

"Glynarra of Mattaca and Mark of Earth, approach me."

Call his manner snobbish then some, but then again, maybe all royalty acted that way. The guard bowed and left, closing the door softly behind him.

"Glynarra, I have heard of you," the king said once we had privacy. "You were supposed to have arrived in my kingdom a few days ago. I was informed that an intermediary, an individual named Handlee, would perform such a function."

"Forgive us, sire," Glyn said, keeping her eyes to the ground. "Something unavoidable arose. While Handlee fulfilled his role, we were unfortunately detained elsewhere, and Handlee is no longer, er...around."

Kott received her reply without batting an eye. He leaned back, tapping his forefinger against his lips. "In matters such as these, I very rarely see someone without having an intermediary intercede on their behalf."

Glyn bowed her head. If humbleness was a person, it would be her. "I am well aware of that, sire, but Handlee was slain by the King of Worthington's soldiers, and due to us being detained, we were unable to secure another intermediary in time. Therefore, my situation compels me to pursue a more direct course of action."

The king stroked his chin. He didn't seem very concerned with Handlee's passage into eternity. "I see. Very well, since you are here, we will speak more. To get straight to the matter at hand, I have heard that you have a most unusual ability that you wish to offer me, is that correct?"

Oh, he was all about the business. He knew about Glyn and what she could do. Apparently, my girlfriend knew what his mindset was as well, and she responded accordingly.

"Sire, while I do have special abilities, they are not what I wished for. They simply happened. The nature of this world gives and takes, does it not?"

Her answer, carefully worded, seemed to please him, as a faint smile flashed across his face. "While you are young, you are also worldly and intelligent. If my wife were with me now, perhaps she could offer more words of advice for you as well as solace for the loss of your parents."

I wondered what had happened to his wife, and I decided not to ask. None of my business seemed the operative plan here.

"Perhaps she would, sire," Glyn answered ever so politely. "Perhaps she would also allow me to live here in freedom instead of being hunted."

There it was—the request. Kott gazed at her through shrewd eyes, eyes that had seen earnest faces and ears that had heard earnest pleas for sanctuary and mercy. As the ultimate politician and power broker here, he had the power to grant Glyn what she wanted.

The only question was, would he?

"Glynarra, I am not unsympathetic with your plight," he finally said after tapping his fingers on the armrest of his throne. "If your powers are as great as I have heard they are, then they would, indeed, be a boon to this kingdom."

He swept his arm around to indicate the room and its furnishings—or lack of them, thereof. "As you can see, I do not live extravagantly. I have never believed in it, and I have devoted most of my monetary resources to my people. Still, having someone with your, er, abilities would be worth paying for."

"Would you like a demonstration?"

His eyes lit up. "I would."

I moved out of the way while Glyn did her stuff. She went through the motions and a window formed, one that led to Suidara.

Kott leaned forward, and his jaw sagged. "That is another world?"

"One of many that I have been to," she replied.

"Marvelous," he breathed.

Glyn shut the window down, and he nodded. "It is true what they say about you, Glynarra. You have great ability."

While that sounded positive, my hopes for Glyn were soon dashed when the king added, "However, I must weigh your needs against the needs of my people. While your power is, indeed, great, employing your abilities would eventually bring war to my kingdom should King Lensa discover that I am sheltering a refugee, as it were."

Glyn lifted her head to look him in the eye. "But, sire —"

"I have not finished."

He held up a hand for silence, and she glowered but said nothing. "War is something I have assiduously avoided for a number of years. I have expended my own personal resources in making my kingdom secure, mainly my fortune, left to me by my parents."

Glyn gazed at the aged furniture. "This castle of yours —"

"Is halfway ruined. I do not have the resources to pay for its renewal, and I will not tax my people just to live in luxury," Kott finished.

My respect for him went up a notch, but it dropped when he said, "My army is strong, but I am not prepared to sacrifice any of my people for the sake of one person."

This was total BS! "But you'd use her power, wouldn't you?" I asked. "You'd want to use it, right?"

Kott stared at me in the way a scientist would stare at a particularly ugly insect. "I did not give you permission to speak."

Screw being passive. "I don't live here. And I don't need your permission."

The king's face turned a dark blue. Clearly, he was pissed. But if he was angry, so was Glyn, and she put her hand on mine to stop me from speaking while she responded to his attitude with an edge to her voice. "Sire, I came here asking for mercy. I came here with a genuine offer to help. All I ask for is refuge."

"Were you not listening?" the king asked. "Were you not?" Kott was now truly angry, and he sat bolt upright to stare us both down. "I must think of my people first and foremost, not some child from another kingdom who might be a traitor."

At that, Glyn flared, and the anger practically leaped from her eyes. "Traitor? You dare call me a traitor?"

In a quick move, he stood up and thrust his finger at her. "Yes, traitor. You can open portals to not only any place on this planet but also to other worlds. How can I be assured that you will not bring Lensa's army here or some invaders from a land or world that wishes to destroy us?"

"You cannot," Glyn replied, her body shaking with suppressed rage. "But if you knew my character, you would also know that I am not that way."

Mini speech over, she took a step back and bowed, polite to the end. "Let's go, Mark. This was a waste of my time."

"King's a waste of space," I muttered.

That earned me a look of wrath from Kott as he took his crown and slammed it against his throne, splintering the wood. "Visitor, you might do well to learn better manners. Glynarra's outburst can be forgiven. Yours cannot. This meeting is ended."

And, just like that, our audience with the king was over. We would not be coming back again. Dejected, we left the room, and the guards, who'd been waiting outside, accompanied us to the exit. There, they bowed out of respect.

"We are sorry," the lead guard said. "I heard every word our king said. It would have been better if he had shown you greater favor."

"It is not your fault," Glyn replied with supreme sadness after she'd returned the bow. "You are only doing what your king commands. Be careful and guard your king well."

With that, Glyn bowed once more and turned away, taking my hand in hers. Once we were out of range, she performed her portal-opening ritual and a window immediately formed.

"I'm sorry, Glyn," I said. "Me and my big mouth."

She shook her head. "No, you backed me up. You said what was right. I have to deal with this on my own — and with your help."

"You've got it."

I climbed into the window with her. "Where are we going now?"

Her face brightened, as if she'd just gotten the idea of the century. "When we were on Suidara, the water sprites helped you. You said that they gave you an edge in our race."

I thought back to our little competition. "Oh, yeah, that's right."

Glyn leaned her head against my chest. "Well, I need an edge, and I think I know where to get one."

Chapter Seventeen

The Favor

"Where are we?" I asked as we went through the window. As with all the other times, it vanished as soon as we walked through, the panes collapsing upon themselves and disappearing in a burst of light.

"Near where we want to go, I think," Glyn answered. "I may have to ask for help. Hang on while I look around."

We'd arrived in a forest, one so thick and dense with trees that I couldn't see more than a few feet in front of me. I looked up and could barely see the sky. While my girlfriend looked around, I took a seat on a nearby log to mull over what had happened so far.

I missed Suidara, our watery beach refuge. If I could live anywhere, that would have been my first and only choice, but apparently it was not to be. Still, for the first time in a long time, I'd felt relaxed and safe, and the kisses from Glyn hadn't been bad, either.

Oddly enough, I didn't miss Earth that much. It was sort of a 'been-there-done-that' kind of thing, but it was still my home, no matter what.

However, while I had a home, Glyn didn't. She couldn't escape her curse, and neither could I. No matter where we went, there was that sword of time dangling over our heads. It would never go away, it would never shift its position and it always threatened to drop.

All that meant leaving, running to another haven then another. To be so rootless, it must have cut into her soul. She had no place to call her own. It wasn't her fault, naturally, but all the same, my heart ached for her.

Still, we'd made—or rather, *she'd* made—the choice to return to Tellkar, and that meant facing up to and probably facing off against Lensa. But we needed an edge, and only Glyn knew where to get it.

"We're almost there," Glyn answered, breaking into my reverie. She sounded hopeful. "At least, I think so."

Her words didn't comfort me at all. A few insects buzzed around us. They were harmless, Glyn said. "I'll ask one of them if this is the right place."

'Scuse me? "Ask an insect?"

"Sure."

My girlfriend let out a sound that was a cross between a bird's cheep and the squeak of a mouse. One insect landed on her hand and gazed at her calmly.

It resembled a dragonfly, except that it had four sets of wings and two praying mantis heads with enormous black eyes. The eyes were speckled with red, and it had a long, thin proboscis that it either used to drink with or impale its victims. I didn't want to know.

Glyn repeated the cry. The insect took off and slowly flew ahead of us. "Follow it," she said.

Buzz-buzz went the bug, and it led us to one tree that stood out from the pack. Reddish-gray all over and with a thicker trunk than the rest, it had to be the leader, and it made me chuckle internally.

A leader tree was freaky, but by now I was used to seeing the strange and different. The insect then returned and tapped Glyn's hand before flying off. She gazed around the area without fear and nodded to herself.

"He was very helpful," she said in a soft voice.

"You mean the insect?"

She nodded without looking at me. "Yeah, him. When I was a little girl, my parents told me about this place. It's called the Hidden Forest. Like I said, when we were on Suidara, you mentioned something about gaining an advantage, and that made me think."

"Think about what?"

She turned to me, and her eyes shone with optimism. "What is it that Lensa has that no one else has?"

That was easy. "He has power."

For that answer, I received a smack on the shoulder and the admonition of, "Nice deduction, but you should try thinking a little deeper about it. Where did he get that power? He wasn't born with it."

Okay, I was beginning to get the idea. "You said he stole it from everyone else, everyone who had abilities."

Glyn had already moved in the direction of the leader tree. Its branches swung down in a defensive posture, but it didn't try to hit her, and, holy crap, these trees were alive?

"You've got to be kidding me," I said. "A living forest?"

"Yes, they're alive," Glyn said in a matter-of-fact voice as she slowly backed away. "Everything has life, and life is in everything. You just have to look for it. Now, before you open your mouth again to ask about something the insect told me, the trees aren't going to hurt us, as long as you make the right moves."

That was easy for her to say, as the trees rustled their branches like a gorilla beating its chest. This was their territory, and they took a step forward as if to assert their dominance.

Stepping wasn't the right word. There had to be some underground network of rolling roots, as the trees moved in our direction. "Don't move," Glyn warned. "They can sense fear."

At that moment, fear was all I had. The plants and flowers swiveled to face us. Photosynthesis was one thing, but this was something beyond strange. Even though it had to be my imagination, I thought I saw them scowling.

While that unnerved me, Glyn's next statement unnerved me even more. "If this works, someone here might be able to help us. We're looking for a woman, and maybe she'll talk to us. But first we have to find her."

She kneeled, gently running her hand over the surface, and muttering to the ground as though it was her friend. It was then that I realized she was talking to it. "Like your mother used to do," I said in wonder.

"Mm-hmm," she murmured as she gently tapped here and there. "That's right. My mother taught me a few spells that relate to nature. One of them is to speak to it. For now, be quiet. I'm not sure I remember it correctly. If I'm right, the trees will part, and they'll show us a way in."

"What if we're wrong?"

"The forest will eat us."

Oh, this is not good.

I inhaled and exhaled deeply, trying to get my now-pounding heart under control. It was a given that Glyn wasn't kidding, so I held my breath and waited.

She murmured something to the grass here and there, ran her hand over the petals of the plants and flowers, and finally, she ended the spell by going over to the leader tree to exclaim, *"Aketro!"*

A second later, the trees stopped and slid to one side. Their branches moved to usher us to a clearly marked pathway. We began walking, with Glyn nodding at every tree, patting their trunks here and there, and whispering her thanks.

"Do the same," she murmured. "This is their place, and you're a guest. Act nicely."

I did as she'd commanded, feeling the rough bark beneath my fingertips, but also feeling a shiver of energy run through them. It was a pulse, their life force.

These trees were alive in every sense of the word. I'd once seen an animated film about going to a magic forest, something about an ill-tempered ogre and his sidekick…

"Something special, isn't it," Glyn stated, breaking into my cartoon reverie as we slowly made our way along the path.

"Uh, yeah, it is."

"Make sure you pet each tree. They might get jealous if you don't."

Right, don't anger the possibly homicidal trees, and I made sure to pat each one, saying, "Thank you."

A few more steps and we cleared the tree line. In front of us was a tiny cottage in the middle of a square field.

It was something straight out of a children's fairy tale, with logs for walls, and a thatched roof. Images of fire and children being roasted on a spit ran through my mind at light speed, and I shook my head to get those images out. I'd read the original Grimm childhood stories, and they were definitely not child friendly.

Then I'd read about the Baba Yaga, and that was an even more unsettling story. "Uh, Glyn, not to diss your choice of allies or anything, but who is this person, exactly?"

"She's what you'd call an ecological witch. Her magic extends to communicating with all the plant and flower life in this forest…and maybe more."

A tiny amount of uncertainty entered her voice. "It's been said that she's so powerful that even Lensa would never dare harm her or send anyone to do so. He's afraid of her, but she doesn't take sides in any conflict, save that of her own. That's what I heard. That, and she only wants to be left alone."

"And we're disturbing her."

Glyn stopped as a troubled expression flashed across her face. "Yes, we are, and it's been said that unwelcome visitors never leave. But I've also heard that she indirectly aids those who have no hope. Perhaps I'm one of those no-hope cases. That's for her to decide."

My girlfriend walked up the door and knocked on it twice. There was no answer at first, and I thought about walking around to the back of the house just in case the person here was gardening or something.

After considering that notion, I changed my mind and stayed where I was. Never attempt to intrude upon a witch's property.

Glyn knocked again, harder this time. "Nyoka, I am here to request a favor of you."

The name came out as Nee-o-ka, with the accent on the middle syllable. Glyn called the other woman's name again, and that did the trick, as a sharp old-yet-not-old cry resounded from inside the cottage. "Who asks this favor of me? Tell me your name first."

"It is Glynarra."

The door opened. A short, rotund woman of indeterminate age faced us. While most of the people here were in the five-three to five-six range, Nyoka barely reached four feet.

Her hair wasn't green, but long and dark gray, and the stars around her neck were faded, perhaps to indicate her age. She could have been fifty years old or one-hundred-fifty.

She stared at me without an iota of fear. It came across as a look of curiosity and nothing more. She then switched her gaze to my girlfriend. "Glynarra...the trees and grass spoke to me of your parent's passage into the great darkness. I grieve with you."

"Thank you, Nyoka," Glyn replied in a flat tone. "You are the only one who has mentioned the word grief."

"People think of themselves first," the old woman answered as she took a quick glance around the area. Satisfied that no one else was coming, she ushered us in. Once she closed the door, she muttered something and turned to us.

"This abode is now secure. I have just invoked a spell to hide my place from the eyes of those who'd wish to find me or you, Glynarra. My magic will protect us, at least for now, but I must know why you are here. Sit, and I will get you something to drink."

Glyn led me to an area filled with beanbags. One of them, a red-green mix, said in an auntie's voice, "Sit here, dear."

Another beanbag reached up to touch my hand. "Over here, dear. I am comfortable."

Uh, right.

Glyn took a seat and the beanbag said, "Oh, you are a nice person. I can tell."

My beanbag said nothing save that I was different. Well, yeah, I was. Nyoka came back with two rough-hewn wood cups of water. "Drink."

Another command, but I sensed she wasn't out to hurt us. If she was as powerful as Glyn said she was, then this witch could have made me into toad food. She could have, but she didn't.

Instead, Nyoka turned to me. Unlike her brief onceover when we'd first met, this time, she seemed to size me up and strip me bare, as it were. If there was a look that could run deep into my soul, she had it.

Nyoka's intense stare dissipated, and she looked at my girlfriend. "Your companion is obviously not of this world. Where have you been, Glynarra?"

Glyn related her story to the witch as quickly and concisely as possible. At the end, the witch clucked her tongue in dismay.

"Lensa's grip on this land is, indeed, a most grievous one. He is not a person to be denied. The only reason he has not captured me is because of my magic and because I reside here."

Her words, said with such sadness, made me realize something. "So, you're a prisoner?" I asked.

Nyoka bobbed her head. "You are perceptive, er…"

"My name's Mark. I'm from Earth."

She turned my name over on her lips, and she offered a smile, but it was tinged with sadness. "You are most perceptive. I cannot leave my house, and if I do, it is only for a short time. Lensa and his vertok would soon find me, and while I am strong, I am not powerful enough to fight both his magicians at once. He has only two, but they are said to be the most powerful in all the world." She added with a hint of resignation, "No one knows of that fact, save you and Glynarra."

Call that a surprise. "I, er, heard that you were the, uh, most powerful of them all."

A mischievous glint came to her eye. "Sometimes a lie is stronger than a spell."

It made sense, and I looked out of the window at the surrounding area. The trees seemed to shift into a defensive stance, although that had to be my imagination. I turned back to face the witch. "So, um, how, I mean, what do you do during the day?"

She shrugged. "I stay here, clean my place, then practice my magic and reinforce it wherever and whenever possible. I also spend time with my friends, the trees and the plants and the flowers. Whatever news they see and hear from the people, they relay it to one another and to me. I am their friend. They sustain me, and they protect me."

Nyoka then impaled me with a laser-like glare, but it held no anger, only curiosity. "And what is your relationship with this girl?"

That was sudden—and forward. "Uh, well, it's like—"

"Yeah, what is our relationship?" Glyn cut in with a tiny smile.

Heat rushed to my face, but now wasn't the time to hem and haw about things. Besides, I thought we'd settled that on Suidara. "We're, um, we're in a serious relationship. More than dating, if you know what I mean."

Nyoka stared up at me. "Do you care for her?"

Direct, wasn't she? Well, being shy about things hadn't helped me so far, so why not tell the truth? "Yes, I care for her…very much. And we came to ask you for help."

A smile flitted across the old witch's face, although she said nothing. Glyn then switched back to the main topic. "We were hoping, Nyoka, that you could offer us a spell that will counteract Lensa's magic."

The witch-woman worried her lower lip between incredibly white teeth before replying. When she did, her answer held nothing but sadness.

"I do not have what you want. I am sorry, Glynarra. You are a good person, but I cannot help you. I have taken a vow not to side with anyone during any conflict between the peoples of this world."

Glyn's lips thinned with disappointment, but she also had the good manners not to get angry. "Then we have come here and disturbed you for nothing. I apologize for doing so. We will go now."

She stepped outside, and I followed her, but Nyoka's hand shot out and latched onto my forearm, turning me around and pulling me down. *What in the hell?*

"Be not afraid," she murmured.

A wave from her other hand closed the door. She stood on her tiptoes to whisper into my ear, "I have one thing, but I cannot give it to your companion. I do this to protect her."

Secrets—we all had them—and, curious now, I asked, "What exactly do you mean that you have something?"

Nyoka's gaze met mine. "I said before that I cannot take sides between the people of this world, but since you are not of this world, then I am breaking no rules."

Clever, this person was most clever. "Thanks."

Her smile was shy, almost coquettish. "I was young once, long ago. I know of feelings for others. Our culture does not place much importance on love."

"Uh, yeah, Glynarra told me."

Nyoka's smile deepened. "She has a special gift, and it is obvious that you have feelings for her. I see how you look at her. That is special as well. Therefore, I shall aid you. I am no friend of Lensa. He has brought nothing but misery to our kingdom. However, if I give you something, then I must also obtain something in return. It is our custom."

I knew that. What did I have that she might like? I searched my pockets and came out with the singing shell. As much as I liked it, if giving it to someone else would help my girlfriend, then I'd give whatever I had. "Please take this."

The witch took it from me. "Most curious. What magical properties does it have?"

"Put it to your ear."

She did, and her mouth dropped open in awe. "This is a most worthwhile gift. It sings a song of the ages, of the birth and death and rebirth of a world. Thank you."

Nyoka reached into her robe to put away the shell and took out a piece of parchment with words written on it in a language that I couldn't understand.

"Mark of Earth, this is for you. It is an ancient spell, written in a language known only to a few. I am one of them. Lensa and his magicians would also know what language this is, although they know not of the spell itself. Take this parchment. Guard it well."

What good was this going to do for me if I couldn't read it? Nevertheless, I carefully folded it up and put it in my pocket. "Kneel before me," she commanded.

I did, and before I could say anything, Nyoka put her palm to my forehead. A shock ran through me, freezing me to the spot. I saw nothing, felt nothing, but her voice echoed in my mind.

"Heed these words well, Mark of Earth. King Lensa is a vain and cruel and stupid man. But he possesses great power. Glynarra, if she faces him, cannot match his strength or his stolen abilities. However, if the king is goaded into issuing a challenge, matters may take a different course."

What was this about a challenge? Glyn had mentioned something about a challenge, but that was like a simple fistfight. This had to be something different, and Nyoka's words echoed more strongly than before.

"It is one of our oldest customs and goes back to time immemorial. If one party challenges another, then they must settle their challenge immediately with no use of powers.

Should one side win, the other side is allowed to make a claim in return. That is how things work here. As for what I gave you, when the time is right, simply hold the parchment and the words will come to you. Speak them as such. They will hold no meaning for you, but they will mean everything to the young woman who is close to you.

Remember, anything acquired can be taken away. A spell, a potion, can be death to the fae. Have no fear and protect Glynarra, for I know she is as dear to you as she was to her mother and father. Say nothing of this to her. It is for her protection – and for yours."

Nyoka released her hold on my mind, and I rose feeling somewhat disoriented, but that soon faded. Odd — Nyoka had mentioned the word 'fae'. That was the first time I'd ever heard anyone mention it here.

When I rejoined Glyn outside, she asked me if anything was wrong. "No, nothing's wrong," I replied. "I'm fine. Nyoka, er, just wanted to know a little bit about Earth."

"I see."

We turned to leave. For the moment, yes, we were fine, but we'd soon meet Lensa again, and the odds were not in our favor.

Chapter Eighteen

Hunting Party

A cool breeze blew against our faces as we walked back the way we'd come. The trees allowed us passage, and I remembered to pat each one gently on its trunk and murmur my thanks. Glyn did the same.

Once we were out, the trees moved like electronic men on a chess table to rearrange themselves and subsequently block off all entry to Nyoka's cottage.

A rustling of leaves here, the sound of branches scraping there, a rumble of roots moving slowly but inexorably under the earth, and soon, it was over. All was as it had been the first time we'd arrived here, but at the same time, a feeling came over me that said we'd never go there again.

It was too difficult to explain that feeling, and I didn't bother trying. The witch's words had sounded like a prophecy, and I wasn't exactly sure what to do, but she was certain that I would do the right thing when crunch time came.

I'd read somewhere that in every hero's or heroine's journey, there was a moment when they had to make that all-important, life-and-death decision. Would I be able to make that decision and carry through when that time came? I could only hope so.

In a way, I had made that decision the first time I'd joined Glyn in this adventure. I'd promised to support her and do what I could. Now, it was time for me to make good on that promise.

We kept going, then Glyn stopped to open a window. "It's time," she said. "We're going to Lensa's castle. It's not far from here, but I don't feel like traveling on foot, not now."

We stepped in, emerging on a dirt road. A large, gray and foreboding-looking structure lay about half a mile away, by my estimation. That was Lensa's castle. We were in plain sight, which didn't make sense, so I said, "I thought you said his seer could locate us."

"I did," she replied while looking straight ahead. A note of determination appeared in her voice. "That's what I want. I hid before. I'm not hiding now."

We started down the road, kicking up soft puffs of dirt. A few people saw us walking, stopped in surprise when they saw me, then they hastily beat a retreat when Glyn looked in their direction. "It is her!" one of them exclaimed.

A look of anger combined with readiness crossed Glyn's face. "Yes, it is me," she answered as she balled her fists. "If you have something to say, say it now or leave!"

They left, the dirt kicking up at their heels. "Pretty rude," I observed as the cloud of dust faded behind them.

Glyn relaxed only a tiny bit. "They know who I am. They don't want to get involved, except to alert the authorities and perhaps claim a reward. I don't blame them, but I don't have to be their best friend, either. After today, I doubt that anyone will want to have anything to do with me."

Walking into danger wasn't my idea of fun, but my girlfriend seemed to know what she was doing. Still, I had to know. "Are you sure about this?"

"Yes," she answered tersely. "The king has what I want—the ability to lift my curse. He wants what I have, my power. I'm tired of this mouse-and-cat game."

"Cat-and-mouse," I replied, gently correcting her.

Glyn shot me a slightly pissed off look. "Got it. Anyway, I'm tired of this. This is my world, my land and my life, and no one is going to ruin it for me. Lensa took away my parents. He wanted to take away my house, and now he wants to kill me in order to get my power. No. No way."

She continued to stride ahead, and I hustled to keep up with her. "Uh, Glyn, you know that if we go to the castle, there are going to be guards."

"I know."

"How do you know they won't kill us?"

Glyn never broke stride. "I don't, but we have an unwritten rule. If someone challenges the king, then they're allowed safe passage. Lensa doesn't have to honor it, but I'm hoping he will."

Oh, right…Nyoka had mentioned the challenge as well. Glyn said nothing more, but she picked up the pace, and I matched her step for step. Then other sounds came through to us, blotting out the buzz of our little winged friends.

"Do you hear that?" Glyn asked.

Thump. Thump. The rhythmic sound of people marching. Men's voices. *Clank, clank*…the rustle of metal against metal. Soldiers were coming to meet us, and my sense of unease grew exponentially with every step I heard. "Glyn," I started, but she waved me off.

"I know."

"You got a plan?"

"Keep them talking and give me your extender."

I handed over my weapon. She tucked it into her robe and traced the outline of a window in the air. A portal formed and she stepped inside. "Keep them talking," she repeated. "I'll handle the rest."

The window vanished and she with it. "Thanks for disappearing on me," I muttered, feeling like the proverbial sacrificial lamb.

Since she'd made her escape, that left me to hold the fort. Keep them talking. How? Those guys weren't into casual conversation.

Tramp, tramp…the clank of metal grew louder. Footsteps — ten soldiers came into view. As I expected, they were armed with swords and clubs. Behind them was a slender, almost wraithlike man clad in a black robe.

Perhaps in his sixties, he walked with a spry step that belied his age. He had to be the vertok, the seer. The lead soldier addressed him as such and with great deference.

"Honored vertok, please stand well away from this place. Death will come here, and I do not wish you to be part of it."

The seer dutifully moved a few yards away and stood with his hands clasped in front of his body. The lead soldier then turned to me.

"We were informed by some people loyal to the king that there were intruders here."

Glyn had been right. Informers and rats were everywhere. The soldier continued speaking as though the words had been programmed into him. "Mark of Earth, we have orders to find the one called Glynarra and bring her to the good king. You, though, shall be executed, here and now."

Stall for time. "On whose orders, soldier?"

Oh, that stymied him for a few seconds. He wasn't used to being talked back to, and when he recovered, he replied with some degree of astonishment, "Our master, of course, the good King Lensa."

Now the pitch and tone of this guy's voice came through, and it sounded familiar. I rubbed my jaw as if considering the matter, then I waved my hand as if dismissing a total imbecile, which this guy was.

"I see. Well, first off, Lensa's a maggot. Second, you little droids don't have any manners. After all, I'm a visitor to your world, and you know what they say about treating the guest right, don't you?"

The lead guard removed his helmet to stare at me. It was Starra, the guy with the eyepatch, our first jailer. I should've figured it out sooner.

At any rate, his answer was predictable. "I do not understand what a 'droid' is, but to answer your statement about treating a guest correctly, the answer is no."

No. Unarmed and out of my league against ten soldiers, I took a step back, searching for something — anything — I could use as a weapon. And, of course, there was nothing. All right, I'd have to do this hand-to-hand, even though they were armed.

A fool's choice? Undoubtedly. But then again, I'd almost been killed by the Underworlders. I'd been threatened by a guy with two faces, and after facing off against them, these hired guns were nothing.

Mr. Eyepatch waved three of his men forward. "We will find the girl, but you will die first. I have not forgotten the trick you and that girl played upon me in the king's castle."

Oh, did this idiot have things messed up! "I think you forgot about the part where you tossed me and Glyn into jail and denied us water until we were half dead. I think you forgot about the part about being decent. Well, get this straight. You were stupid enough to fall for our trick. Now, you're butthurt. Too bad."

Starra growled something incomprehensible, then yelled, "Kill him!"

The unholy trio advanced, standing one behind the other, then they stopped. A collective gasp came from them. They shook and shivered, began to quiver...

And a blade exploded through the chest of the lead soldier, sending out a great gout of blood that missed me by mere inches. He gave me a look of surprise, managed to say, "What?" and when the blade withdrew, he fell on his face. His two comrades in arms fell like dominoes behind him.

Three soldiers down, seven to go. I looked behind the rest of the men. A window was open, and Glyn called out, "Hey, over here, you pathetic poltroons," before vanishing into it.

Pathetic poltroons? I'd heard that on a comedy show once and thought it funny, but listening to it here made it sound ultra-serious.

Naturally, they whirled around at the sound of her voice. I picked up one of the swords a dead soldier had dropped and started swinging. While I didn't know jack about the finer points of sword fighting, I knew enough to chop with the blade and stab with the sharp end.

One soldier lifted his chin in an act of defiance. That left an opening between metal and flesh, and I whipped my sword around, cutting deeply into the man's throat. When I yanked out the blade, a mighty river of blood flowed out and he collapsed.

I'd never killed anyone before, and my gorge rose, but this was a matter of life and death—and in this case, I chose life.

Mine.

Six to go, and of course, the remaining lackeys got their swords into position. "Prepare to die," another soldier said.

"You said that before," I answered, getting ready for more combat.

Out of the corner of my eye, Glyn appeared on the right, just behind the soldiers. She had the extender ready, and I pointed in her direction. "Guys, before you start slashing, look over there."

Oh, the stupidity of mankind—three of them did. Glyn pressed the button on the side of the extender. Like a coiled snake, it shot out, but unlike a snake, the extender had no fangs, only a sharp blade, and it skewered the unlucky trio. They toppled over without a sound.

Death was something that came in many forms, either from monsters or from people. While I wasn't inured to it, I knew that I had to put it behind me and compartmentalize it and think about it another day. It was the only way to stay sane.

"Now, we're down to three," I said. "Glyn, you'd better leave. Window and all that."

She slowly shook her head and sat down. A moment later, she lay down. "I'm a little tired. You can handle them, right?"

Are you kidding?

Glyn tossed me the extender, but Mr. Eyepatch moved quickly to bat it away. "Mark of Earth, you have only your sword to defend yourself with," he said. "I have my orders from the king to dispatch you with my blade. Prepare to die."

Was that threat number three? He lunged at me, but he did so awkwardly. Hot and tired though I was, I twisted out of the way just in time and aimed an equally awkward slash at his neck.

My blade whistled through the air, he parried it and I gripped the handle with both hands for additional power. This wasn't baseball, but by swinging the sword back and forth as fast as I could, I managed to keep him off me.

Starra was good, though, and he blocked my swings easily. After another thrust-parry combination, he backed off and circled around me, bringing his sword up to shoulder height in a lateral position, a sneer on his lips.

"You have no skill, strange visitor. You were fortunate that my man was a poor fighter. I am not. However, I have just decided to leave the honor of slaying you to my men. They need the practice."

While he was talking, I glanced out of my right eye to see if my girlfriend was going to do anything.

Glyn didn't rise. In fact, she seemed to be speaking to the ground, her lips moving rapidly and soundlessly. Like, I was about to get sliced and diced here, but she was talking to the earth. *Glyn, if you're going to do something, do it now!*

"Men, advance and slay this intruder," Starra ordered.

Both of his men came at me, and I looked at death. However, before they could raise their swords to strike, the grass from either side of the road shot out and wrapped itself around their wrists and ankles, causing them to drop their weapons.

"This is a trick," Starra said, anger in his voice. He'd also been seized by the grass. Wriggling his body proved futile. Although he struggled mightily, the grass lengthened and subsequently wound itself farther around his wrists and ankles in response.

Once it started to pull them down, though, a note of fear entered his voice. "What manner of sorcery is this?"

"Mine," Glyn said with a sense of extreme satisfaction.

The grass yanked even harder on their extremities, and fight though they did, they couldn't overcome the power that Glyn wielded. They fell on their backs, their helmets bouncing a few feet away, and they cursed the magic that assailed them.

My girlfriend got up to walk over to them, stone-faced and silent. She watched as the grass rapidly knitted itself over their prone bodies, forming a thickly woven blanket that went from their necks to their toes, building up layer by layer.

Although the grass had started to obscure their faces, I recognized two more of them — the twins. They stared at me with fear and hatred in their eyes, although neither of them spoke.

Glyn knew who they were, but at that point, she probably didn't care anymore. Neither did I.

"I told you before that my mother taught me a couple of spells," she said to me in a quiet voice.

"Yeah, you did."

"One was to communicate with nature and ask for its benevolence."

She then kneeled and whispered something to the ground. It began to twist and writhe, and some blades under the bodies of the soldiers crept upward. "The other was to ask nature to act as a tool of vengeance."

Starra got the message, and his lone eye bugged out in fright. "Mercy," he croaked. "If you have any decency, you will have mercy upon us. *Please*."

"Mercy," Glyn echoed, and her voice got an edge to it, the edge of anger and hate, and the tone of one who sought revenge. This was a revenge that could not and would not be denied. "Your king had none when he ordered his men to kill my mother and father. Even though you were not among those who slayed my parents, you have killed before, have you not? Do not answer. I am sure you have."

She indicated me with a wave of her arm. "You and your two friends captured us. Do you remember that?"

"Yes."

Her eyes grew hard. "You were there when we were jailed, were you not?"

If Starra knew that Glyn was going to snuff out his life, perhaps he'd have chosen his final words more carefully. Then again, no. He had nothing but hate inside. "I remember it all," he stated with defiance. "And I would do it again, without changing a thing."

Disgust combined with rage coated Glyn's next words. "You tortured us, and you enjoyed it. Now, you want to kill my friend. He is my most special ally and companion and my love. His death, I cannot and will not allow."

She turned away. "Goodbye."

In a flash, the grass wove itself over their mouths and noses, then around their throats, choking them. They struggled, but they'd been bound good and tight, and there would be no escape for them, not today.

While they couldn't speak, their death rattles told the whole story. I couldn't look and went over to join her. She was shaking. "I didn't want to do that," she whispered. "I didn't want to, but they left me no choice."

I risked a look behind me. The men had stopped moving. "You could have left them tied up and—"

"And they'd have gotten free. Then they'd have tried to kill you. I care for you, Mark. I knew that back on Horror World. I couldn't let you die then. I *won't* let you die now."

She reached up to gently caress my cheek then pivoted around to face the vertok, who was staring at us in disbelief, his hands over his mouth. "Seer, what is your name?"

He took his hands away from his mouth and replied in a faint voice, one that spoke of all hope gone. "I am a vertok."

Glyn waved off his answer. "I do not care what your rank or ability is," she said tiredly. "I wish to know your name."

He began to shake in fear. "It is Wartten. Please do not kill me. I am not a fighting man."

My girlfriend stepped over to confront him, and she sounded almost kind. "I will not kill you. That is my promise. Instead, I want you to take a message to the king."

I'd never seen an elf sweat before, much less pee itself. He didn't do the former, but he most certainly did the latter, and the smell of ammonia cut through the air.

He didn't seem to be ashamed of it though, and he bobbed his head rapidly, like that toy bird that bobbed up and down, pecking at water in a glass. "I shall do as you request. Anything."

My girlfriend shoved her face a few inches away from his. Her voice lost its tone of decency, replaced by firm resolve and underscored by rage.

"Go tell your king that I am coming for him. I am with my most special companion, Mark of Earth. We will be upon your castle soon. Leave now and tell him."

"I will."

Wartten ran off, his robes flapping. Glyn waited until the seer was out of sight then turned to me. "Are you injured?"

"No, just tired," I said, wiping sweat and blood from my face. "What now?"

Glyn walked over to one of the dead soldiers. He had an animal skin attached to his belt. She jerked it off, opened it and poured some water down her throat.

Once done, she returned to my side, handed the skin to me and I finished off the water. We sat and said nothing for a few minutes.

Finally, she got up and pointed to a spot beyond the trees. "Lensa's castle is over there. If we walk quickly, then it should take us about ten minutes."

"Don't you want to rest more?"

Glyn shook her head. "No. By now, the vertok's probably told Lensa that we're coming. I want the king to think about that, and I also want to meet Lensa while I'm still pissed off. That'll help."

Fine with me. I found the extender and picked it up, securely tucking it into my belt loop. As for the sword, I tossed it away. The extender would have to do. "Then let's go meet the king."

Chapter Nineteen

Showdown

Glyn and I approached the castle hand in hand. Her pace was steady, her face set. Not a muscle moved or twitched, and her breathing was even. Talk about ice! She could out-freeze a glacier with that attitude, and that was something I envied.

If she felt scared or hesitant about taking on Lensa, then she was putting on a great act. I did my best to emulate her, but inwardly, my heart was slamming against my chest wall. If it were a bird, it would have taken flight long ago.

As we walked, she asked calmly, "Are you ready?"

Are you serious? No. Even though I was unsure, I couldn't let her down, so I lied. "As ready as I'll ever be."

After uttering that statement, I kicked myself mentally for using such a stale cliché. Still, she didn't laugh, only pointed in front of her.

Naturally, we were up against superior odds. The sight of the guards on patrol around the castle didn't do much to quell the uncertainty that ran through every fiber of my being. They were armed with swords, and it was a given that they weren't in a mood to parlay.

"You still have the extender, don't you?" Glynarra whispered as we got within range. She let go of my hand.

"Uh-huh," I murmured out of the corner of my mouth. I had the weapon behind my back and all I needed was to get a few feet closer. "Ready."

"Halt, traitor," one of the guards said as he and his co-soldiers marched straight toward us, their swords out and bodies tensed, ready for battle.

The barrier didn't seem to be up. I put out my hand, felt around and encountered nothing. Perhaps the king thought it unnecessary. Or maybe he'd thought himself so powerful that he believed no one would ever attack him.

If he'd actually thought that way, then he'd made an extremely poor tactical decision, and we were going to make him pay for it. I took a step forward, and the guard ordered us to halt again. He extended his arms from his side in a gesture of thou-shalt-not-pass, while two of his men lined up behind him.

"Traitor," I said to Glyn out of the corner of my mouth. "Are they talking about you?"

A grim smile adorned her face. "Most likely, yes."

"You are to surrender now," the lead guard said. "Will you come quietly?"

For supposedly well-trained soldiers, they weren't very bright. I whipped out the extender, pressed the button on the side, and the sharp metal tip automatically shot out ten feet, going through guard number one and impaling guard number two in the process.

Neither of them had time to scream. As they fell, the remaining guards did an about-face and fled inside the castle, yelling about a strange invader. I figured the soldiers would show a tad more courage, but anyone would lose their nerve after seeing their friends lose their innards.

"A strange invader," I mused. "Guess they were talking about me this time?"

A mirthless laugh came from her. "Yes, most definitely. Are you going to leave your weapon here?"

"Yeah."

I didn't bother pulling the blade out. Up against magic, it would be useless. We walked across the drawbridge and into the main hallway where we faced no less than fifteen armed and armored soldiers who stood shoulder to shoulder to form a wall. All of them had their swords out and raised.

"Halt," one of them said, and we did. "The other soldiers have already informed us as well as our king about what you have done. It is a most grievous infraction of our rules."

What a polite way of saying I'd just stabbed two of their men to death. "Ain't that a shame," I replied with all the sarcasm I could muster. "Ready for more infractions?"

One soldier began to move forward, but the lead guard ordered him back, and the man returned to his place, grumbling.

As for Glyn, far from being cowed by their presence, she stood her ground to state her case. "We are unarmed. My name is Glynarra. Your king knows of me. I am here to challenge him. Although I am not well-versed in the ways of royalty, I understand that if a challenge is offered, then I am to be allowed safe passage. Is that not correct?"

She was taking a big chance, but considering Lensa wanted her abilities, he wouldn't kill her. On the other hand, I was neither royalty nor a citizen of this world.

All the same, her tone, quiet and yet stern and uncompromising, got their attention. The guard who'd spoken, nodded. "You are correct."

"Then I repeat my challenge to the king and claim safe passage for myself as well as for my companion," she replied coolly, indicating me with a wave of her hand.

Silence ruled, and sweat dripped from every part of me as I looked at death from their weapons. After fifteen interminable seconds, the lead guard turned to his men, ordered them to sheathe their swords, and they proceeded to escort us into the courtyard.

In sharp contrast to Kott's castle, this place was large and beautifully appointed. While the interior of the castle was impressive enough, here, a magnificent garden dominated the landscape.

Every corner had been artfully designed with strategically placed trees that offered the maximum shade. Row upon row of brightly colored flowers dotted beds at the edges of the garden.

Ostentation was the name of the game, and the king certainly believed in it. Many of the royal families on Earth thought the same way.

A circle of greenery stood in the center of the garden, and a golden throne sat just outside it. Lensa walked around inside the circle, muttering to himself. As he moved, he rolled his shoulders and swung his arms like a boxer warming up for a championship fight.

The area itself was large enough for two people to move around freely, and I wondered what his endgame was. He commanded magic, and he was far more powerful than I was. Glyn was also no match for him in terms of casting spells or magical ability.

When the king spotted us, he ceased his mutters and his demeanor brightened. "Ah, Glynarra, you have come. I assume you are here to demand your freedom?"

She nodded. "Yes."

He crossed his arms over his chest. "I am pleased by your presence. And you have brought that individual, Mark of Earth, with you. Charming."

Charming—in his case, I'd make an exception, and I walked to the throne to lean against it and give him my command. "Lift the curse, Lensa."

Wow, there, I said it, and one second after I'd said it, a few classic tropes ran through my head.

Give us freedom.

Give me liberty or give me death.

Let my people go.

Doubtful that Lensa had ever watched a biblical movie in his life. Oh, wait, they didn't have television here. They didn't have the Internet or telephones. In many respects, they were backward in terms of development.

What they weren't backward in was magic and the command of it. Moreover, my words failed to have much of an impact on him. In fact, he received my four-word command without batting an eye.

Most rulers would. After all, this was his turf, his home field, and he had the advantage. If his personality ran true to form, he'd probably throw his head back and utter an evil laugh.

Of course, he did. It was odd to see a short, green elf toss his head back, crown and all, and give a deep and loud belly laugh, but he did it. To his credit, the gesture didn't come off as comical as I thought it would.

Lensa had two cohorts with him, two large and thick-set men clad in armor. They chuckled inside their helmets, adding to the ridiculousness of the moment.

In contrast, Glyn said nothing, and after Lensa finished laughing like a hyena on uppers and calmed down to a shaking-his-head-at-my-idiocy level, he wiped his eyes and offered a genuine smile.

"That, Mark of Earth, is one of the most amusing things I have heard in a long time. You wish your freedom?"

His question came out with all the arrogance of someone who had power and had never known deprivation. Well, he was about to get a lesson in the latter.

"No, I already have my freedom," I replied. "I can go back to Earth if I want. What I want you to do is to lift the curse on Glynarra."

A wicked smile adorned his face. "If I lift the curse, that will include you, will it not?"

Sadistic jerk. "Yeah. But this is about her, not me. Let her go. You have a kingdom. What else do you —?"

"Need," he finished for me, and his voice turned savage, as did the expression on his face. It reminded me of a feral dog. "What else do I need? I need her power. I need her ability to open portals to other realms so that I may invade if I choose, conquer if I choose and rule in those realms, if I choose. I may even enter your world."

Is that right? I took a step in his direction. "Take away your magic, Lensa, and you don't stand a chance.

241

You're short, underpowered and pathetic. Up against someone from my world, hand to hand, you're nothing."

Lensa's face flushed a deep blue, and his air of joviality vanished. "Take care in how you speak, visitor. You are in my kingdom. When I allowed you entrance, it was with the express purpose of letting you live, even though you have killed two of my soldiers and Glynarra has killed more. Think about that and about your position."

I didn't have to, but Glyn took over for me, holding me back. Her voice sounded nothing if not supremely withering. "Mark is correct. Without your magic, you are less than a bug to be squashed. I am but a peasant, but I offer a challenge. Anyone could beat you hand to hand, as an adult would best a child."

Glyn continued to insult his lack of fighting prowess and lack of manhood, and I wondered what she was talking about. Then it hit me. Nyoka's words of, "He must make the challenge," echoed in my mind.

Make the challenge? Hmm…challenges worked better when someone was angry and not thinking straight. He was already wound up, so why not send him over the edge? I patted the armrest of the throne and sat. "I think I'm going to like it here."

Lensa's facial color went from blue to purple. "Invader, vacate that seat immediately."

Yes, I'd angered him, and it was time to dig a little deeper. I wiggled my butt on the golden surface as he approached, a storm cloud on his face. "Yep, who needs Earth when I can rule here? You're finished, Lensa, so step aside…"

His slap came without warning, and it sent me flying off the throne. For a small man, he was exceedingly strong. "You dare to defy me? You are *nothing*! I will take any test and destroy you!"

Immediately, he clamped his mouth shut, but the damage had been done. There it was — the challenge. He'd invoked it. Even his two henchmen stiffened. They knew. Lensa looked around, his eyes wild, then he calmed down, even though he had to know how badly he'd screwed up.

As I got up, his seer appeared at the edge of the combat circle. Thankfully, he'd cleaned up and changed his clothes. "Sire, I felt a disturbance in the air," he said carefully. "Have you invoked the ancient rule?"

Lensa nodded, his visage grim. "Yes, I have."

"But, sire —"

"And I welcome it. Make the introductions," he ordered.

A sharp clap from the king's hands sent the bodyguards to opposite sides of the circle. "By the rite of Valla, by the rule of Vorra, we have a challenge," the seer intoned. "It shall be done now as it was in the old times. No weapons, no magic and no outside interference."

His words galvanized Lensa, as he took off his crown and placed it on the throne. Then he pulled off his robes to reveal a lithe, well-muscled form, clad only in a loincloth. "I am ready. Mark of Earth, are you prepared?"

In fact, I was, but this wasn't my fight. "I'm prepared to watch you lose. Glynarra will be doing the fighting. It's her world, her curse and her life."

A sneer crossed Lensa's face. "So be it. Shall we, Glynarra?"

Glyn, stone-faced, calm, ready to fight or die, patted my hand. She then strode to the center of the circle. I backed off to the side and waited.

The seer watched as both combatants warmed up then bowed politely to each other. He then clapped his hands once more and yelled, "Begin."

It was on.

Glyn got in the first blow by rushing ahead and nailing Lensa with a clean shot to his nose. He staggered back, his eyes wide, then set his stance. Both fighters feinted, tried a few kicks, all in the name of feeling each other out.

Lensa, though, was somewhat larger than my girlfriend, and he went on the offensive, lashing out with well-timed combos to her chest and face, sending her tumbling in my direction. For his age, he hit hard and fast.

"Pick her up, Mark of Earth," he said with a sneer. "She is but a child and not much of a fighter."

Glyn got to her feet without my help, wiped blood from her nose and mouth, and with a yell she bore in with a salvo of her own. Her wild, windmill type of attack had lots of misses at first, but then she found her range.

A series of chops and kicks to the king's neck sent him staggering. Glyn then threw a shot to his jaw that knocked him out of the circle. His bodyguard had to lift him up.

"You aren't much better," Glyn replied and spat blood on the ground. "In fact, you're worse."

So far, they seemed to be evenly matched, but then a dark shadow emanated from Lensa's form. It burst into a giant cloud of shadow locusts, blotting out the light and swarming Glyn.

She gave a cry of surprise, and her fists came through the blanket as she swung wildly. When the shadow disappeared, Lensa charged in to clip her with a shot to her jaw that sent her down.

Not for long though, as she got up with a snarl and went on the offensive again, throwing punches left and right. The wily king countered by splitting his body into three different versions of himself. They subsequently beat and kicked her all over the place. The final kick hurled her in my direction.

Lensa recalled the clones into his body and stood in the center of the circle, hands on his hips, and laughing. "You are a fine fighter, Glynarra, but you are no match for me."

Piss. Me. Off! "You're cheating," I yelled, pointing at the vertok. "Hey, buddy, whatever happened to fighting fair? You got rules, and—"

"That concept means nothing to me," Lensa interrupted, breathing regularly. "This fight is to the death, but before I kill her, I shall take that power from her that I need so dearly."

With a look of alarm on his face, the seer stepped forward, arms raised as he tried to intervene. "Sire, the rules of combat demand that no magic be used. This is—"

"My wish and my will," the king yelled while waving his man back. "If the powers of this world wish to take it up with me, they can, but I will have what I want!"

As he spoke to his seer, it gave Glyn a brief respite. She got to her feet, spitting out a river of blood as she did so. "I can... I can win," she said. "Wait."

She started forward, but I grabbed her shoulder. "Glyn, he's using his powers to beat you. Cheating, you know?"

"I know. I can still beat him."

With a primal scream, she rushed him, scoring heavy hits on his face and body, and with another scream louder and angrier than the first, she kicked him between the legs. "You...witch," he groaned as she sank to his knees. "That is cheating."

"The same as you were doing to me," Glyn snarled as she grabbed him by the throat and hurled him over his throne. He hit the ground hard with a loud thump.

A moment later, though, he got up, swiped blood from his face, and smiled. His breathing was still regular, and like time-lapse photography, his injuries healed at an accelerated rate.

In contrast, Glyn looked like she was ready to fall. Her breathing was labored, and her body seemed to cave in. Blood and bruises covered her face. I had nothing to offer, and if I went after Lensa, he'd use his acquired abilities to wreck me as well...

Wait.

Acquired. The witch's words came back to me. *Anything acquired can be taken away. A spell, a potion, can be death to the fae.*

Hurriedly, I searched in my pocket for the piece of paper she'd given to me. Where was it...yes! I took it out and with trembling hands, looked at the gibberish written down, only it wasn't gibberish to me, not now.

Like lightning, the pronunciation made itself clear in my head, and I read out the incantation. *"Triy nattaa sennto verena!"*

Lensa had been on the verge of rushing Glyn, but at my utterance, he stopped in his tracks and gasped. "What…what have you done?"

I said nothing, only watched as his body shook and twisted as if an invisible force had gripped him. Phantoms flew from inside him, wraithlike black shadows that emitted cries of pain and relief as they went.

Lensa cried out as well, reaching for the wraiths as though attempting to pull them back, but it was no use. All his powers, all the abilities he'd wrenched from others, all those souls, they were now free, and they melted into the ether.

Glyn stood tall as she got her second wind. "It seems like your power has left you, sire," she said mockingly. "And we're not done yet."

The sudden loss of acquired strength and magical abilities left Lensa staggering. Now, the odds had been evened. While Glyn may not have been the greatest fighter around, she had the edge in youth and rage. She also had a reason to fight.

He didn't.

"Come to me," she taunted. "Our battle isn't done."

Lensa obliged her by making a desperate lunge, but she sidestepped his rush and chopped him on the back of his neck. He went down face first, and she kneeled to do a rat-a-tat on his head before he flipped over, covering his face.

It didn't help, as she aimed a knife-edged thrust at his throat. A gasp of surprise and pain erupted from his lungs, and his hands automatically went to the injured area.

Bad move, as she straddled his chest to hammer his face. It was fist fighting at its most primitive. It was crude, and it was extremely effective. Glyn couldn't kill him, but she could maim the living hell out of him.

And she was doing a fine job of it. A low moan of anger-anguish burst from her throat, and it quickly segued into a bellow of pure fury. "Give me my freedom," she yelled as she smashed his mouth in. "Lift the curse upon me. Lift it upon my friend."

More punches caused his eyes to swell, then she leaned over to bite into his ear and tear half of it off. With a sound of disgust, she spat out the mangled flesh. "Lift the curse. Do it *now*!"

"Mercy," he cried. "Mercy! I accede to your demands!"

With that, some unknown force levitated Glyn off Lensa's prone form and returned her to my side. "It is done," the seer said. "The ritual of combat is over."

Bleeding, battered and beaten, Lensa struggled to his feet. One bodyguard started in his direction, but the king waved him off.

His life's essence dripped from a broken nose, shattered mouth and numerous cuts on his face. His mangled ear also poured blood down the side of his neck. Perhaps he still had some of his healing ability. It didn't matter, not now.

"You lost," Glyn stated in no uncertain terms after she spat out more blood and wiped her face. "Are you going to honor your promise?"

Breath whistling through his mangled mouth and smashed nose, Lensa nodded. He was beaten, he knew it, and so did his sycophants. Abject defeat wasn't a pretty thing to witness in anyone, but in his case, I'd make an exception.

"I concede," he said, slurring his words. "I will lift your curse, Glynarra, but if I do, I have the right to claim something in return."

Customs — they had to be observed. She bobbed her head. "Name it."

Lensa staggered, but he regained his balance and stood as tall as he could under the circumstances. "My terms are simple. I shall lift your curse, but in return, you will never be able to visit or stay in this realm again. That is the price you must pay. Do you accept?"

Glyn's face fell, but then her expression set like cement. "So be it. Lift the curse, and I shall depart within the hour."

Lensa snapped his fingers and his two magicians materialized five feet away. Apparently, he still had some magic left over. "The spell of release," he mumbled.

The magicians put their heads together, spoke a few words, then as one, they turned to their leader, nodding. "We are ready," they said in unison.

The king raised his hands, muttering something that sounded dire as well as evil. His disciples did the same thing, their voices rising as one. A few seconds later, their chant rose to an unholy-sounding crescendo. *"Ni'k a Yal. Ni'k a Yal. Butaini ni'k a yal!"*

Lensa then dropped his hands at his sides. I expected smoke to drift up, fire to blaze above or a shudder to run through my girlfriend's body. It was a little anticlimactic when nothing happened.

Nevertheless, the king stated, "It is done. The curse upon you and your companion is gone. Perhaps you will live in your companion's realm. Perhaps you will choose to live elsewhere. It does not matter. I have my kingdom, and I still rule." The beaten ruler paused to once more spit blood out. Two of his teeth came with it. "Leave this castle, Glynarra. Our business here is concluded, and I no longer wish you to be in my sight. My guards will not oppose you. Go."

With that proclamation, Lensa turned and limped away. His soldiers came over to support him, and soon, they disappeared inside the castle.

While Glyn had her own problems, I had the feeling that good ol' Lensa was going to have more troubles of his own, considering that he'd broken the ancient rules.

However, that was for the forces of this world to decide. Since there was nothing else to say, Glyn and I took our leave and walked to the exit. Once there, the guards made way and let us pass without incident.

Safe from attack, she opened a window and we climbed through it, emerging a few yards from her house. She led the way inside, and once there, she collapsed into a beanbag chair and held her head in her hands.

"I never thought I'd have to leave my world," she said as she began to sob. "Never. Now…I don't know what to do or where to go."

I moved over to kneel beside her and hesitantly put my arm around her shoulders. She stiffened then relaxed against me. "Well, you could come back to Earth."

"With you? And what would I be there?"

"My girlfriend, and, if, um, you care for me enough, when we're older, my wife. I mean, I still have to finish school, think about university, but yeah, I want you with me."

The last part surprised me. While it was a lot for me to say, considering that I'd never had a girlfriend before, much less thought about marriage, I meant every word.

After all, having known this wonderful person for around two months, but only recently gotten to know her in the last two weeks, I wanted nothing more than to be with her for the rest of my life.

Someone once said that if you found someone who completed you, then you didn't throw that part of you away. I didn't intend to, now or ever. "You are sure?" Glyn asked. "If you are, is your world ready to see me as I truly am?"

Call that the ultimate buzzkill question, but it couldn't be ignored. In many ways, Glyn knew more about Earth's culture than I did, or maybe she simply knew about human nature.

Whatever the case, if she ever showed her true face, not to mention demonstrate her abilities, then we'd never have a moment's peace. Disguises could last only so long. One slip, people would catch on, and that spelled disaster.

Horror ran through me at the thought of what the government could do. Quarantine her, for one thing. Imprison her, for another. Neither of those options appealed to me.

Still, there was one person who believed in her, and that was me. "My world may not be ready to see you as you are, but I am."

Glyn got up. "I have to wash my face. Wait."

She walked into another room. I heard running water, and when she came back, her face was clean. After a quick trip to the kitchen, she returned with two glasses of water and handed me one. "You'll need this. I do as well."

I drank. It was cool and refreshing, and I felt some of the tension from the fight leave. Glyn drained her glass in one go, then put it down and kneeled beside me, gently winding her arms around my neck. "I have to ask you one question."

"Yeah?"

"Do you love me? I know you fought for me. I fought for you, too, but here, love isn't considered a priority."

If there was one thing that I was sure of, it was that I cared for her. "I'm from Earth, Glyn, and yes, I love you. And before you ask, I'm very sure that I do."

She put her lips to mine. "Then that is all the proof and assurance that I need."

Chapter Twenty

One Last Window

Since there were no more enemies to fight, the question of what we'd do from now on surfaced. There was no right or wrong answer, only our choice to make. It was that simple and that complex.

Glyn worried her hands together. "I...I have another question."

"Okay."

I could only hope that she'd ask me the question that I wanted her to ask, and she did. She sounded much surer now. "If we don't go back to Earth, would you come away with me?"

Her question was a simple one, and yet it carried so much meaning and many more implications to it. Perhaps the way she'd asked it made me reassess my priorities. Why did I have to return to Earth? What power could compel me to?

Since I was now legally an adult, that meant making adult decisions. It didn't necessarily mean that they were the right ones, only that they were the best options for me at that time.

If I went with Glyn, it meant giving up my old life. On Earth, while my existence wasn't perfect, I had a home, some structure to my life and it was a safe and secure, although boring, existence.

It was also a lonely one. I had one good friend, but as for my mother, would she ever change? Maybe, maybe not—it was up to her.

Finally, what would I do wherever Glyn wanted to go? I hadn't finished high school, had no great skills…would I be able to cope?

On the other hand, all I'd been doing was coping ever since Glyn had opened her first window. With her at my side, I felt that I could do anything. After thinking things over, I said, "Yes, wherever you go, I'll go, too."

Glyn smiled and touched her forehead to mine. "Since that's settled, I have an idea of where we can go, but first, I'd like to say goodbye to Nick."

A fine idea. "Uh, are you going to go in your old form or as you are now?"

"You choose."

A half-smile flitted across her face. In a flash, she assumed her Tellkarian form, green eyes to glowing purple ones, rounded, human ears to the sharpened Satanic-looking type her people had, and back to having six fingers.

In the end, did it really matter what she was? To me, no, but to the law, to those who sought to use her power for their own ends, it mattered a lot.

"Transformation over," she said softly. "What do you think?"

Glyn reached up to caress my face, and her lips, soft and warm, met mine briefly, my tongue entwining with hers. She leaned against me, then, her body supple and warm and willing, but I was the one who pulled back.

"I think you're beautiful, Glyn, but if you want to go, we'd better go now. I'm not sure if Nick's family is home yet, but you know Earth people as well as I do. You know that they'll never understand things."

A tiny smile emerged. "As you said, you do. That's enough."

It would have to be. Glyn quickly threw some robes and other things into a sack, then she went outside. I heard her intone something, then she came in to address the carpet. "Fennimur, I have to go away. You have been a good friend, but you will have a new owner one day."

He didn't ask her why, only answered with a catch in his voice. "I shall miss you."

A tear slipped from her eye. "I shall miss you, too."

She wiped her face, opened a window and a second later, we emerged near my house. From the sun's position, it was around four. "What did you say back on your world?" I asked.

"It was a spell of release," she replied. "It took away the protective magic around my house. Now, anyone can live there, and I don't want Fennimur to be lonely."

Always thinking of her friends — that was Glyn. She gazed around the area. "Are we going to your house? I mean, don't you have to pack?"

Right, good idea. "Uh, yeah, but that can wait. You wanted to say goodbye to Nick, so we're going to his place. C'mon."

"I'm…I haven't shifted," she said with alarm. "Wait."

I stopped her hand when she began to move it. "If you don't mind being with me as I am, then I don't mind being with you as you are. Let's go."

As we walked down the block, the few people we saw reacted appropriately—with shocked stares and some titters. No one, though, said anything or came near us, although we did hear the obligatory comments about it being too early for Halloween.

Naturally some of them followed us. Among them was Joel Catton. Ah, this would have to happen, but here, Glyn was ready and so was I.

Joel ran around to confront us, his smirk on full display. "Hey, Cornish," he said. "What's the deal, here? First, you don't show up for the last few days of school, and now you're with some Hollywood extra?"

Mental sigh time—blast him or not? While it would have been gratifying—at least, temporarily—to put him down, it really wasn't worth it.

Glyn, on the other hand, gave me her things, sized him up and asked him if he wanted to eat a dirt pie. At the sound of her voice, not to mention her saying 'dirt pie', he froze. "Glenda…is that you?"

"It's Glynarra," she answered with that customary edge in her voice that meant imminent violence was about to happen. "That's my real name."

"What are you, some kind of freak?"

Uh-oh, bad judgment call, as she lashed out with a hard right hook that sent him face down onto a nearby lawn and into la-la land. "Enjoy your meal."

As for the rest of the crowd, they grew quiet and hung back. Glyn murmured that she could always ask the grass here to form a wall or mummify them. "Remember, magic is everywhere. I can do it."

"Is it worth it?"

She chuckled as she took her sack of goods from me. "No. It isn't."

At Nick's house, I rang the bell, and when Nick opened the door, he dropped the massive sandwich he was eating. "Jesus! Mark? Glyn?"

He bent down to clean up the mess. It looked like a BLT sandwich, heavy on the bacon and lighter on the veggies. His hands full of meat and bread, he jerked his head to the side. "Hey, you're…you're back," he said haltingly. "My parents are still at work. Come in."

"Just for a bit, Nick," I said. "We wanted to say goodbye."

We walked in, and he took the remains of the sandwich into the kitchen while I closed the door. Those people who'd been following us had stopped at the end of the driveway, and they had their smartphones out, filming away. There wasn't much time.

When Nick returned, he looked upset over the loss of his food, but his face brightened when I told him about some of my adventures with Glyn and our plans.

"It's all true?" he asked.

"All true."

His eyes shone, but they lost a bit of their luster when I said that he had company. I also mentioned that Glyn's picture was probably on the internet by now. A sad smile suffused his plump features.

"It doesn't matter. I can handle them, but you guys… Are you ever coming back? I mean, you got your lives and all that, but I thought that maybe I could see your world, Glynarra."

Her expression matched his. "Nick, I can't go back to my world, either. It's a long story. But I can show you a few other worlds. That is, if you want."

A spark of hope appeared in his eyes. "Really?"

My girlfriend and I exchanged glances and she nodded. That meant it would be so. To put his mind at ease, I said, "Yeah, really. We'll come back for a visit, show you the universe. No sweat."

My best friend seemed about to cry, but Glyn walked over to hug him and deliver a peck on his cheek. "We're just a pane away," she said. "You know that, right?"

He wiped his misty eyes, sucked in his gut and puffed out his chest. My guess was that it was only the second time a girl had kissed him — and both times, it had been Glyn — then I thought about my relative lack of experience. "Yeah," he said, his lips barely moving. "Only a pane away."

There didn't seem to be much else to say. Nick and I gave each other a bro-hug, then Glyn opened a portal. "See ya, Nick," I said as I got halfway in.

"Later, man."

My last image of my best friend was of him waving goodbye. And just as quickly as we'd come, it was over. We emerged in my room. "Your aim is getting better," I kidded.

Glyn smiled. "I try."

She took a seat on my bed while I grabbed a suitcase from my closet and began tossing clothes in, along with some textbooks. Then I got a few toiletries, just in case. Wherever Glyn decided to go was fine, but it didn't mean that study time was over.

Once I was done, I sat with her, and she asked, "Do you really need me?"

I gazed at her steadily. "Yes. Why?"

She shrugged. "As I told you, in our culture, love isn't what's considered important among our people.

It's personal station, ability, health and the possibility of having children."

Having children? "Uh, Glyn, we haven't, you know, done that yet?"

Her gaze went from needy to something deeper, more primal. "No, not yet, but soon — if you stay with me."

Well, how could I turn down that offer? "Er, is inter-species marriage common with your people?"

"We'd be the first."

And what would our children look like? Five fingers or six, shifting ability, ability to perform magic or what humans perceived as magic, language…there were too many factors to consider.

While going over the pros and cons of such an arrangement, someone opened the door downstairs. "Mark?"

It was my mother. Part of me wanted to stay silent, and the other part wanted to freak her out by showing her my girlfriend.

But that was just as bad. I'd be using someone different for shock value, and Glyn meant a lot more than that to me. She gestured at the door. "Who is that?"

"My mother. Do you want to meet her?"

A look of uncertainty told me all that I needed to know. "Considering what you've told me about her, maybe it's not the best idea, but it's your choice."

Choice didn't seem to factor into it, as my mother's footsteps got louder as she mounted the stairs. Once she got to my room, she stuck her head inside. "Mark, I called you at least six times. I left you messages, and…oh."

At the "oh" part, she froze and pointed to Glyn. "What…what's going on here?"

Face-palm time, and I promised myself to keep calm. "Mom, this is Glynarra," I said, indicating her with a wave and trying to sound as casual as possible. "She's from Tellkar."

My girlfriend smiled at her. "How do you do, Mrs. Cornish. Mark's told me all about you."

Call our replies to my mother a cheesy introduction and a horrible cliché, in that order. 'Hi, Mom, here's an alien that I've been living with for the past two weeks and we're going to get married one day.'

My mother's jaw dropped about a couple of inches, and if this had been a cartoon, her jaw would have fallen entirely from her mouth and it would have run screaming from the room.

But this wasn't a cartoon, and my mother stabbed an accusatory finger at my girlfriend. "What is that…thing?"

My mother's trip to 'rotten first impression land' continued. Was that racist or what? "She's not a thing, Mom. She's a person. I told you where she was from."

In a monotone, my mother repeated, "Tellkar? Are you serious?"

Glyn got up, all pretense of niceness gone, and she bared her teeth in a snarl. "What your son said. I'm not a thing, Mrs. Cornish. Tellkar is my world. I don't care what you call me, just don't call me a *thing*."

My mother had already started to back away. "I'll call the police. That's what I'll do. Mark, move away from…her."

Well, at least she hadn't called Glyn a thing again. "No," I said, trying not to break my promise of losing my temper—and only half-succeeding.

"No, Mom. Listen. We're together. You just came back long enough to tell me you're going on another trip, right?"

My mother's face turned bright red. She didn't have to say anything. I already knew. "We're leaving, Mom. Thanks for all you've done for me."

Her voice came out in a strangled croak. "Leaving?"

I pointed at my suitcase. "Yes, leaving. I turned eighteen a few days ago. You remember when my birthday is, don't you?"

My mother said nothing except to offer a helpless shrug. She'd forgotten. It figured. "That means I can come and go when I want, and now, I'm going."

Her face collapsed. "After what I've done. You owe…owe me, after all I've—"

"Done for me," I finished, getting up to stand beside my girlfriend. While what I said next hurt, my mother had to know. "I owe you. You drummed that into my head from day one. You gave me a home. Thank you for that. You helped me with my education when I was a kid. Thank you for that, too."

The anger then boiled over and my voice rose. "What do I owe you? Tell me. What do I owe you? You were never here for me to talk to. You never had time for me. We both know that, so don't give me this 'I-owe-you' garbage." My head felt as though it would split from sheer frustration, but I forced myself to speak normally. "Just…don't."

"Mark—"

"Save it."

The sound of leather being slapped came through, and I realized that it was me. I'd been unconsciously slapping my suitcase and stopped. Anger wouldn't help here. She had to know. It just about killed me to tell her that, but there would never be a better time. So, I softened my tone.

"Mom, I don't care about money or getting the latest smartphone. I never cared about living in a better place. I just wanted someone to talk to after Dad died. I was four."

I bit my lip. Continue telling her? By now, I was past the point of no return. "Your job was always more important. It took precedence. That's what you said to me all the time, so what was I supposed to think?"

My mother's mouth quivered. It was almost comical and yet, not. In fact, it was downright sad that it had come to this. Still, when she spoke, she sounded defiant. "All right, since you've given me your thoughts, here are mine. You're eighteen, so you have the choice to stay or leave. If you stay, she can go back to where she came from. If you leave, then don't bother coming back."

That was it, the ultimatum. I'd already given mine, and she'd given me hers. I looked at Glyn. "Are you ready to go?"

She'd already put her arms up and closed her eyes. "Give me a second."

My mother looked around wildly. "What…? Mark, what is she doing? Is that some kind of satanic ritual?"

"My girlfriend's opening a window," I replied. "Be quiet."

While what I was doing amounted to disowning my mother, this was how it had to be. She would never see reason. She'd never admit to being wrong, never apologize, for it wasn't in her nature.

And all this time I'd been hoping against hope that my mother would change, that we'd be a family, be good friends—but now I knew that it was impossible. I ignored her pleas and closed my eyes, mentally adding my nonexistent psychic power to Glyn's.

A moment later, my girlfriend said softly, "Mark, open your eyes."

Glyn's hands moved as though she were playing a harp, she uttered a guttural sound and, like so many times I'd seen before, a window began to form in front of us.

On the other side, water lapped against a beach. I knew where that was. It would be an adventure, of that I was quite sure. Our lives would…

"Mark?"

I turned around to see tears streaming down my mother's face. "Yeah, Mom?"

Her tough façade collapsed, and she begged, "Please, don't go."

Pleas and begging—I wasn't good with either one of them, although I'd never seen my mother beg for anything. But the way she sounded now was definitely a plea.

For a nanosecond I considered it, but then the notion left my head. Had my mother said that earlier, had she been around more, even the past year or the past six months, perhaps I'd have stayed.

But she hadn't, and now it was too late.

Glyn tugged on my arm. "The window is ready. Should I open it?"

My heart skipped a beat. "Yes."

Glyn then uttered another guttural sound and the window swung open. She looked at my mother with sympathy. Their eyes met, but then my mother turned away.

That was how it was going to be. My girlfriend grabbed her bag in her left hand, stepped through first, then turned around to offer a smile. "Mark, come on. You're going to love it here."

I already was. My mother spoke my name once more, but my left foot had already gone through the window. I took my suitcase and followed my girlfriend through to the other side.

We landed on soft sand, and a hot sun shone overhead. It was the most beautiful of beaches, a true paradise, and it contrasted sharply with the drabness of my world. The ocean's waves were choppy, so our swim would have to wait.

As for my mother, the last image I had was her slumping against the doorjamb. Then the window closed, and my world—at least the world I knew, that of having a single parent and school and all the other things that were, by now, so mundane—vanished.

Tears stung my eyes. Part of me felt that I'd done my mother wrong, but the other part said that I had to do what was right for me. It was right and wrong at the same time, and I knew it would take a while to work through this.

"Are you going to be all right?" Glyn asked.

Now she was asking the questions. I wiped my eyes. "No, definitely not. I'm acting like a wuss, aren't I?"

My girlfriend slung her arm around my waist. "No, you're dealing with loss. I had to deal with it when my parents died. I'm still dealing with it. At least you had Nick to talk to. None of my so-called friends ever came around to offer their condolences." She hugged me tightly, and her voice was very soft. "I'm sorry about your mother, Mark. I thought that when I beat Lensa, I'd get closure. I didn't, so I'll have to work through that, too."

"Yeah." I couldn't say much else.

She let go, then, and with strong fingers, she latched onto my face and pulled me down to face her. "If it makes you feel any better, if you want, we can always go back to Earth and visit. We'll see Nick, and we can talk to your mother, too. She might change her mind, you know."

My heart, which had been so heavy before, felt lighter now. "You'd want to talk to her after the way she criticized you. After what she said? You'd do that for me?"

My girlfriend shrugged. "She's your mother. That's all I'll say. Family isn't something you throw away. I'd do anything to bring my parents back, but...but they're gone."

Her voice caught and I pulled her to me. Glyn shuddered, and she clung to me like a child who'd just been found by its parent after being lost, but then she took in a deep breath and whooshed it out slowly. "I'll deal with it."

I let go, and Glyn turned and swept her arm around in a panoramic gesture. The weather was perfect, and a sand hut had already formed a few yards away. A voice boomed from the sky as well as the sea. "You are back. I am glad to see you. Your accommodations are ready."

Xithantus was a most gracious host. "Thank you," we called up simultaneously.

A blue light came from the sky, bathing both of us in its rays. Once the light faded, Xithantus said, "I see no abnormalities in either of you. Will you be staying long?"

"As long as we're welcome here," Glyn replied, a radiant smile working.

A deep, rolling laugh came from everywhere. "You are always welcome here. Avail yourself of this world's beauty."

With that, the ocean became calm. A smell like fresh coconut came our way. If that wasn't an invitation, what was?

Glyn turned to me after putting her bag down and shucking her robe. "We came here once before, but we never saw the whole place. Or would you rather go swimming first?"

I dropped my suitcase and quickly shed my clothes. The sand formed a gentle wave to take our luggage and togs over to the hut. "I could always do a few laps."

With that, Glyn grasped my hand, and we took our first steps toward the beautiful ocean that was part of our new world.

Want to see more from this author? Here's a taster for you to enjoy!

Port Anywhere
J.S. Frankel

Excerpt

Randorran Galaxy. Sometime around noon.
Earth Year, 2134

"Is that griddle clean, yet?"

Nerfer's call emanated from the storage room, a question that went past impatience but stopped just shy of outright anger. Deep and harsh, his voice sounded like it belonged to a giant, but he stood on the short side of one-hundred-sixty centimeters. His actual height was contentious at best, as he was essentially pink jelly encased in a clear plastic containment suit. But the commanding tone was unmistakable.

In days gone by, people would have called him Spam-In-A-Can. Perhaps calling him 'crushed fruit in a suit' would have been more appropriate. But after thinking about it…no. It wouldn't have worked.

With a sigh, knowing he wouldn't believe me, I answered, "Yes, it's clean. So are all the other tables. Come see for yourself." I doubted he'd take my word for it. Nerfer was notoriously difficult to please.

"I will. Give me a second."

He could have a second—or ten. My journey to spotlessness on the bridge continued. The bridge itself took up a third of the total space, with a captain's chair and a console in front of the main viewing window, an interstellar communicator, which sat on the console to the left of the captain's chair, and helm controls to the right.

Behind the helm was the other two-thirds of the bridge. That was the restaurant. The glass that made up our main window to the stars was spotless, and it offered an incomparable view of the heavens.

If the view was incredible, so was the restaurant, in its own way. My late father had designed it after looking at countless vid-photos of diners from the mid-twenty-first century. For some reason, he'd had a fascination with that era.

Our restaurant had plush leather booths—ten in all—a counter with eight stools and a syntha-fridge that could synthesize any kind of food, but only in its raw form. I still had to cook it. We also had a combo grill-fryer where the food got prepared by me, Rick Granger, co-captain of *Port Anywhere*, our ship's name.

This place was where I belonged, where my focus was. As the co-captain of this ship, I had a duty to guide our ship among the stars as well as to be on guard for anything that might threaten the safety of—

"Coming out," Nerfer said, interrupting my dreams of a full captaincy.

The door to the storage room opened. It housed numerous old food crates and doubled as his sleeping quarters. He came toward me, his semi-solid body undulating in his containment suit as he moved along. From what he'd told me, he was a member of the Gliddod race. His people came from a distant galaxy, one so far away that no one really knew where it was.

He'd shown up here six months ago in a spacecraft that had fallen apart after he'd docked with ours, and he'd asked my father for a job. My father, being the decent person he had been, had given him the position of running this restaurant while he went off to attend to the daily mechanics of operating this ship. Oh, and he'd also made him co-captain.

Did that piss me off? There was an old saying — 'Did a one-legged duck walk in circles?' In a private moment, I'd asked my father, *"Dad, why'd you hire this guy? You don't know where he's been or if anyone's chasing him or what. Weren't you training me to be the captain and the head cook?"*

"When it's time, you'll be both," he'd answered.

Thanks for your confidence in me, Dad.

After a while, though, I had to admit that our new pink crewperson had proved to be an excellent cook, and after my father's death from Bridorran Fever, Nerfer had also ended up being a more than capable captain. It still bothered me at times, though, being relegated to the 'also-ran' position.

In a quick, economical motion, Nerfer moved around to check each table. Finally, he finished his inspection with a grunt that sounded like a bubble popping underwater. "Good job, kid."

Finally, a compliment. A pseudopod shot out from his suit — the suit was porous in a sense, and it allowed him to do that — and he pointed to a table. "Number six has a spot on it. We got Janoorians comin' in soon, and they hate dirt."

Compliment given, compliment withdrawn — and with that, he went back to the storage room. Fine, I'd clean the table — again. We had only ten, but he'd spotted a tiny imperfection one-fifth as large as my pinky fingernail on one of them. In days past, people had called it being anal. These days, people called it attention to detail.

Our vessel, an Earth-class freighter, had been converted from a freighter-slash-exploration vessel to an exploration-vessel-slash-interstellar restaurant. So, when we entered a new galaxy and if some alien life forms contacted us, once they found out we weren't armed, they'd either drop in for a meal or tell us to keep moving.

Usually, they partook of a meal with us, we chatted, then they departed after paying us whatever they could. You could call it a precarious living, because we never knew who'd come our way. My parents had always believed in randomness, and my existence here was as random as it got.

We called our ship *Port Anywhere*, mainly because we went everywhere, to every galaxy and beyond. We had self-sustaining ion-conversion engines, and the great thing was that they left no radioactive residue upon the stars, unlike other ships. Recycling was cool. 'Go green,' the old saying went. We were in space, so, 'go non-radioactive'.

Our journey had started two years before, just after I'd turned fifteen. We'd lifted off on a bright, sunny day in June from a flight field located near Salt Lake Flats, Utah. A sudden surge, the G-forces had pulled me back, and soon, we'd been in space.

After that, our voyage to wherever continued unimpeded. The ship didn't have a wormhole device, not exactly. Unlike other, newer ships, it couldn't go very fast, but it had a recyclable fuel supply, it was safe and from that point on, I'd learned almost everything there was to learn about spaceships and fixing them.

My parents were first-rate engineers as well as designers, and they'd willingly taught me everything I needed to know about the ship, save the engines. *"They're self-sustaining,"* my father had once said. *"All you have to do is keep the place clean."*

Of course, I learned about other things, such as basic repairs to the hull, space walking, electrical wiring and more, but, by and large, my parents handled things.

The first six months had been cool. Outside of my cleaning and service duties, charting the stars and training against battle droids had taken up most of my time. On occasion, we'd touch down on distant worlds, but like desert nomads, we were always on the move, except we moved among the stars and not sand, although the grains of the universe were always there.

On the surface, everything was wonderful — up until my mother had died from cancer a year ago, just after I'd turned sixteen. Modern science could cure a lot of things, but it still hadn't gotten around to curing that.

The picture in my cabin showed a tall woman with long, flowing brown hair, a pretty face and a pleasant smile. My father had also been tall, around a hundred and eighty-two centimeters, with an aquiline nose, short brown hair and brown eyes, traits which I'd inherited, although I wasn't quite that tall — yet.

In all honesty, I'd never thought much my looks. After all, there were no girls here to date, and the closest I ever got to female companionship of my age was watching old holo-vids. Decades back, they'd been called movies.

"I'm sorry about your mother," my father had said to me after her funeral. He'd encased her in a metal coffin, we'd said our goodbyes then he'd pressed the button that ejected her into space. *"She was a good person."*

Yes, she had been, and from that point on, he'd rarely spoken of her. Grief was a powerful thing. Still, we'd soldiered on, and our lives had continued among the stars…

"Rick, you wiping those tables down again?"

Nerfer had poked his head out of the storage room to ask me that question. I gave him the standard answer. "Yes, captain."

His standard grunt came my way. "Fine."

He moved to the captain's chair while I finished doing the tables and gave the grill another touch-up job as well.

We'd been in the Randorran Galaxy for three days. It was the home to Janoorians, Melattans and Sillosians, among others. They were traders, they got along with each other, but they didn't keep company very often. Something about a guild operating here…

"Rick!"

Nerfer's voice — loud and stern — made me jump. I'd been spacing out — literally — and while it made me laugh silently, it also confirmed that I had to pay attention more. A good captain paid attention to everything. "What?"

"Check the computer. Company should be coming soon."

Sure enough, the interstellar com-link device crackled to life. "This is Vadda, of the Janoorian people. We have a reservation. Your Captain Nerfer agreed to this."

Captain Nerfer. Captain. What about me? However, I had to act professional. "Acknowledged. Co-captain Rick Granger speaking. How many in your party?"

"Three. We requested that you prepare one of our planet's delicacies. We will bring the raw form of it. Can you make it to our satisfaction?"

If there was one thing I could do, it was cook. I checked our onboard computer's database. They'd asked for tenlos, a plant of sorts.

"I'll do my best, sir. Sending coordinates for docking procedures."

"Acknowledged."

The com-link fell silent. Nerfer swiveled around with a grunt. "Was that Vadda?"

"Yeah. They're bringing tenlos aboard. That's what they want for lunch."

He nodded. His version of a nod was to bob back and forth, his semi-solid body making a swishing, squishy sound. "Good. You'd better let me handle it first, though. I know about tenlos. It's alive."

Nerfer had to be kidding. "Alive?"

Bob-bob. "Yep. You have to kill it first. After that, fast fry it with oil, then slice and dice it. Trust me. I been around," he said in his usual not-quite-correct way.

Aw, whatever, already! I went to the airlock and waited. Vadda and his friends would be coming soon, and…there! Their ship, a small vessel maybe twenty meters in length, was inching its way over to the landing dock.

Seconds later, a tiny thump accompanied by a vibration indicated a successful docking procedure. I punched the airlock intercom. "When you're ready, please enter the airlock for decontamination procedures."

"Acknowledged," a deep voice said.

The door on their side slid open and three blobs squiggled their way in. One of them carried a sack slung around its neck — or was that its waist? I couldn't tell. The sack was wriggling. Nerfer would have to be right. Anyway, I started the decontamination procedure. Ten seconds later, a beep signaled that everything was clear.

Once the door opened, three black semi-solid puddles of ink roughly fifty centimeters in height and around sixty centimeters in circumference faced me. A low thrum of a voice spoke from the middle puddle-blob. "I am Vadda. You are the one we spoke with before?"

I nodded. Ordinarily, communicating with an alien species—weren't we all?—would have been difficult. However, my father had designed a universal translator that operated on interpreting sounds and breaking them down into something understandable. The device was tiny, roughly the size of a pinhead. It was implanted behind my left ear.

"Uh, yes, sir. My name is Captain Rick Granger. I'll be preparing your meal. This way, please."

I gestured for them to follow me to the dining hall. They didn't walk, just squidged along, sort of like a snail moving at a faster pace but leaving no slimy trail behind. Inside the restaurant, I waved my arms at the seats. "Any booth is okay."

Vadda and one of his crew immediately went to the closest table to our position. The third member of the party, the one that carried a sack, went to the grill area where Nerfer was waiting. The sack was writhing furiously, and the puddle said in a high-pitched voice, "Be careful. The tenlos must be killed first by crushing its root."

"Got it," Nerfer said.

Two pseudopods shot out of him and took the bag. He opened it, and immediately, a gray plant around a meter long leaped out and hit the ceiling—literally. It hung there, waving numerous spindly branches around and screeching an unearthly sound.

Well, if I were about to be roasted or grilled, I'd scream, too. "C'mere," Nerfer said, and his pseudopods quickly grabbed the plant and crushed its root. It gave one final shrill cry then let go.

"You're on, kid," Nerfer said as he tossed it on the griddle that already had a coating of oil on it. "Start 'er up!"

Showtime, and I went to the griddle to take out a knife and a spatula and start cooking the mess. A horrible odor came from it, and why couldn't alien plants or meat smell decent like bacon and eggs…or grilled cheese? Rhetorical—they couldn't.

While I suffered through a stink that was a combination of wood alcohol and crap, the Janoorians went wild over the odor, undulating their squishy bodies this way and that. "Ah, the young man is a master chef," one of them said. "He knows our tastes!"

They could have their tastes and keep them. Once it was done, it resembled fried rocks. I divided the portions just so, slid them onto plates then served our guests. Did they use utensils?

No, they simply bent over the mess and ingested it…noisily. Once they'd finished, Vadda leaned back. "A fine meal! The tenlos is a foul plant on our world. It attacks our people from time to time, so please, do not feel bad for killing it."

I didn't feel bad for cooking it up. I would have felt bad, though, if I'd had to eat it. Vadda then got up and pointed to the door. "We are sorry not to spend more time here, but we must be on our way. We are delivering cargo to another sector in the galaxy."

"Not a problem," I said, attempting to keep my stomach's contents inside.

His friends also rose, getting ready to leave. Vadda slid a pseudopod inside his body, took out a red jewel and handed it over. "Take this as payment, please. Should you visit this sector of space again, we will most certainly partake of a meal with you."

Oh, please don't.

But I said nothing and led them to the airlock. While I waited for it to pressurize, I asked him about the jewel.

"It is called *energa*," he said.

Energa? "What does it do, exactly?"

"It has the property of reflection and is considered valuable on our world. Please use it as you see fit."

Reflection? Maybe it was a mirror. It was shiny, anyway, and I bowed, out of respect. "Thank you."

They departed, and once they were free of the ship, I checked out the jewel. It sparkled, but that was about it. Out of curiosity, I walked into a storage room nearby, found a small hand-laser and did my best to slice off a tiny piece. The beam simply deflected away and burned a hole in the door. "Oh, so that's what it does."

Interesting…and a call that came over the ship's intercom interrupted my thoughts. "Prepare to shift. Prepare to shift."

Why now? The computer never gave a reason, although the sensors detected another vessel approximately four thousand kilometers away, its purpose, unknown. No communication came from it, so…

"Shift occurring. Shift occurring."

With all haste, I ran to the restaurant where Nerfer was in the process of putting all the dishes and cutlery away. "Get ready," he said. "Shift's in forty-five seconds."

"Right."

I parked my butt in a booth, wrapping my legs around the table support. The shift was simply the interspatial move of this restaurant-vessel from one quadrant of space to another. I had no idea why it happened, and neither did Nerfer. It simply did. After my father had died, the shifts had begun.

And when we shifted, talk about massive! The energy of the movement flung us far and wide, and if I weren't sitting down, I'd end up on my back or head at the far point of any room I was in.

Good thing we had our interstellar computer. It held all the information on the various galaxies we'd visited thus far. Our ship had no weapons, but it had powerful sensors that could map out any planet's dimensions and details almost instantaneously, and while it couldn't tell us about the inhabitants' culture, it gave the basics on what to expect. It could also translate any language instantly.

Still, face-to-face communication had to be done, and in my almost two years on this interstellar barge — a flying brick that was one-hundred-twenty meters in length by seventy-five meters in width—I'd seen sludge, rock-people, lizards and other life forms that were too difficult to describe. I'd spoken with them all, and it was interesting to learn their ways. But I still missed Earth.

Nerfer's race—so he said—could learn languages much faster than humans could, within a couple of hours. Very useful for him...

"One," the computer said, bringing me back to reality.

Then it came, that great heave from here to wherever. I kept my head down on the table and waited it out. "Hey, Nerfer, how are you doing?"

"Still in one piece."

When we stopped shaking, I asked the computer for more information.

"We are currently in the Madlia Galaxy," it said in its tinny voice. "Scanning. We are orbiting a planet known as Rattan One."

"Display information on the planet."

Whir…click. "Displayed."

A hologram popped up with the pertinent information. The planet was similar in size to Earth, with approximately fifty percent of its surface covered by water. Oxygen-nitrogen atmosphere, suitable for breathing. Rich vegetation.

As for the people, they were around two meters in height, slender yet muscular, with oversized hands and feet. Hairy all over, they resembled the cavemen on Earth that I'd studied when I had been younger. Two mouths, one on top of the other. Tiny ears. A slit for a nose. Gray-skinned. In a word, ugly. I wondered if they were warlike and if our entrance into space would provoke them…

"Unidentified vessel, respond."

The crackling of the interstellar com-link and the voice—deep, raspy, and unfriendly—made me jump. "This is *Port Anywhere*," I answered.

"What is the nature of your vessel and your visit?"

"We're a, uh, a restaurant ship. My name's Rick Granger, and I'm in charge of—"

"You are in orbit around our planet. We have the right to inspect any alien spacecraft or repel it if we wish."

Jerk. If I'd had a space cannon, I would have decimated that slime, but we had nothing to defend ourselves with. "Understood," I answered, striving to enhance my inner calm. "I'll send the coordinates for our docking site."

"Does your ship not have a landing bay?"

It did, but it had only enough room for one of our ships, a reconnaissance vessel. "We do, but it's probably too small to accommodate one of your ships."

Silence…then, "Very well. Send your coordinates."

The voice cut out, and I dutifully sent the coordinates to our—*ahem*—hosts. Nerfer was hard to read, mainly because he didn't often form expressions. He invariably relied on his voice to make his thoughts and intentions known, but now, his mushiness formed itself into a frown and his voice was full of grave misgivings.

"Rattanians don't take no for an answer. Deal fairly with them and they'll be nice, but if you cross them in a deal, then you won't be worth *vellora* spit."

In space, vellora were akin to maggots, the lowest of the low. "I'll be careful."

He bobbed back and forth. "Good. Did they tell you what they wanted to eat?"

"No, they only wanted to look around." That was what bothered me.

Nerfer grunted. "Fine, they can look around, for all I care."

Yeah, that reminded me. "How do you know everyone, Nerfer? You never told me, and you've been in charge here for six months."

His frown deepened. "My world no longer exists," he said after a time. "A plague hit us. It broke down our cellular matrixes."

"Which means…what?"

"It means we dissolved into organic ooze. There is no treatment, no cure."

Geez, no wonder he was impatient and angry much of the time. Even though I hadn't seen Earth since I'd been just past fifteen, at least I had a home. He didn't. Nerfer continued in a voice devoid of self-pity.

"I got out, just in time. After that, I became a courier. I delivered goods and sometimes arms to other worlds. Had my own ship, did well, but then I pissed off a warlord and he blew my ship out. I managed to make it here, and…"

The com-link crackled. "Alien vessel, this is Commander Kulida, leader of the Rattanian space forces. We are nearing your space dock."

Nerfer shut down his bio, formed a finger and punched the intercom-link button. "Understood. Our representative will meet you at the airlock. You are welcome here."

He clicked off, and had he had eyes, he probably would have rolled them. Instead, he only muttered, "Welcome like hell. I don't like this one bit. Kid, you be careful."

Kid, it was always 'kid'. I'd turned seventeen about a month before, and he still thought of me as an infant. It was enough to make me scream in frustration.

A few seconds later, a dull thud signaled that Kulida's ship had docked with ours. I ran to the airlock and punched in the command for the airlock doors on the visitor's side to open. Three tall beings wearing gray containment suits entered. Two of them carried a large metal crate. They looked around the eight-by-eight-meter room with interest.

There wasn't much there, only the walls and some *shodokutan* lights which used concentrated light to destroy any possible pathogens from alien races. I pressed the button to start the decontamination process. Their world may have been similar to Earth, but pathogens were pathogens.

"Activating decontamination procedures, Captain Kulida," I said. "Just a few seconds."

"Acknowledged," he responded.

After ten seconds, the process finished, and the readout showed no pathogens. I opened the door to my side, and three massive men stepped out. "Thank you for allowing us aboard your vessel," said the person who didn't have his hands on the crate.

He took off his helmet to reveal a gray skull of a head with deep-set black eyes and a visage so gaunt that it appeared that he was suffering from malnutrition. Perhaps everyone on his world looked like that.

With a sniff, he examined the ceiling of the hallway then turned his gaze upon me, as though he were viewing a particularly ugly species of insect. "I am Commander Kulida. I come bearing cargo. We need to talk."

About the Author

J.S. Frankel was born in Toronto, Canada, a good number of years ago and managed to scrape through the University of Toronto with a BA in English Literature. In 1988 he moved to Japan and started teaching ESL to anyone who would listen to him. In 1997, he married the charming Akiko Koike and their union produced two sons, Kai and Ray. J.S. Frankel makes his home in Osaka where he teaches English by day and writes by night until the wee hours of the morning.

J.S. Frankel loves to hear from readers. You can find his contact information, website details and author profile page at https://www.finch-books.com

Sign up for our newsletter and find out about all our romance book releases, eBook sales and promotions, sneak peeks and FREE romance books!